'Krügel successfully pulls off a difficult balancing
act between profundity and hilarity, catastrophe
and absurdly over-the-top comedy...This book
will make you laugh and make you think.'
Frankfurter Neue Presse

'A simple, heartfelt story that you just inhale—
with a wry sense of humour in just the right places.'
Myself

'Moving from the very first page.'
54° Nord

MAREIKE KRÜGEL lives in Schleswig-Holstein with her husband and their two children. She has received numerous literary awards, including the Friedrich Hebbel Prize. *Look at Me* is her fourth novel, and the first to be translated into English.

IMOGEN TAYLOR is a literary translator based in Berlin. Her translations include *The Truth and Other Lies* by Sascha Arango, *Fear* and *Twins* by Dirk Kurbjuweit, and *The Trap* and *The Stranger* by Melanie Raabe.

LOOK AT ME

MAREIKE KRÜGEL

Translated from the German by Imogen Taylor

TEXT PUBLISHING MELBOURNE AUSTRALIA

textpublishing.com.au

The Text Publishing Company
Swann House
22 William Street
Melbourne Victoria 3000
Australia

Originally published in Germany under the title *Sieh mich an* by Piper Verlag GmbH, München/Berlin, 2017
Published by The Text Publishing Company, 2018

Book design by Imogen Stubbs
Cover illustration by Helena Perez Garcia
Typeset by J&M Typesetting

Printed and bound in Australia by Griffin Press, an Accredited ISO AS/NZS 14001:2004 Environmental Management System printer

A catalogue record for this book is available from the National Library of Australia.

Print ISBN: 9781925603354
Ebook ISBN: 9781925626391

In the end, it all boils down to one thing.
You can suffocate or you can starve,
but everyone has to die once.

J. K. A. MUSÄUS, VOLKSMÄRCHEN DER DEUTSCHEN

I DON'T WANT TO DIE and I don't want to walk through this door. School doors are the entrance to hell. But there's nothing for it—my daughter needs me.

The door is heavy and opens outwards. I'm immediately met by that particular school smell—a smell common to all the schools I know, except the music school where I work, which smells of dust mites and rosin. It's always made me feel sick, that smell, and it doesn't seem to get any better with age. I've come to collect Helli countless times, but my stomach continues to rebel.

The corridor, which is decorated with students' artwork, leads straight ahead, then around one corner, and another, until there you are at the glass door dividing the smelly, linoleum-floored part of the school from the more comfortable carpeted part, which smells of coffee. I spot Helli immediately. She's sitting on a chair outside the secretary's office with strange little horns sticking out of her nose. It's unusual to see her sitting still. I quicken my pace.

When I was about as old as Helli is now, I suffered from symptoms nobody was able to explain. Every few weeks, without warning, I'd be struck by a vomiting attack at school. After a few mortifying scenes in class and at break, I learnt to read the subtle signals my body sent me, and from then on I made it to the toilets in time. Not until I was pregnant did I experience anything like it again—I'd throw up noiselessly, over and over, and even once I'd learnt to read the signs, I felt in those moments as if I were going to die. My brain told me it wasn't possible, but the feeling was there and never lost its horror—I'd be shaky for hours and even days afterwards, overwhelmed by the least stimulus—all light too bright, all voices too loud. I felt like a zombie, not quite alive but not properly dead. Carrying on with everyday life seemed more than I could cope with. It was as if a promise was broken with every attack—as if I'd only survived at a price I wasn't prepared to pay.

As I approach, the little horns in Helli's nose reveal themselves as ragged screws of tissue, stuck in her nostrils to serve as tampons. They are already soaked bright red and fall out when she jumps up to greet me.

'You took your time,' she says.

'I was doing the shopping. I couldn't get here any quicker.'

Helli's nose is dripping. She leans over and bleeds purposefully onto the carpet.

She's different from me. She doesn't mind puking or bleeding or causing any other kind of mess or inconvenience.

I hand her a packet of tissues I've brought from the car

and she fiddles about with it. Eventually she presses a scrunched-up wad of paper to her nose, and I turn my attention to the floor to gauge the damage. Helli's shoes have not escaped unscathed, and a bloody trail leads all along the carpet from the glass door to the school office. I follow this trail, knock and poke my head around the door to tell the secretary that I'm here and am taking my daughter home.

'Mrs Theodoroulakis,' calls the secretary, whose name is something so boring that I always forget it—Lehmann? Kaufmann? Neumann?

'Yes?'

'Would you come and have a look at this, please?'

I'd been fearing this. Leaving Helli waiting in the corridor, I step into the office, where Mrs Neumann is squatting on the floor with a cloth.

'I can't have your daughter bleeding all over the place like this, Mrs Theodoroulakis. I don't have time for this kind of thing. I don't see why I should have to spend all morning scrubbing stains out of the carpet. I'm not a cleaning lady, you know.'

Helli must have stood at Mrs Neumann's desk for quite some time—she's left an ornate pattern of drips on the floor in front of it. I have a vivid image of Helli standing there, leaning over and dripping away gleefully while Mrs Neumann frantically dialled my number, rummaging in the desk drawers for tissues with her free hand. On one patch of carpet I spot a small white heap. Mrs Neumann has evidently tried to get rid of the bloodstain with salt, as if it were red wine.

'You need cold water to get blood out,' I say.

I've become something of a stain pro since Helli's been around.

Mrs Neumann straightens herself and holds out the cloth to me.

'You do it, then, if you're such an expert. I've had enough of people like you. Full of bright ideas, but only ever stand and watch.'

Somewhat taken aback, I accept the cloth, which is no use at all because it's warm. Mrs Neumann has folded her arms and assumed a stern look. Although she's small and round, there's something menacing about her.

I don't know what to do. All I know is that out in the corridor, Helli is waiting, still dripping away impatiently— and that the bloody trail doesn't stop at the glass door, but leads all the way to one of the classrooms, deep in the entrails of the school, where it smells of vomiting attacks. I know that the bell's about to ring and that the teachers are about to emerge, and I certainly don't want to be mopping up blood under *their* feet. Just now I can imagine little worse.

Mrs Neumann is standing in front of me, clicking her tongue in annoyance because I still haven't got started. She's right, of course. She isn't a cleaning lady and maybe she's no keener than I am on crawling about on the floor in front of the entire staff. I feel sorry for her, but it isn't my job to clean the carpet either. My job is to look after my daughter. I thrust the cloth back into Mrs Neumann's hand and make a rapid exit. Outside I snatch up Helli's schoolbag and jacket, grab her arm and pull her along behind me.

'Hey,' Mrs Neumann calls out after us. 'Come back here,

please, and get rid of this mess. I'm not a cleaning lady!'

Helli and I begin to run, around one corner, then the next, down the long corridor and through the heavy door, until we reach the car, which, in spite of all the no parking signs, I've left directly outside the school. We bundle ourselves in.

'Quick, drive!' Helli shouts, laughing. 'Otherwise the stupid bitch will chuck cloths at us out of the window.'

She's sitting in the front passenger seat. I look at her with raised eyebrows. Her nose has stopped bleeding—it probably stopped the moment we left the building.

'Into the back with you,' I say.

'No.'

I can't tell for certain whether the movement I see out of the corner of my eye is the school secretary climbing out the window to remind me, again, that she's not a cleaning lady, but I decide I don't have the time to argue with my daughter. I step on the accelerator.

Though the windscreen is steamed up and it won't be long before I can't see out at all, I drive away from the school as quickly as I can, only feeling safe when we reach the bus stop down the road. I park in the bus bay, leaving the engine running and the heater on. The fan is blowing at full tilt. It seems to be fighting a losing battle, but the hot air always wins out in the end.

'What was the matter with Mrs Neumann?' I ask. 'She isn't usually like that.'

'Her husband's gone. She's been a bit mad ever since,' says Helli.

'What do you mean, *gone*?'

'Run off or died—one or the other.'

'It's not quite the same.'

'Well, at any rate, he's gone. Her name's Mrs Kaufmann, by the way.'

'I suppose it doesn't make much difference in the end whether someone's died or run off,' I say, but the moment I speak the words I know they're wrong. It makes a huge difference. Run off but still alive is, generally speaking, the better alternative.

Helli nods, as if she understands what I'm saying. It's even possible that she does.

I get out my phone and find the kindergarten number. My music class, which is only half an hour long, is due to start in three minutes.

Kirsten picks up.

'It's Katharina,' I say. 'I can't come today. My daughter's hurt herself—I have to pick her up from school. An emergency.'

'Not much notice, is it?'

'I may have to take her to hospital. I'll make the class up later if the parents want. But not until after Christmas.'

'I'll pass that on,' says Kirsten and hangs up. She's only nice to our boss and the children's parents.

Two clear patches have formed on the windscreen, large enough for me to see the road if I lean forward. I flick the indicator on and pull out of the bus bay. Helli has discovered the ice scraper I threw into the footwell of the passenger seat this morning. It's in a kind of beaver-shaped glove that's supposed to keep your hand warm while you scrape. Helli thrusts her hand into the beaver, making it dance like a puppet and talk in a nasal voice: 'I'm afraid we have to go to hospital, like, totally fast, Mrs Kindergarten. My daughter's brain is bleeding out of her nose and she's getting stupider by the minute. I'm *so* sorry. Honest.'

Helli looks like something out of a low-budget horror film. There's dried blood on her pale, round face—blood on her chin, blood on her nose. The top she's wearing has splodges of blood the size of coins just over the place where little hillocks of breasts are beginning to form—whether first signs of puberty or leftover puppy fat, I find it hard to tell. There are splashes of blood on her trousers too, or whatever you call them these days—jeggings or treggings or sausage skin. Her hair is lank and could desperately do with a wash—it's even more colourless than usual.

I suppose it would be easier for Helli to be unattractive if we hadn't called her Helena, like the beautiful Helen of Troy, with her 'face that launch'd a thousand ships'.

Costas is an olive-skinned, black-haired Greek, and our son, Alex, takes after him—in personality too. He'd certainly be too dignified to give himself a minor haemorrhage just to get off school a few hours early. But unlike her brother, Helli has a magic blood vessel in her nose that responds to vigorous poking. When she gets bored in school, she prods at it until the blood begins to flow. And flow it does—it wells up and drips and runs, and within minutes she has half the school running around like headless chickens.

It's the fourth time in two weeks I've had to pick her up because of a nosebleed. Lately she's been fabricating dizzy spells and headaches as well, making the terrified secretary more anxious than ever that I hurry. I could simply turn the car around now and drive Helli back to school so that she doesn't miss this afternoon's lessons, but her nose would probably start to bleed again immediately. Besides, I'm afraid of mad Mrs Kaufmann.

Maybe I should take Helli straight to emergency, just to teach her a lesson. I could even put paid to the whole business once and for all by having the trained blood vessel cauterised. But the thought of Helli's screams when she saw the doctor bearing down on her with a soldering iron is enough to make me reject the plan. Helli and doctors is a tale in itself and one reason that I don't go to the doctor anymore. Over the past eleven years, Helli has more than exhausted my capacity for medical encounters. Still, I can't resist getting a bit of revenge for the ice-scraper beaver's silly remark.

'We really are going to the hospital,' I announce. 'It's time we sorted out this thing with your nose. There might really be something the matter.'

She bursts into tears. I didn't want that, of course. I reach out to stroke her, but she dodges my hand, gives a dramatic sob and flails out at me.

'All right, no hospital,' I mumble.

She gives another couple of sobs, then suddenly shouts: 'Look what a stupid hat that man's wearing,' and I know the crisis is over. Helli's moods, Costas always says, are like the weather. If you don't like the look of things, just hang on in there.

We're working our way through the suburbs and along the

tree-lined stretch of road that takes you across the country-side, past wind turbines and farms and through villages. I'm deliberately driving the long way round because there's less traffic here. We come to the outskirts of town—red-brick houses with gardens, the same as everywhere. The sky is bright and open, and at the edge, where it looks paler, is the sea—the end of the land.

My phone rings. It's Costas, so I don't bother pulling over but pass the phone to Helli. She's pleased—she loves talking on the phone.

'Hello, Dad!' she shouts. Then she listens for a while. Then: 'No, we're in the car—she's just picked me up. Nosebleed.' Then: 'Yes, *again*. But it's stopped now.' Then: 'Yeah, of course, everything's fine. What about you?' Then: 'Okay. See you.'

She begins to fiddle around with the buttons on my phone and seems to have forgotten all about me.

'Helli?' I say. 'What did Dad want?'

'He was, like, worried. Because you hadn't got in touch or something. Anyway, I told him everything's fine here.'

I'm almost touched that she thinks it fine that I've can-celled my music class because her nose has ruined a carpet, and that we've had to run away from a school secretary who's gone mad with grief.

◊

If it's fine you're after, it's not a good idea to have a husband who's almost impossible to get hold of except by phone. Since Costas started working in Berlin, we've been fighting a lot.

Fights are the price you pay for a weekend relationship. A fight makes it easier to say goodbye—even after a relatively harmonious weekend, he and I will dredge up a few last-minute things guaranteed to start a fight. Then we spend the following week making it up by text and email and Skype and phone, until we're so desperately looking forward to seeing each other again on Friday that it can only be a disappointment, and we have one almighty argument when Costas gets home. This is followed by a lull—Saturday is generally peaceful and we don't fight again until Sunday evening, when Costas is about to leave to catch his train—just in time to give ourselves something to make up in the days to come.

This time, though, we have longer than usual—until the weekend after next—which means that our reconciliation is also more drawn-out. Right now, we're somewhere in the middle, which means that I don't immediately reply to Costas's texts and keep our phone calls brief and strictly informative. Not that there isn't plenty we could discuss—what's going on with Helli, for one thing. There's also the Christmas shopping list I gave him—a long list of things I assume it will be easier for him to get hold of in Berlin.

Still, at least Costas has noticed that I'm being short with him and seen it as cause for concern—he wouldn't have rung midmorning if he hadn't. All I'd really wanted, though, was that he realise I was annoyed—I didn't want him worrying. No one need worry about me.

Helli has tired of the phone. She tosses it in my lap and it slides off into the footwell. But her fingers never stop. They turn up the heating, adjust the air vent, flick on the warning lights—and all the time she's watching what they're doing, the way a mother watches her children scurry around in a sandpit. Finally she switches on the stereo. The CD that starts up is Josef Protschka and Helmut Deutsch's recording of Schumann's *Dichterliebe*, which I slid into the player earlier this morning. I have to be careful to keep my eyes open when the music begins—I usually close them, sucking in the air through my nose with an audible hiss. Protschka is singing the third song: 'The rose and the lily, the dove and the sun...'

When I first realised—years ago, as a student—that this song was a reference to Dante's *Divine Comedy*, it was like a revelation. I probed every word, every chord, and saw that whatever scholars and critics might want me to believe, this little poem clearly wasn't about flowers and birds. It was about Christian imagery and the possibility of loving somebody so much that you're prepared to let go of everything that has sustained you in the past. In those days I had the time to read difficult texts—now I count myself lucky if I get to skim the newspaper at some point during the day and fall asleep over a second-rate novel at night.

When I really began to listen, the connection between Heine and Schumann and Dante became clear to me. Things which had been drifting about in my head, unconnected, were in fact related to one another, and this realisation kept me in a state of excitement for days on end. These days I can't decide whether everything's connected, or whether it's quite the reverse and all connections are a mere figment of my imagination—a longing for a kind of logical order to objects and events, or at least for some sort of meaningful relationship between them. Schumann certainly tried to interweave his life and work so closely that one is inconceivable without the other—it can hardly be coincidence that the motifs are so similar. This has always impressed me, and I'd love to have done the same, but in my case there's nothing to connect. There's no work—only life. Now the fifth song is starting, the one about the lily's cup. It's a wonderful opening—tender, rich, intense. Costas thinks I talk about music the way other people talk about food.

'Fuck, Mum!' Helli shouts.

There's a bang and an ugly grinding noise on her side of the car. I brake and open my eyes. The car has mounted the pavement and Helli is screaming at me.

'What are you doing? We could have died!'

She points accusingly at a street lamp that we must have grazed with the wing mirror.

◊

I've always thought it would be useful if we knew how we were going to die. It would be an unbeatable way to treat phobias. At this moment, for instance, I know I ought to be upset and at the same time deeply relieved—after all, something terrible could have happened—but instead I just sit here and feel myself shrug inwardly, because I know what my own end will look like and it has nothing to do with a car accident. I've known for two weeks. That's when I discovered the something. Since then, all has been clear to me. The something is in my left breast and isn't behaving the way I'd like it to: it isn't getting any smaller, isn't moving and doesn't hurt. It is what it is. But then it isn't its job to give me hope.

I suppose your average woman in her early forties has a gynaecologist she can trust. Not me—as I said, I don't do doctors. That will change now—I'll have to learn to be like Helli, because I'm going to make a mess and cause people trouble. I'll gradually fade away, becoming fainter and fainter, until the person I am now has almost disappeared, and everyone else will finally begin to understand what I already know. Things have been heading this way for a while, after all—heading towards death.

I know that, but I'm not ready to deal with it yet. On Monday I'll be sensible and make an appointment with a gynaecologist. On Monday I'll set the machinery in motion. Mondays are days of transition. Today's Friday, though, and Friday's job is to let the week wind down gently. It has to be kept free of trouble. Thoughts have to be squashed before they start hopping about like fleas, jumping from tests to diagnoses and from diagnoses to operations, chemotherapy, radiotherapy and other ideas that have no business ruining the weekend.

Helli gets out of the car, shouting that we could have died, or at the very least got whiplash. You have to give it to her— she knows how to milk a situation for maximum dramatic effect. She lays into me, telling me that I'm irresponsible, that I don't drive half as well as Dad, that we might have to pay for the lamppost, and that she's never getting in a car with me again—ever. She puffs little clouds into the cold air—a small, chubby, pancake-faced dragon.

I remain in my seat, clutching the steering wheel. Behind us, a four-wheel drive with Bamberg number plates stops and disgorges an entire family. Probably holiday-makers come to see the Baltic in winter, or on their way to catch one of the giant ferries to Scandinavia. A shaggy dog barks furiously as Helli is surrounded by a flock of eager children. The young mother appears, swathed in an oversized scarf and wringing her hands. She tries to wipe Helli's bloody face clean with a tissue but doesn't get anywhere, because my daughter isn't through with raging and won't stay still. The father, who looks far too young to have so many children, peers through the window at me and asks, 'Are you all right? What happened?'

'Schumann,' I say, 'and maybe a bit of black ice.'

'Ah, of course,' he says, and laughs.

In the end, I too get out. I forge a path through the thronging children to Helli, who is waving her arms about, her face as red as a beetroot. I take her in my arms. She squirms and struggles but eventually calms down. The young mother is still holding out the tissue. I take it, smiling thanks.

'She had a nosebleed earlier,' I say, by way of explanation, but the woman only gives me a sceptical look.

Her husband, meanwhile, is inspecting the damage. He stoops down and hands me the wing mirror that was sheared off by the lamppost.

'On the newer models, the mirrors fold in automatically,' he says. 'Yours is one of the last where things break off.'

While his wife herds the children and the dog back into the four-wheel drive, he comes over to Helli and me and gives us both a hug. Perhaps that's what they do down south.

'You should drive straight back home and have a rest,' he

murmurs into my hair. 'Car accidents are like visits to the dentist—they weaken your immune system. You mustn't be surprised if you feel a cold coming on tomorrow.'

'Thanks,' I say faintly.

The kids wave out of the windows as the four-wheel drive goes on its way. Helli too waves cheerfully and laughs.

◊

Back in the car I hand her the sheared-off mirror. She frowns and turns it over, then has a good look at herself. I half expect her to ask who is the fairest of them all.

'Can you even drive with only one wing mirror?' she asks.

'Of course,' I say, starting up the car again.

You can do all kinds of things if you have to.

When Helli's had enough of her reflection, she notices the music.

'What is this crap you're listening to?' she asks. She pushes a button and the music stops dead. My heart lurches, the way it always does at such times—after all these years, it still hasn't got used to the constant chopping and changing, the way nothing is allowed to run its course before giving way to something new. My heart likes to hear a song play out, wants to hear its final chords.

Helli's fingers find the radio dial, twiddle it until she's found a station, twiddle it some more until she's found another and then turn up the volume. I stare at the road and concentrate on driving—I'm not going to let myself be distracted by those scurrying fingers, and even less by the music blaring out of the speakers. Helli is clearly enjoying it—at least enough to abandon her twiddling and let her fingers drift to the window crank.

The song is one even I have heard often enough to recognise, though I couldn't tell you who sings it. Helli's body jerks almost imperceptibly to the beat. I can see her mouthing the words to the chorus: 'You're so hot, it makes me wanna cry/ Nothing can ever stop you and I.'

In my notebook I have a list that I'd like to add to now. It's headed *Grammatical errors in pop songs that could be avoided if someone in the studio understood enough to put the songwriters straight.*

The list is a whole page long.

The last bars of music segue straight into 'Last Christmas'. I'm glad when our house comes into view shortly afterwards.

Helli rattles at the glove box, then leans over to adjust the digital displays behind the steering wheel. I glance at the clock as I turn into our drive: *10:32.* I see the time vanish and the temperature appear in its place because Helli has found the button that makes it do just that: *−3°*. After that, I'm informed that my average fuel consumption is 5.4 litres. Then at last I can cut the engine and silence George Michael. I pick up my phone from under my seat and put it in my coat pocket. Helli gets out, leaving behind her on the passenger seat the ice-scraper beaver, a bloody, scrunched-up tissue and the wing mirror.

INSIDE, TODAY'S TO-DO LIST is waiting for me on the kitchen table beside a cup of cold coffee. It says:

Things to do before Kilian comes:
- *vacuuming (upstairs too—essential!)*
- *washing (unload, reload, dryer)*
- *make up spare bed (iron sheets—or is that bourgeois?)*
- *shopping (see separate list).*

That ought to be doable, even with Helli and Alex at home—Alex finishes school early today.

I check on the rats and open their hatch so they can go out. They live autonomously in this respect, making up their own minds when it's too cold for them. Then I bring the shopping in from the car. Helli walks beside me, looking to see what I've bought. In the kitchen, I rummage through the bags for the frozen lasagne and head for the freezer.

Helli takes a bottle of vermouth out of the basket and

asks: 'Are you going to get drunk because Dad's out at a party without you?'

Costas drinks very little—it's no wonder she's struck by it. Funny, though, that the sight of a bottle of vermouth should make her think I'm planning to get pissed. It's a long time, I suppose, since we've had friends round in the evening for a civilised glass of wine.

'Kilian's coming this evening,' I say. 'And I don't have to drown my loneliness in alcohol just because your father's going to a party by himself.'

My plan for the evening is to park Helli in front of the television, with or without Alex, so that I can devote myself to Kilian, who is coming to see me for the first time since we were students together a good fifteen years ago. I don't yet have a strategy for the moment when I switch off the TV, which tends to trigger a fit in Helli—one of the more severe kind, affectionately dubbed 'grand mal' by Costas. The only way of avoiding it is to let her watch TV for so long that she ends up falling asleep on the sofa. That might even work tonight, because she has her riding lesson later on. With a bit of luck, she'll wear herself out.

After a while she loses interest in the shopping and wanders off to her room to text her friends. They'll still be in class, and smartphones are forbidden at Helli's school, but she'll try anyway—you can bet she won't come up with anything else. I think wistfully of the mornings I spent lying on the sofa when I was allowed to stay home from school as a child. I had a kind of sick library made up of books I knew and loved so well that I'd read them even with a headache.

Helli only reads books if she's sure there's a TV series with the same name she can watch afterwards or in parallel, filling in anything her brain skipped while she was reading.

I strike *shopping* from my to-do list. It feels good to strike something off a list because it's been dealt with, and recently it also feels good to turn straight to the next chore, something normal and everyday. Anyone who claims that normal is boring is probably either very young or having a midlife crisis.

To-do lists and shopping lists are the only lists I leave lying around for anyone to see. All the others go in my notebook; I'm pretty sure my children have no idea they're there. I only ever write in secret. If I can't make a note of something because I'm being watched, I imagine myself walking through all the rooms of my childhood house, depositing one item from my list in every room. Later, when I find the time, I walk through the house again, collecting the items from the rooms, one by one, and write them down. We lived in a three-storey terraced house—I go up and down a lot of stairs.

I put the vermouth in the fridge because I assume you're supposed to cool it. Maybe what I said to Helli wasn't true. Maybe I *am* going to drown my evening without Costas in alcohol.

'I've got to be seen' were his precise words when I raised the subject of his idiotic office party last weekend, at the eleventh hour, just in time for a full-blown parting fight.

I've got to be seen. I can't get over those words. They seem to sum up all the superficiality and lack of critical thinking in our society. That Costas, of all people, should speak those words almost physically pains me. Superficiality and a lack of critical thinking are two of his greatest bugbears.

'It's not just a Christmas party—it's an obligation. Everyone who's important to the firm has to make an appearance.'

He always says 'the firm', like in a thriller.

'But you're not important to the firm. You say so yourself at every opportunity. You're just another slave—or whatever you call yourself.'

'Whore,' says Costas darkly.

'Well, they do pay you, I suppose. And hanging around making sure people see you is all part of being a whore, isn't it? But what does that make me? Your pimp? The one who sends you off to work, takes care of the day-to-day stuff and pockets a share of your income in exchange?'

'Don't be ridiculous. I don't want to argue. Not about that kind of thing.'

'Is there even a word for someone who's married to a whore, keeps house for her, drives her children around and generally keeps things running at home while she hangs around at parties being seen?'

He got angry. I suppose that was something.

'Firstly, I asked you to come with me. Wives are expressly invited...'

I sputtered.

'*Partners* are expressly invited,' he said. 'No one's forcing you to stay at home while I go out, leaving you in charge of everything. But you can't imagine that it won't all come to a grinding halt without you, can you? That things might actually be all right here, even if you took a night or two off?'

'And secondly?'

'Secondly?'

'That was firstly. What's secondly?'

Costas stared at me and I felt a small thrill of triumph. He's so much bigger than me, so broad-shouldered and dark-haired and altogether imposing (from my perspective, at any rate), that I always take pleasure in getting the better of him. But I knew what I was letting myself in for. Everything has its price. If I decide to leave the facts behind and corner Costas, things get loud.

'I don't care about secondly. But if you think going to this fucking party will be any fucking fun, you've got no fucking idea.'

'Then don't go. Or come home on Saturday morning, at least. It isn't all that far.'

'The party's on Saturday and I still have a whole pile of work to get done. They give me enough funny looks as it is, because I'm always heading home for the weekend. I can't afford to lose this job. One of has to earn some serious money, Kat. Do you fancy trying to live off what you bring in? Playing the triangle with a bunch of kindergarten kids two or three times a week. We can't even feed ourselves on that.'

He'd put on his coat with the shoulder pads—the taxi was waiting outside to take him to the station. In the half-dark of the hall he looked like a wounded bear, swaying slightly with pain and anger. He hates conflict more than anything and thinks that if a husband and wife yell at each other, they've reached red alert—the last stage before couples therapy—so this last year has been awful for him. I'm different. I'm not afraid when Costas turns into a swaying bear. But such, perhaps, are the sad little pleasures of a housewife whose daily effort produces no lasting result, brings in no profit, knows no end and receives no recognition—at least she can provoke her husband to visible effect.

He rarely scores a direct hit when he fires in my direction. When he tries to be nasty, he does it so clumsily that it's almost funny. Maybe that's because, unlike me, he isn't really nasty. He only pretends to be nasty, trying to wound me because he thinks it's expected of him, but invariably missing. Snide remarks about my kindergarten kids and my pathetic contribution to the family income aren't enough to make me angry. There are some truths so self-evident that there's no sting in them at all.

'I'm not the one calling you a whore! You're the one who bitches and moans every Saturday about having to leave again the next day to go and sell your soul. So what if I'm just playing the triangle? At least I know I'm doing something meaningful.'

'And what I do is meaningless? Is that what you're saying? I work, I feed my family. And I create homes for people...'

'You create offices, not homes. You design ugly spaces for ugly people and make our cities uglier and uglier. You've said so yourself.'

'What choice do I have? Do you want me to quit? I'd love to live in your world, Kat, where you can have everything just the way you want it.'

'You're welcome to join me here in my world—any time. And I'm happy to assure you that we're all very grateful to you for prostituting yourself for us, if that's what you want to hear. But don't come to me for sympathy. I'm not going to be your madam and pat you on the cheek or stand around in a minidress, forcing a smile at your ridiculous Christmas party.'

Costas didn't reply, and refused to look at me. He fumbled for a moment with the buttons on his coat, then gave up and stormed out into the cold, tails flapping and hands bare. I'd have liked to pull him back, to hold him tight, to keep him here with us. It frightens me that he's going to be away for so long. And it feels wrong not to have him close to me just now. But I can't tell him that. Maybe someone should do some research sometime into why being nasty helps relieve fear.

◊

My phone is beeping in my coat pocket in the hall. As I take it out to read the message, a second text arrives. Alex writes: *What's for lunch?* Sissi writes: *Can I call you later? We have to talk.* I stand in front of the hallstand, laboriously tapping away at the small keys: *Hello Alex, I haven't decided yet. Maybe soup. See you soon. Lots of love, Mum.* Then I write: *Dear Sissi, Why don't you call me on my mobile at about 3? Helli has riding then so I'll have time. Much love, Katy.*

My stomach is rumbling because it's too long since breakfast. I've read that a lot of people in our affluent western society no longer know what it is to feel hungry. I suppose they're not the mothers of schoolchildren. The rumbling, which I'll deal with later—I have a list to work through first—is joined by a familiar tweak in the region of my diaphragm that always strikes when the children are ill and keeps me checking up on them at regular intervals. It's not that I think Helli's nosebleed is anything serious—the fact that she's in her room right now, when she should be at school, is enough. And Alex texting me to ask what's for lunch is enough to set my stomach rumbling.

Sometimes I think I'm a kind of spider in a web—a web of threads reaching out to all the people who are important to me. When one of those people moves, the thread quivers or jerks too. The image isn't quite right, of course: spiders spin webs to trap their prey, so if a thread jerks, it means there's something to eat. But I feel like a spider all the same—I've spun all the threads myself and respond to their every vibration. Without this web of mine I'd be homeless and lost. The same goes for the others—if it weren't for me, they'd be doomed to lie there waving and calling, with no one to come and check up on them.

◊

I feel ambivalent about doing the laundry. On the one hand it's the most maternal of all household chores—all those little playsuits, all the favourite trousers and best shirts you're responsible for over the years. On the other hand, it never fails to fill me with dread.

I wish I could put it off, but I have no excuse. We keep the washing machine and tumble dryer in the bathroom, which is, for some reason, on the ground floor of our house, and I'm already in the hall at the coatrack. Not feeling like something is no reason for not getting a job done—that's the first lesson you learn on the way to adulthood and a principle you internalise at the very latest when you have a small baby to care for. I put the phone down a little too roughly and go and tackle the laundry.

In the bathroom, I squat down in front of the washing machine, my knees cracking. One load is already finished—a little light is on, telling me I can open the door. First I load the tumble dryer, then I pull over the laundry basket, fill the washing machine again and start the cycle. The floor shudders, water rushes, the machine throbs.

Since I'm in the bathroom, I have a quick pee. This morning's coffee will make itself felt sooner or later—maybe I can head it off, before it gets urgent. 'Last Christmas' is jingling away in my head. Christmas is something else I feel ambivalent about.

My mother didn't tell us at first. It was only when she could no longer hide it—when she had the operation and soon afterwards the first course of chemotherapy—that she reluctantly admitted there was something the matter with her. She didn't ask for help and somehow managed to get the essentials done, so that although I worried about her, I gave no thought to the bigger picture. It wasn't until she suddenly had to go into hospital for a longer stay that the extent of the problems became clear. My father couldn't even boil an egg and certainly wasn't going to try. Sissi was only thirteen, but she already lived in her musician's world, where mundane things like doing the dishes were no more than burdensome distractions from what really mattered. I couldn't ask any of my friends—least of all Ann-Britt, who was as clueless as I was and had no intention of bothering herself with anything as boring as housework.

Cooking, shopping and vacuuming were easily learnt compared with doing the laundry. I'd find myself in the basement, despairing in front of a mountain of clothes, a machine that was far too small for them, and a rickety clothes horse. The washing took days to dry down there in the colder months. Back then there was no internet to provide advice in a couple of clicks, so I embarked on a drawn-out series of experiments. I tipped washing powder into the various compartments, twisted the dials and tried out all the programs, one after the other. My father didn't remark on the matted, ridiculously shrunken socks in his drawer, and I passed no comment on the holes in his underwear. I bought softener and detergent that I knew from TV, and after an amazingly long time I noticed that there were labels in the clothes with washing instructions on them. Until then, I'd assumed that sixty degrees was a moderate temperature that you couldn't go wrong with.

It was a lonely battle I fought with the laundry, down there in the basement. The perpetual look of concern on my father's face was a clear signal to me that he didn't want to be bothered by frivolous questions like *prewash or no prewash?* He visited my mother in hospital every day, usually after work or in his lunchbreak, and at home all he wanted, if possible, was peace and quiet. Sissi too wanted to be left in peace—or at least she didn't want to talk about anything but music. To keep a conversation going at dinner, I'd throw her tempting morsels that she snapped up eagerly. We spoke about the relative merits of Liszt and Brahms, about fidelity to the original score, about old performance techniques and how relevant they were, and whether Rostropovich's interpretation of Bach's cello suites was beautiful, or pure kitsch and totally misunderstood. I could soon draw Sissi out of her shell with that kind of thing. We were just two teenagers chatting, of course—our discussions weren't particularly well-informed, let alone original, but they served their purpose. Unable to withdraw into a world of my own like the others, I couldn't bear sitting there in silence at the dinner table.

My mother sometimes came home for a few weeks, but she always went back to hospital. Were there complications? Did she need monitoring? I was sixteen by then and should have taken an interest in the details of her illness, but I didn't. As soon as talk turned to medical matters, I switched off. I think I assumed I wouldn't understand anyway.

Perhaps medicine has moved on since then. I have no idea which diagnoses are a death sentence and which are considered a mere challenge these days. It makes no difference, once you've reached your use-by date. Your body will always get the better of the doctors eventually.

Although she had promised Sissi and me, our mother didn't make it to Christmas.

◊

'Did you buy tampons?'

I jump. Why didn't I hear Helli galumphing down the stairs? Since when has she been able to sneak up on me like that? At least she's got changed and washed, I suppose.

'Is your nose bleeding again?' I ask, pulling up my trousers and flushing the toilet.

'Not for my nose.'

'For down there?'

I mean it to sound funny, but instead it sounds uptight. When Helli was born I resolved to talk to her frankly and easily about these things, unlike my own parents. And now I've gone and ruined it all by saying 'down there'.

'Ha ha.'

'Do you need one now? Or are you just asking for future reference?'

'Now.' She flings open the cupboard and begins rummaging around.

'Stop that,' I shout. 'Stop messing everything up and talk to me. We have to tell each other if something important happens, do you understand? I'm not a mind-reader.'

I sound like Mrs Kaufmann who thinks she's not a cleaning lady.

I should probably be grateful to Helli's friend Cindi for helping her out yesterday afternoon when, as Helli now tells me, her period started while they were watching TV together. But I'm not. I feel as if Cindi has robbed me of something. It sounds as if she knew what she was talking about too— Helli's only response is a patient smile. I show her the box on the bottom shelf and she inspects the contents and nods sagely. Then she pats my shoulder and vanishes into her room, galumphing audibly this time. I stand in the bathroom feeling completely superfluous, my arms dangling at my sides.

◊

To put off cooking, which I hate like nothing else, I go out into the cold and check the letterbox. Along with a bank statement and some junk mail, I find a postcard from Ann-Britt. It shows a group of tattooed Maori men, making big eyes and sticking out their tongues. I'm about to turn the postcard over to read what Ann-Britt has written when I see something out of the corner of my eye that attracts my attention.

My breath hangs briefly in the air before me like mist as I turn my head. Theo is standing in the middle of the garden next door, waving. Some distance away from him, its engine puttering, is his ride-on lawnmower. I don't suppose he's intending to mow the lawn in this frosty weather—it's more likely that he's pursuing his favourite pastime of repairing and revamping old electrical appliances and machinery. I don't let him near our things anymore—not since he tinkered with our toaster and it emitted a six-foot high flame in the middle of the breakfast table. Theo shouts something I don't catch—the puttering is too loud. Standing at the window, behind the net curtains of the consulting room, Heinz too is waving. He smiles and nods, while Theo's waving has given way to a kind of flailing that looks more like a cry for help than a greeting. I put the post back in the letterbox, hurry down the front steps, cross the drive and jump over the low lattice fence separating our gardens. When I reach Theo, I see what's wrong: he's missing his right thumb.

'Theo,' I say, gently turning him towards me so that he's looking into my face. 'Where's your thumb?'

He stares at me with a pained expression—his eyes have a slightly glazed look to them.

'Gone,' he says, gesturing helplessly with his mutilated hand. He seems not to feel anything yet.

'Let's get your hand bandaged, all right? Then we'll look for your thumb. Give me your hand, Theo.'

He holds it out to me as if to shake my hand. I reach up and touch my neck, but today of all days I'm not wearing a scarf, although I rarely fail to wind one around my neck in the winter—I have a whole collection in my wardrobe. I leave Theo's hand hanging in the air and take off first my jumper and then the sleeveless shirt I'm wearing underneath as a vest. I register the cold, but it doesn't bother me; nor does the fact that I'm standing in my bra in full view of the neighbourhood. It doesn't seem important. Still, I do pull my jumper back on before folding the shirt and binding it tightly around Theo's hand. He's not bleeding heavily yet—the blood vessels are still in a state of shock, but that could change at any moment. I keep talking to Theo as I'm bandaging—it calms us both.

Helli and Heinz arrive almost simultaneously from different directions. A glance at Heinz's bewildered face is enough to tell me that he isn't going to be much help.

'Heinz, you call an ambulance,' I say. 'Tell them you can't drive because you're in shock. Helli, we're going to look for Theo's thumb.'

While Theo stays where he is, a confused smile on his face, and Heinz heads back to the house, Helli starts to crawl around the frosty lawn on all fours, looking for the severed thumb. I watch Heinz go. He moves rather strangely, then turns purposefully to one side and pukes into a miniature cypress before disappearing into the house. I go over to the ride-on mower and turn off the engine, plunging us into a silence that roars in our ears. That can happen around here. It's so quiet sometimes it's almost a relief when a bus drives past on the road. I too get down on the lawn and begin to hunt. If I'm right in supposing that the mower is to blame, the thumb could be anywhere. Time is against us—though perhaps the cold weather is an advantage. Aren't severed extremities best kept on ice anyway? Or does that increase the risk of irreversible frostbite? I recall a newspaper article I once read about donor organs that had shut down while they were packed in an ice chest. In one case, it said in the article, a shocked kidney had refused to work for weeks. I have no idea how something as simple as a thumb would react.

Theo says something, but too quietly for me to catch it. He says it again, keeps saying it, and eventually it gets through to me: 'Please don't go to all this trouble for my sake.'

I get up and rub his back. Heinz re-emerges from the house with his strange waddling gait, his eyes red-rimmed, and says huskily: 'They're on their way.'

Theo is still mumbling to himself: 'Don't go to all this trouble. I'm so sorry.'

Helli has stuck with her search for a few minutes, which isn't bad going for her, but now bursts into tears and throws herself full-length on the ground, shouting, 'There's no point, I can't find it anywhere!'

I don't know who to comfort first.

By the time the ambulance arrives, everyone has more or less calmed down, but the thumb still hasn't turned up.

The paramedics have a soothing influence—they radiate kindly competence. I wonder why it's always men who drive ambulances, while the hospitals are teeming with female staff. Is it the old-fashioned idea that women are in charge of everything that takes place between four walls, while the outside world belongs to men? There must be some other explanation—maybe it has something to do with education— but really I shouldn't be thinking about such things right now. My mind has a habit of wandering off, being distracted by silly questions that stop me from focusing on what needs to be done. It's selfish, really, to be so caught up in your own thoughts, as if they're all that matters.

◊

The paramedics lead Theo to the ambulance. On the way he half turns, giving a friendly wave with the hand that's swaddled in my shirt. Heinz stays behind with me. We persuaded him not to accompany Theo to hospital, and I promised the paramedics I'd take care of him. That seemed the best solution. He and Helli trot along behind me like goslings as I climb back over the lattice fence into our garden.

Now Alex is coming up the drive. No idea why he's finished early today—probably one of those staff training days or something. It's not a good sign that I'm surprised to see him. Only an hour ago I knew what day of the week it was and when I could expect my children home. Through the open door I hear my mobile ringing. I feel a knot of tension at the back of my neck, perhaps the beginning of a migraine.

'What's going on?' asks Alex cheerfully.

He's always cheerful. And even when he isn't, he has an almost unbelievably agreeable way of being bad-tempered. He's what people call a mother-in-law's dream—always has been. It's a pity I'm not his mother-in-law.

The tension in my neck would ease off, I know it would, if I could just be alone for a moment and make a list. Any list.

AFTER CHECKING TO SEE who the missed call was from—
Sissi—I stand by the stove and scribble a hasty addition to my
to-dos: *Ring Sissi back (urgent—no excuses).*

Alex saunters past, glances at the list and takes the pen
out of my hand. He writes: *Nota bene: call Rentokil about the
monsters in the cellar.*

We don't have a cellar and my lists are out of bounds to
everyone except me, but I forgive Alex because, for a start,
he's a seventeen-year-old who knows his Latin acronyms in
an age in which most teenagers haven't even mastered their
own language.

There's a painstaking way of making vegetable soup and
a time-saving way. You can chop fresh vegetables and add
them to the boiling water at intervals, carefully judging their
different cooking times. You can make the stock with real veg,
preferably fresh from the organic farmers' market. I know all
that. I might even manage to do it myself sometime—it isn't

as hard as all that. But not here and not today and probably not in this life. I pour boiling water from the kettle into a saucepan and strew it with vegetable stock powder. The stock powder floats on the surface and little discs of limescale from the inside of the kettle circle at the bottom of the pan. I'm hoping they'll dissolve along with the powder if I only stir hard enough. Then I cool the water down with a thick lump of frozen veg. Now all I have to do is wait, keeping an eye on the pan and giving it the occasional stir. In the meantime I can get on with a hundred and one other things—I suppose that's why soups and stews have been so popular with women for generations.

When Costas cooks, it's quite a different story. It wouldn't enter his mind to put the shopping away in the cupboards, vacuum the living room, ring the bank or even wipe the bench while he was getting a meal ready—however much time he had on his hands. In my place, he'd probably make a salad while he waited for the soup or some simple but exquisite pudding. In the past, Costas often cooked dinner for the four of us if he got back from work in time, and it was always amazing—sumptuous, aromatic, fresh and very garlicky. The children adored his cooking—all that meat he put in front of them, all that Greekness. They admired him for it, were proud of it—until, that is, Alex became a vegetarian and it dawned on him that his father had been born and raised here in Germany and must have taught himself to cook Mediterranean food from recipe books. The absence of anything but pasta at his granny's in Bochum should have aroused his suspicions rather earlier, but it never struck him.

Costas's parents moved south to be near his brother when his father retired. The house up here was too expensive and too much trouble to keep up. They'd had enough of the Baltic—enough of the cold wind and the slanting rain, the oily, rusting ships. My father-in-law never passes up an opportunity to remark that he doesn't want to see another harbour as long as he lives. After thirty years working on the docks, the mere sight of container cranes and passenger terminals is enough to give him heartburn, he says. Bochum is nowhere near the coast, so it's perfect for him. There's a family myth, perpetuated on both sides, that we visit him and his wife down there about twice a year. In fact it's been three years since we last went to see them. Now that Costas is working in Berlin, I'm less inclined than ever to waste our precious holiday time together visiting Bochum. It's a shame for the children that their grandparents live so far away, but perhaps my something and I can shake this family up a bit. Even small changes can open up new possibilities—so who knows? Heinz, who is a great believer in what he calls 'family constellations', has told me a lot about it.

While I've been cooking, Heinz has installed himself on the sofa where he can look pale in peace. He's one of the things I can be taking care of while the water comes back to the boil.

◊

To get to the living room, I have to go through the hall, passing my phone and the perpetually smelly rat cage. Through the bathroom door I hear the satisfying sound of the washing machine—the drum turning, the clothes being cleaned, the water pumping, everything going at full tilt. The layout of the ground floor is unconventional—like a maze. I know the set-up of the houses next door, which were built at a similar time, and I never fail to marvel at how much more competently they were designed. The only pretty and practical things in our house were built by Costas.

I presume that most architects are reasonably handy about the house. They have to build models—at least during their studies—and they know about materials and measurements and how to make the best use of space. On the other hand, I don't suppose anyone would expect a surgeon to be particularly skilled when it came to carving the Christmas goose, or a dentist to be especially proficient at extracting Lego bricks from down the side of the sofa. Costas, though—whether it's because he's an architect or not—is resourceful and industrious. He put a lot of work and imagination into our little house in the first few years after we moved in. At some point, of course, that was bound to let up, but these last years he hasn't even dealt with the most basic repair work. In the autumn I put my foot through one of the patio steps, it was so rotten.

Like many of the houses round here built in the seventies, our house is red brick with a black roof. It looks tiny, especially compared with the generously proportioned thatched houses on the country farmsteads, or the glass-fronted nouveau riche seaside villas which are so plentiful in these parts. It has an unmistakable weatherside where the moss grows more quickly than you can scrub it away, and it's set back from the road so that any visitors have to crunch their way up a long gravel path. No one with a decent gravel path needs motion detectors or burglar alarms. The front garden is full of conifers, which makes it look forbidding in a north German way without the bother of unfriendly walls or fences. I often have the feeling that the house prefers its own company and likes to stand aloof from worldly affairs. Costas grew up here. We bought it from his parents when they moved to Bochum. Alex was just two, and it was our chance of a house with a garden near Lübeck, where Costas had a job and I was doing my PhD at the academy of music. My thesis, which I'm officially still working on, was entitled: *When the Piano Knows More Than the Voice: The Relationship Between Poetry and Musical Adaptation in the Song Cycles of the Romantics.* It was going to be about something quite different, but I'm more than used to seeing the stubborn reality of life get the better of my plans. When I went to see my supervisor to discuss my chosen topic with him, he laughed at me.

'Clara Schumann?' he said. 'Do you seriously think that's original? Every PhD student in a skirt comes to me wanting to write about Clara Schumann—you do realise that, don't you? If you want to write about women, then do a PhD in gender studies. But if it's art you're interested in—serious art, and especially music—you can't expect to find any women.'

Upstairs, in my old desk, more than eighty pages of thesis are mouldering away, just like our patio steps, which were built at about the time I condemned my manuscript to the drawer. I still sit at my desk sometimes, reading and answering emails, writing postcards to New Zealand or making notes for my music classes—and I try to ignore the triumphant voice of my professor whispering in my head: 'You see, Mrs Theodoroulakis? I told you so.'

◊

Heinz is pleased that I go and sit with him. He takes my hand and puts it in his lap, where he kneads it untiringly as he tells me about Theo. He talks as if a sluicegate has opened.

Theo's problem, Heinz explains to me, is that he can't free himself from traditional assumptions about gender roles. He thinks men are cowboys or macho-types who mess around with motorbikes, while women want children, wear pink chiffon scarves and like boy bands. This is hard to get your head round if you know that Theo used to be called Susanne—while Heinz was once Franziska. Franziska was already living next door, with a husband and their little boy, when we moved in. When the husband left, taking their son with him, Franziska stayed on and gradually metamorphosed into Heinz. At some point, Heinz introduced us to Theo, whose metamorphosis was still to come. That gave the neighbours something to puzzle over. Then, four years ago, they had a big barbecue to celebrate Theo's official transition to life as a man.

Most of his life, Heinz explains to me, still kneading my hand, Theo tried to be a good girl. He let his mother wash his hair without screaming, played with Barbie dolls, handed in flawless schoolwork, did well in his exams and trained as a geriatric nurse. He'd always done his best. And the moment Susanne became Theo, he did his best to be a real man. Unfortunately he thought that involved repairing electrical appliances and working on engines.

The ride-on lawnmower had been Theo's birthday present to himself, only this autumn, just before the end of the mowing season. Heinz was against it. He pointedly gave Theo a pair of woolly socks and some shaving soap on the morning of his birthday and refused to go along to the garden centre to help choose the pièce de résistance. Sometimes, you see, Heinz gets a feeling—almost as if he's clairvoyant. He says that's what makes him such a good homeopath. So Theo mowed and mowed—it was an unusually dry autumn—and was happier than he'd been for ages. The only thing that bothered him was the built-in safety switch that cut the engine automatically when you got off. But for someone like Theo a measly safety switch was no obstacle. He'd soon figured out how to override it, and now he can leave the engine running as long as he likes—it doesn't cut out just because he climbs off to move a rake out of the way. What he was doing on his mower on a day like today, though, is as much of a mystery to Heinz as it is to me. They'd already had rather a rough morning, apparently, so perhaps Theo sought out his mowing machine for therapeutic reasons—because nothing soothes and comforts Theo like a nice bit of maintenance or repair. This, of course, leaves Heinz feeling partly to blame for the lost thumb—and, indeed, when he drops his eyes to his lap at this word and catches sight of my hand, all five fingers present and accounted for, he has to get up and make a dash for the toilet.

I seize my chance and hurry into the kitchen just in time to catch the soup attempting a breakout. The pan lid is rattling so violently I'm afraid it's about to fall off, and the soup is foaming and hissing in an alarming manner. At least no one expects a perfect meal from me. I turn down the heat and, without enthusiasm, dip a spoon in the stuff to try it. I'm not expecting it to be delicious—all I'm aiming for is *acceptable*—but it's sad and insipid. I run my eyes along the spice rack in search of inspiration. Then I add more vegetable stock, a pinch of nutmeg, some pepper and half a teaspoon of a herb mixture my sister once gave me, which goes by the enchanting name of Sibylle's Magical Culinary Secret. I decide it tastes better after that and begin to lay the table.

◊

We make for a strange family when we sit down to lunch. Heinz came out of the bathroom just as I was calling up the stairs, and Alex was kind enough to bring his sister down with him. Calling her is pointless—you have to shoo her out of her room and not let her out of your sight until she's reached the kitchen. When Alex is at home, he usually assumes this duty without having to be asked. He's humming to himself as he sits down, and I try not to listen. The tunes in his head are catchier than mine and I can do without them.

Helli has brought her phone with her and doesn't even raise her eyes from the screen to locate her chair. She just sits down and by some miracle her bottom ends up on the seat. I suppose I could do that too if I practised for long enough, but I'm not sure it's a skill worth striving for—doing so many things at once and none of them properly or well. The older you get, the more you try to make each moment count. There's a thriving industry of coaches and motivational speakers and self-help authors who live off us ageing people—people who sense time slipping away from them and hope that by stopping and scaling back they can make what remains more precious. That's one reason I refuse to give up my clunky old phone. I don't want to be in constant contact with everyone I know, or to read articles or watch videos every time I have a few minutes to spare. I have to keep distractions at a minimum, or else these brief moments of respite become superficial—no longer restoring, sustaining or uplifting but merely diverting. All the same, I keep an ear out for my phone because I'm hoping Costas will be thoughtful enough to send me a lunchtime text. That doesn't mean I'll soften towards him, or let him off the hook, because the thing is, punishing him gives me a sense of control I don't actually have—over him *or* his text messages. But of course I hanker after him, and wait anxiously for his texts. The longer he's gone, the younger he grows in my imagination, so that by the time he gets home, I'm expecting the Costas of our student days, and I get quite a shock when I see him at the door the way he really is. The shock fades, but the whole thing begins all over again every time he leaves—I never seem to learn.

Heinz, who is no longer chalky white after his trip to the bathroom but does smell strongly of a men's cologne I seem to recognise, is sitting on his chair, legs apart.

I dole out the soup and say a loud 'Guten Appetit'. Then I throw Alex a glance: his signal to say something that might lead to an interesting conversation.

'Did you find Theo's thumb?' he asks.

When Helli looks up, I hold out my hand to her, palm

up. She's so distracted that she surrenders her phone without protest. She shouldn't really even have it with her at the table, but since she tends not to stick to this rule, and Alex and I are keen to avoid tantrums and long, tedious arguments while we're eating, we've come up with this trick of distracting Helli. It has to be Alex who asks a question or raises a topic, because Helli looks up to him and still finds him more interesting than her phone. I'm afraid the same can't be said of me. The trick would soon wear off if we used it every day, but we don't usually eat together except on the weekend. During the week it's harder to nab Helli's phone, but I take my chance whenever I can and try to keep the thing away from her as much as possible. She's still only eleven, and at that age there's a limit to how much time you can spend sending your friends inappropriate photos and cyber bullying your enemies—or at least there should be. If I miss my chance to catch her unawares and have to resort to playing the authoritarian parent and insisting on the rules, I risk serious collateral damage. Once when I'd confiscated her phone Helli grabbed every object within reach and threw it out the open window. Half an hour later she was almost dying of remorse and in need of some heavy-duty comforting. She started to help gather up the projectiles, which was something, but she didn't keep it up for more than five minutes. I had to put everything in front of the heater to dry, because it was pouring with rain. From start to finish, the whole business cost me about two hours of my life.

'No,' says Heinz. 'His thumb's still lying around outside somewhere.'

'Could it be sewn back on if it turns up?' Alex asks.

Heinz shakes his head with regret.

'Maybe it won't turn up until the spring,' says Alex. 'Do you think Theo will want it, or might I be able to keep it?'

'What do you want with someone else's thumb?' I ask.

'Ew, gross,' says Helli, and I'm not sure whether she's joining in the conversation or commenting on the soup. It's a mystery to me how she's so chubby—she seems to regard anything I cook as inedible.

To be fair, though, the soup really does taste so vile that I wouldn't blame anyone if they decided to share a taxi down to the harbour afterwards to fill up on chips.

I try not to feel too relieved when Helli gets up and shuffles out of the kitchen, her phone still safe in my pocket.

◊

I love Helli a little bit more than everyone else in our family does. It's not that she's easy to love—far from it—but I suppose I've just turned my love for her up a bit hotter and a bit fiercer to make up for it. Right from the beginning she looked so red and angry and screamed such a lot that I put up a kind of shield of maternal love to stop the censorious world from so much as thinking of making any idiotic remarks. The birth was torture for us both—Helli was a 'sunny-side-up' baby who refused to turn right way round—and when at last she did slide out of me, she didn't mew in surprise as Alex had done, but gave a roar of outrage that didn't subside even when the midwife laid her on my belly. I felt helpless, and also slightly annoyed. I was there and our bodies were touching and this should have been a beautiful moment, but she wouldn't stop screaming. At the same time, I felt a certain respect for her stubbornness. She clearly hadn't liked being born and wasn't going to let anyone change her mind in a hurry. She was a fat, noisy bundle of life, and that filled me with delight.

That mixture of feelings marks our relationship to this day: helplessness, irritation, bewilderment and admiration. I'm puzzled by her anger but in awe of the tenacity with which Helli insists on her right to be herself.

There were few occasions for joy, though, either during her infancy, most of which she spent emitting ear-splitting screams, or in her wilful pursuits as a toddler. She was an expensive child—a regular at the emergency ward and a strain on our finances. If it was quiet while Helli was at home, it usually meant trouble. She might, for instance, have decided to surprise us by laying the breakfast table, but for some reason abandoned her plan and started pouring beautiful and intricate patterns onto the carpet from a bottle of olive oil. She was insatiably curious and always had to have proof of everything—she wasn't content to conclude that since her own quilt was filled with feathers, it was likely that the other quilts in the house were too. I still don't know where she got hold of the scissors and knives and other tools she used to slash things open, bore holes in them or carve them up to examine their insides, because I was very conscientious about locking away anything sharp or pointed. Even as a tiny tot, she could empty a cupboard faster than I could dash up the stairs. I was always watching her, always keeping track of where she was, or so I thought, and yet she fell off every piece of furniture in the house. When she fell off the kitchen table, I was standing right beside her and could have sworn she was sitting behind me on the floor, drawing in a patch of flour. She got concussions and cuts and extensive grazing, was bitten by dogs and swans, and managed, with the assurance of a sleepwalker, to find the rotten branch in every tree she climbed.

Helli had meltdowns long before the word made its way into the parenting books that I obsessively worked my way through over the years. As she grew older, my already complicated feelings about her were joined by a desperate longing for peace and quiet at any cost—a longing inevitably accompanied by pangs of guilt. Just as Helli careened back and forth between rage and exuberance, sheer joy and deepest despair, good intentions and sombre plans for revenge, I whizzed about between my feelings for her like a ball in a pinball machine. Sometimes I loved her for her vitality and envied her lust for life, but at other times, listening to the seconds-long silence that followed a loud crash before the howls of pain set in, I'd secretly wish those howls would never come. There were days when grieving all my life for a dead Helli seemed almost easier than having to take care of her for another twenty-four hours.

We traipsed from doctor to doctor, but none of them could find anything the matter. I should take a firmer hand with her—that was the general consensus. It was also the opinion of her kindergarten and school teachers, whose only solution was to send her out of class, or to call and ask me to pick her up if she really got out of hand. By then I'd long since abandoned my PhD—and with it all hope of a part-time post at the music academy, or in fact any job that required my uninterrupted presence.

I had high hopes when Helli started high school. Her marks were good, in spite of it all, and I knew she was proud of that. I managed to persuade myself that she was growing up and finally starting to show some common sense. But of course everything carried on as before—she continued to come home with mountains of work she hadn't finished in class, forgot all her homework, lost every pen in her pencil case in a ridiculously short space of time, and told her teachers such outrageously tall tales that the first parents' evening was like running the gauntlet. Eventually, only a few months ago, her German teacher put me on the right track, and I made appointments and talked to people and booked Helli in for tests. There's one intelligence test still outstanding, because the first time round she abandoned the questions halfway through and began to colour in the empty spaces in the letters instead—but the diagnosis is as good as certain: Helli has attention deficit hyperactivity disorder—ADHD. Where we'll go from here and what it will mean for her, I don't yet know. I'd like to discuss it with Costas, but lately he's waved me away whenever I start to talk about Helli. He doesn't have the energy for an extra dose of Helli in his life.

What do you do when you have a something in your breast and your daughter might have to be taken out of school if her behaviour doesn't change? You can't just go and die when everything's up in the air like this.

◊

Heinz thinks the tests we're putting Helli through are a lot of nonsense. He's been waiting for her to leave the kitchen so he can have a serious talk with me—I can tell from the way he watches her leave and looks to see if she's out of earshot. I could get in first and cut him off, but I think it would do him good to preach at me for a bit. He's had a stressful day—he needs cheering up.

Alex excuses himself, takes his plate to the sink and goes into the hall, humming. I hear him all the way up the stairs. Even when he hums it sounds beautiful—with a voice like that he could do anything.

Heinz turns to me and I lean back, ready to provide him with a good audience.

'I saw you drive off to pick up Helena earlier,' he says, by way of an opening.

Of course he did. He spends every spare minute of the day at those net curtains of his.

'Has she been in trouble at school again?'

It's a loaded question. Heinz thinks I'm a spineless dupe being preyed upon by evil doctors who make their living pumping innocent children full of drugs. Still, I nod, because I want him to forget his worries.

'You ought to try her on aurelia,' says Heinz. 'Just to see if it makes a difference.' He always talks about his remedies as if their names and effects were common knowledge. I don't know if it's a clumsy attempt to impress others with how much he knows, or whether he's so caught up in his own little world that he has no idea that most people won't have a clue what he's on about.

'The real issue here is that Helena's being asked to adapt to a system that's not right for her. I'm afraid it's all too common in our schools. Children who don't fit in are given therapy and made to fit in—or else declared *unfit*. It doesn't occur to anyone to change the system to fit the children the way they are. It would be just as feasible to create a learning environment to suit Helena, but no, that costs *far* too much and it's *far* too much trouble, and goodness only knows where we'd be if we started down that path!'

I think about making us both coffee, but decide to stay sitting down, as he's just starting to hit his stride and I don't want to put him off. He's critical of caffeine in any case.

'Before you let them saddle her with some trendy diagnosis, you must consider the alternatives. Just give it a go. We could start with a full patient history, if you like, but I'm pretty sure I'm on the right track with aurelia.'

Heinz is a big fan of human testing, although he wouldn't put it quite like that.

'We all sing a song, Katja,' he says, and now I'm intrigued. I've never heard him say that before—he must have read a new book. 'You only have to listen carefully. The longer I practise homeopathy, the more important these songs seem. I'm going to give a talk about it in Kiel soon.'

So this is a rehearsal. At least I get to hear the talk free of charge, I suppose—if you don't count the time I'm spending here at the kitchen table with Heinz when I could be working through my list.

'I tell you—up here on the Baltic we're all coastal plants. We're saltwater people. If you're not, you won't stay long. The climate's too harsh and windy and the winters too long and dark. The only people who stay are the ones who really belong, whose songs are coastal songs. Over the past few years, I've prescribed a striking number of sea remedies. It's a wonder I didn't notice earlier. We all sing water songs up here. We are all of us—from a homeopathic point of view—sea creatures, minerals, algae and so on. Six weeks ago I had a patient who sang the song of the great black-backed gull—absolutely no question.'

And he launches into one of his incredible success stories, which, like everyone, I love to hear. It's heartening to think that healing can be so simple—and doctors so kind and under-standing. We all need stories like these, with the newspapers so full of doom and gloom.

'I really had to dig deep—there are a hell of a lot of species of gull in the world—but in the end there was no doubt. It was the great black-backed gull. The only trouble was that there was no remedy available—not even in India. I'd have to make it myself, but great black-backed gulls are rare on the Baltic. So I wrote to the people at the University of Bremen, who got in touch with ornithologists on the North Sea islands, and eventually they were able to send me a feather. A few colleagues and I crushed it to a powder—a process that goes on for hours. We were exhausted by the time we were done. Then I made globules out of the powder. What can I say? Two days after starting treatment, the woman was so much better that even I could hardly believe it. She'd been covered in abscesses, her hair was falling out and she'd been so depressed she hadn't been able to work for years. But then the globules began to take effect, and suddenly her skin was smooth and clear, her hair shone, and she felt amazing. Free as a bird, she said. It's possible that the glaucous gull or lesser black-backed gull might have had the same effect, but I think my research paid off. You always see at once when a remedy hits the mark, but this was a bullseye.'

'How do you hear the song, Heinz?'

'*That* is the art.'

'And what is aurelia?'

'The moon jellyfish,' he says solemnly. I suppose I shouldn't be surprised that my daughter should make him think of a jellyfish, but I'm offended all the same.

'There's something I've been meaning to ask you for ages,' I say, which is a lie, because I've only been meaning to ask it for two weeks. 'Could you also cure serious diseases with globules? Broken bones? Psychoses? Cancer?'

I don't say: severed extremities.

'At the end of the day, my dear Katja, a tumour is nothing more than cells multiplying. To all intents and purposes a pregnancy, too, is a tumour, but as I'm fond of saying, it's a while before you find out whether or not it's malign.'

He laughs at his own joke and I smile encouragingly.

'In most cases, malign tumours are a sign of unresolved conflicts, and in that sense homeopathic treatment can be a very good idea indeed. Unresolved conflicts are, you might say, my speciality. I help the body help itself. Conventional medicine is far too one-sided: its strategy is to identify a target and then send in the heavy artillery to bombard it with everything they've got. If you end up killing the enemy, that's chalked up as a success, even if you've destroyed everything else in the vicinity. Doctors need to listen. They need to hear the songs their patients are singing. Cancer cells in the liver tell a completely different story from cancer cells in the prostate. They're messages our bodies send us. You don't shoot the bearer of bad news and hope that's the end of it. But that's the way cancer is treated these days, and it's the sad reason it so often ends fatally.'

'And what song do I sing, would you say?'

'You, Katja, sing the mermaid's song. Beautiful and mysterious, an excellent cook, and a comfort to all poor despairing seamen drifting alone on the high seas.'

He raises a finger, hushing me. From outside comes the sound of crunching gravel and slamming doors. Theo has come back in a taxi.

WHAT SONG DO I SING? And what message is my left breast trying to send me? Haven't I been woman enough to please it these last years? Didn't I breastfeed my children for long enough? Am I so oppressed that my body has decided I should stride the world like an Amazon in future, one breast cut off so I can move more freely? Or have I simply worn my bras too tight, used the wrong kind of deodorant and not eaten enough fruit and vegetables? Do I sing the same song as my mother and cousin and perhaps also my grandmother? The song of the bladderwrack? Whatever unresolved conflict I owe this something to, I feel little inclination to deal with it. I don't know what I'd find worse, chemotherapy or facing up to my problems. I'm too exhausted for either. Really, I have only one wish: that the something is either completely benign or else already so far advanced and furiously metastasising that it's clear I'm hurtling straight towards death. I'm too tired for hopes and fears.

As Heinz bursts out of the door to welcome Theo, I creep into the hall to my notebook and turn to the page headed: *Epitaphs for my gravestone*. It says:

> *Katharina Theodoroulakis—*
> *She didn't want to go to university anyway*
> *This wasn't at all the way I'd imagined things*
> *If ifs and ands were pots and pans…*
> I add: *She sang the song of the bladderwrack.*

A phone rings—the landline this time. Or rather, it doesn't ring—it jingles. Ringing phones have been out of fashion for some years, and I sorely miss them. Our phone plays a dire electronic version of the theme song from some cartoon show the children know and I don't. You'd think I'd have some say about the sound the phone makes in my own house—after all, I'm the one who's here most and has to listen to it. But the other jingling noises we could choose from were no better, and at least this way fifty per cent of the family are happy. Costas abstained from the vote. I wonder what his phone in Berlin sounds like and whether he got to choose the ringtone himself, and I catch myself feeling a twinge of envy at such independence.

The display shows a number I don't know. I pick up and say my name, at the same time looking down at myself and deciding that I'd better get changed after this phone call. Not only am I sweaty and wearing nothing under my jumper—I'm also stained with blood and spattered with vegetable soup.

'Good afternoon,' says a male voice at the other end. 'This is Lorelei Müller's father—Lorelei from your music class.'

I sigh, angling the phone away from my mouth and hoping he doesn't hear.

'Lorelei says she hasn't been given any homework, but I thought it was best to double-check with you. She's been so forgetful lately.'

'No, Mr Müller, that's right,' I say. 'There's no homework in the preschool music class.'

When I was starting out, I gave my music groups for children cute names, like 'Singing Frogs' and 'Musical Mice'. Numbers have gone up considerably since I started using pedagogically accurate labels: 'Preschool Music Class', 'Basic Introduction to Music'. Though they're not all as bad as Mr Müller, my classes attract precisely that species of pushy parent the media are always going on about. I'd be dealing with quite a different parent if I gave classes called 'Working in Clay' or 'Exploring Nature'.

'You shouldn't feel shy about giving homework,' says Mr Müller. 'Lorelei doesn't know what to practise for next Thursday. She's very upset about it.'

'But that's the whole idea, Mr Müller,' I say.

'That she should be upset? Why?'

'No—that she doesn't have anything to practise. The children aren't supposed to feel pressured. If they're having fun, they'll practise the things we've worked on in class anyway. They'll sing the songs at home or clap along to music or teach their brothers and sisters the dance steps they've learnt. And if they don't, that's all right too. They have to learn at their own pace.'

'I appreciate that,' says Mr Müller. 'But we don't even have notes in Lorelei's folder to give us some idea of what she's doing. My wife and I have no way of knowing whether she's singing the songs correctly, for instance.'

'There's no need. There's no wrong way to sing a song.'

'I have to disagree with you there, Mrs Theodoroulakis. I'm not sure you even understand what I mean.'

'Believe me, I understand very well...'

'The class isn't at all what we'd imagined, to be honest.'

'Research has shown...'

'I think I'll ask whether the music school has anything else on offer in this area. Many thanks for taking the time to talk to me. I can see more clearly now where the problem lies. Have a nice weekend.'

'Mr Müller,' I say, 'you're welcome to...' But he has hung up.

I sigh, loudly this time, now that I don't have to worry about Mr Müller's feelings. Perhaps I should give him Kirsten's number—she's a trained kindergarten teacher and I'm sure she'd be only too delighted to set homework.

'What's wrong?' asks Alex behind me.

I start—perhaps I also squeak a little in fright. I do that sometimes. Alex doesn't call out 'Boo!' or leap out from behind the sofa these days, but he's never lost his enthusiasm for making me jump. He does it so casually now, though, that you wouldn't think it was deliberate.

'Who was that?'

'The father of one of my preschool kids.'

'Which one?'

'Lorelei.'

'Poor girl,' says Alex. 'And poor you. I can imagine.'

I ask myself what a family therapist would have to say about the fact that my seventeen-year-old son knows the names of my pupils and takes an interest in their emotional ups and downs—and mine.

'Did you want something?' I ask.

'Just seeing if you'd finished on the phone.'

'You're expecting a call? On the landline?'

'My mobile's dead,' Alex mumbles. He isn't usually interested in phone calls—you don't need to be a detective to put two and two together.

'Tell me. Who is it?'

'A girl.'

He stares at the carpet. He looks so embarrassed, it must be serious.

'In your class?'

'The year above.'

'Do you just have a crush on her, or are you actually going out?'

'We're going out.'

The day is full of surprises. I should be pleased for Alex, but instead I feel numb. For years I assumed my son was gay. He didn't seem all that interested in girls, which I found hard to understand because I'd stumbled from one crush to the next at his age. I'd have had a suitable spiel ready if he'd come out to me, but now I don't know what to say. First I hear that my daughter has started her period, then I hear about my son's first girlfriend, and all I do is stand there looking on.

◊

There are thousands of different ways to annoy your parents. The most straightforward is to find out what they really care about and trample all over it, doing the opposite of whatever it is that they want you to do. That's how artistic careers are spawned in the households of petty bureaucrats and mohawks sprout in families where great store is set by what other people think. If I'd been asked years ago to name my Achilles heel as a parent, I'd have cited my hopeless romanticism. It wouldn't have surprised me if Alex had grown up to be a cynical womaniser, sleeping around recklessly, impregnating minors, uploading sex tapes to YouTube starring himself in the lead role—or if he'd announced grandly that he didn't believe in true love and was convinced that, biologically speaking, humans were not monogamous creatures. But I was wrong: my sore spot has turned out to be music. Serious music.

Alex always did sing nicely. He could carry a tune and mastered even quite complex melodies at an early age. Enrolling him at music school was the obvious thing to do, and he had violin lessons and then guitar lessons, both of which he loved—he never had to be bullied into going. Once he could play the guitar, though, he began to sing along to it in his room, and after a while he announced that he wanted to give up guitar lessons and take up singing instead. It was then, if not before, that I should have put my foot down. Alex was twelve—it was bound to go wrong. Since then he's been taking singing lessons from a mountain of a woman with earrings down to her shoulders and jangling bracelets—and wants to sing in musicals. I can imagine little worse. *Cats* and *The Lion King* or, God forbid, *The Phantom of the Opera*.

'The phone's free now, anyway,' I say. 'I'm going to get changed. You can manage?'

It's a rhetorical question—Alex would manage just fine even if our little town were besieged by a horde of the undead—but it's a question that mothers have to keep asking. If you don't, you might miss the moment when the answer is 'No'. You'll never know what's going on with your children just by watching them.

◊

In the hall I have a quick look at the rats, who rustle in their cage and only stare at me in astonishment when I appear, as if to say: 'What do *you* want?' I leave them in peace. They don't need me, and today, more than ever, that's a reason to like them.

Then I check my mobile and see that I have a text from Costas—I must have missed the beep. *Boring here*, he writes. *I miss you all. Did you have a good lunch? Canteen fare without pudding for me. Lots of love, C.*

He's a hypocrite. He knows perfectly well that he'd have been as unimpressed by my cooking as the others. And the fact that he assumes I'd bother to make a sit-down lunch for myself when Alex and Helli are, as far as he knows, both at school, is a sign of just how little he knows about my everyday life—even without the severed thumbs, bleeding noses and wombs, never-ending to-do lists and heaps of dirty laundry.

I take Ann-Britt's postcard into the bedroom. I'll get changed in a minute—there's soup on my jumper, after all. But first I'm going to enjoy a bit of peace and quiet.

I sit down at my desk and open the old laptop, which is all mine these days. It used to be the family computer—we let the kids use it to play educational games, watch children's television or write the occasional email to my father. Since they've acquired smartphones, though, I have the old thing to myself. Costas has an expensive wide-screen computer in his deserted study, but it's out of bounds to everyone else because it's a valuable tool of his trade and would presumably lose its aura (and thus its inspirational powers) if it were to be contaminated by the programs Alex and Helli like to watch. Why my husband still has a study at home when he's had an office in Berlin for a year now (presumably equipped with another expensive tool or two equally uncontaminated by children's shows), while I make do with a desk in our bedroom and the ancient family laptop—that's something I prefer not to ask. There are some questions that would bring so many others in their wake that it's easier to ignore them. Life isn't perfect, and as much as I'd like to be treated as an equal, fighting for the same rights and privileges as a man is hard work—and who has the energy for that? I've always thought it was a mistake to make women's liberation entirely women's responsibility. You can't say *Just do what men do* and leave it there. Men have to be prepared to make some slight concessions too. In this life, I'm happy just to have found a man I could love sincerely. If I happen to be granted further lives, I'll be only too glad to try to wangle a study of my own out of my future partner—and society at large.

Ann-Britt would laugh at me, but she never was much good at putting herself in other people's shoes. That's a big part of why I appreciate her friendship—and all those miles between us. She shows me what another life might look like, and I feel happier about the choices I've made when I realise that I'm not really jealous of her. I need Ann-Britt to feel good about my life, and I suspect she feels the same about me.

I look at the Maori men on the postcard for a while, letting the suspense build. Then I turn the card over and read:

Dear Kath,

The first signs of summer are here and I'm going to miss my jumper, which is sleeping out the summer at the back of the wardrobe. Lately I've taken to growing orchids in my windows. They look as if they're made of plastic and are very low-maintenance—they'd be just your thing. How's the Baltic? Is it frozen? And you? Have you woken up your jumpers for the winter?

Love as ever, and from Rob and Leyla too,
Anni

Her handwriting is neat and elaborate—something I've often observed in people who grew up in the east before the Wall came down. Ann-Britt adores writing and takes forever over it, and she's deliberately cryptic in her letters, thinking it's sophisticated. It was the same when we wrote each other messages to hide in our private postbox on the way to school, first my turn, then hers—one letter a day, which we'd pick up and read on the way home. We saw each other in class anyway, of course, and had ample opportunity to talk, but writing made us feel grown-up. We were proud of our 'correspondence' and adored putting in allusions and code words that no one else could have understood. Ann-Britt invented nicknames for the boys I was in love with, dubbing them silly things like 'Polo Neck' or 'Gel Head'. One was called 'Sleeping Pill', and another 'Asparagus Tarzan'. I didn't let it get to me—I knew she wanted me all to herself, but I was never close enough to any of those boys for it to constitute a real danger to our friendship. These days Ann-Britt and I write each other sporadic postcards and slightly more frequent emails. Ann-Britt sends me photos of her cat, Leyla, and of her house, which she's always having improved in some way. I send her pictures of myself with the children, in which I'm invariably a blur because I'm busy keeping Helli still until the photo's been taken.

Ann-Britt knows very well that orchids aren't my thing— or if she doesn't know, she ought to, after all these years. How could she not? You can't misconstrue someone for thirty years—not even Ann-Britt could manage that. I suppose she's only joking.

We've known each other since our first year at of high school. She had moved to the area—'from somewhere quite different,' we were told. It was only later that I discovered she had emigrated with her family from East Germany. She was average in everything, except perhaps her looks, but then we all were pretty in our different ways, simply because we were young and made an effort. She was slender as a beanpole, not boyish but delicate, even nymph-like. She liked drawing and sport, and was what people generally describe as 'bright'— the word we use when someone is blessed with a quick wit but 'intelligent' seems too strong a word. She was incredibly conscientious and always put her full effort into everything she did. I smiled condescendingly at this, surprised at the time she spent on even the most trivial tasks our teachers set us. I didn't see the point in doing any more than you were supposed to.

There was much that she envied me, and it seemed to me that she was right to do so. After all, my parents had a house with a garden, while she lived in a flat, and I had plenty of pocket money, whereas she had to work to finance her teenage desires: an angora jumper that needed washing by hand, a small television set for her room, cinema tickets and enough left over to go out for a pizza afterwards. I had enough money for all that, and took it for granted, though none of it, except the cinema, was of any interest to me. I ate pizza with Ann-Britt, admired her jumper, congratulated her on her television and understood her envy, which only seemed natural.

She didn't tell me she also envied me my talents—not until later, when we were grown-up and she had outstripped me so far career-wise that I couldn't have caught up with her even if I had harnessed all my talents at once—and I had a few. There was a time when I had trouble deciding which of my gifts to cultivate. I had music lessons from the age of six, playing various recorders, then the flute, and eventually also the oboe. Painting and drawing were among my hobbies, although I only ever painted for myself, because I found in painting a deep sense of satisfaction and inner peace that nothing else could arouse in me. The results were not unimpressive and I was aware of that, but I preferred not to pronounce my pictures finished or to show them to anyone, content to slip from one painting or drawing project to the next. Languages were something else I'd always had a gift for—I could learn whole pages of vocabulary with no trouble at all, and understood grammar without needing to have it explained to me. For a few years I took classical dance lessons and riding lessons, and because I read every book I could lay my hands on, I had a pretty extensive general knowledge. None of my achievements cost me much effort, and I pitied Ann-Britt because she had to sit on her bed swotting in the evenings if we had a test at school the next day. It seemed pretty pointless to me—hadn't our teachers taught us everything we were going to be tested on? Why bother revising?

When we were together, Ann-Britt called the shots, and I never questioned it. She didn't have what I had—she didn't have the house or the riding lessons—and if it made her happy to decide what I did, I was glad to oblige. Wasn't that what friends were for?

But there was one talent she did possess: Ann-Britt could blend in like a chameleon. And she had plans. When we talked about the future, she knew exactly what she wanted. She wanted to live abroad, without children—and preferably without a man. She wanted to wear suits and high-heeled shoes, and have an important job where she was treated with respect. She also wanted a big flat and enough money to do it up exactly as she pleased. Maybe a cat too.

I didn't know what I wanted. Part of me would have liked to travel and see the world. Another part of me didn't really want to grow up. Most of the time I thought I'd like to be a musician and lead a bohemian life—not that I knew the word in those days. At other times I wanted to be a writer or perhaps an opera singer, and sometimes I thought I might be an actor. I certainly didn't want high-heeled shoes or an important job—I wanted to create something or make something happen. It didn't matter what it was.

The year my mother was quietly dying, Ann-Britt went to America on a school exchange program. When she returned, neither of us was the person we'd been before.

Ann-Britt's family didn't have enough money to send her to America, but that didn't stop her. It was the first time I fully grasped her particular talent and saw how much more useful it would be to her than all the gifts I was blessed with. She applied for a government grant, studying for it as if for an important exam. It would never have occurred to me that you could *prepare* to submit an application, that there were criteria you could meet or fail to meet, questions to which you could respond correctly or incorrectly—let alone that my poor, disadvantaged friend, so undistinguished in so many respects, would know exactly which side of herself she had to show to persuade the selection committee that she was better qualified than all the other candidates. Because that's exactly what she did. She outstripped all her competitors and was the only applicant in the entire state to be awarded the grant.

While she was away, Ann-Britt sent me letters from the US. She sounded thoroughly happy and had clearly struck it lucky with her host family. At last she had a house and garden and was living the life she deserved. By then I was struggling with the washing machine and frozen meals—and with the silence and mood swings of my teenage sister, who was making my life even more difficult than it already was by refusing to accept that our mother was dying.

Years later, Ann-Britt's host parents came to visit her in Germany and she invited me round to meet them. They were the most exhausting people I had ever encountered—yet Ann-Britt had genuinely enjoyed their company. In the USA too, then, Ann-Britt's ability to blend in had turned out to be her greatest strength. She always knew what was expected of her and could, if she wanted, be anyone's perfect daughter. I, meanwhile, still didn't see why it wasn't enough to be gifted.

After our leaving exams, for which I did almost no revision while Ann-Britt followed a rigorous and detailed study schedule over a period of several weeks, we went our separate ways, but we began to send postcards back and forth, keeping each other up to date. There were letters too sometimes, phone calls and later emails, but the postcards persisted. Ann-Britt studied English and politics, did internships in London and Cape Town and landed a job at a German organisation in New Zealand. Before long she had a nice flat, wore suits to work and bought herself a cat. She hired a private coach to teach her Spanish, just because she felt like it, set up a reading group and spent her holidays on a Mediterranean island, attending courses in watercolour painting and charcoal drawing. When she was offered a better job that required a residence permit, she rustled up an attractive, interesting, well-educated man who loved her sincerely and made her the proposal she wanted, never suspecting that he was doing anything other than fulfilling his own dreams. She got her residence permit and her job, and wrote to me that although the man hadn't been part of her life plan, he was turning out to be a real bonus. I wrote back, saying that I was working on my thesis, was pregnant again, and looked forward to the weekends, when Costas cooked proper meals for us all.

◊

I re-read the postcard. In a moment of weakness I think of writing straight back and telling Ann-Britt about the something. It seems to me that the information would be safe in New Zealand. But I decide against it, because it wouldn't change a thing, and the something might get silly ideas if it felt it was being taken seriously.

I check my email on the laptop, but there's nothing in my inbox from Ann-Britt. I'll have to make do with the card for the time being. Instead there's an email from the head of the other kindergarten where I give weekly classes, wanting to know whether the music group is going to put on a little performance at the Christmas party—and two emails from parents of kids at the music school, both asking why there's no Christmas party scheduled for the preschool group. I think of all the Christmas parties I had to go to when Alex and Helli were little—all those crumbly biscuits and sticky plastic cups of cordial—at the sports club, at kindergarten, at school, in the town hall. Have these parents gone mad? I take my diary and look to see how many afternoons I have at the music school before Christmas and which of them might work for a party. I wonder whether I'll still be entirely myself by then—or will I already have lost a part of myself, and be on the way out?

I clap the laptop shut without answering the emails. It's almost the weekend—the parents and their questions can wait until Monday along with everything else. Now it's time for me to turn myself back into a good mother and go and shoo Helli out of her room. I take Ann-Britt's postcard with me so I can stick it on the fridge when I get down to the kitchen.

◊

I don't go in Helli's room anymore unless I absolutely have to. If I need anything from her, I tend to knock at the door and sort things out from there. Every few weeks I help Helli to clear a path or two through the mess so that she can get from her bed to the wardrobe or the door without squashing anything. I take a big bin liner in with me and get rid of any mouldy food. That's as much as I have the strength for—and besides, the belief that everyone has a right to privacy is deeply ingrained in me. If you grow up in a terrace on a housing estate, you're always going to be obsessed with privacy. I took photos of Helli's room along to the preliminary consultations before her tests, afraid that they wouldn't believe me if I only described the scale of the mess.

I knock because it's time for Helli to get ready for riding. I've put on a new top—a kind of feminine version of the lumberjack shirt, short and close-fitting, but in typical lumberjack checks and that nice soft flannel that was, until recently, the preserve of the male. I managed not to brush against my breast when I was changing, and to think of nice things. If the urge to feel for the something threatens to overpower me when I'm getting changed, I sing the

glorious trio from *Così fan tutte*—usually Dorabella's part—
which requires so much concentration that the something is
edged out of my thoughts. The same technique worked two
weeks ago when I was soaping myself under the shower—it
really was terribly banal, just like in one of those uninspired
made-for-TV movies—and felt the something for the first
time. I wonder whether Kilian approves of lumberjack shirts
on women of my age. I remember the way he used to make
fun of my shoes because he thought them too sensible. I'll
probably end up getting changed again before he arrives.

I go on knocking—pretty firmly now, so Helli can hear
me even if she's got her headphones on. We have to be on time
and really need to get a move on. We're picking Cindi up on
the way and also need to leave time for grooming before the
lesson begins.

Riding does Helli good. I often wonder why I didn't think
of it earlier. The poor horses at the riding school are just
like her—always being told what to do—and they understand
her impulsiveness. Some are jumpy, others jaded, but none
of them seems to feel the way a horse should. It's possible
they don't even know who or what they really are. They treat
Helli like one of them. One consequence of that, I'm afraid,
is that Helli is occasionally put in her place with a well-aimed
bite. Usually, though, she manages to concentrate for a whole
forty-five-minute lesson, presumably because she's in nonstop
motion and gets a good shaking up. Maybe we should sit her
on a vibrating chair to do her homework.

I keep the riding things in the cupboard off the hall—
partly because they smell, and partly because it saves us having

to spend hours hunting for them under the piles of stuff in Helli's room. Experience has taught me that it's best to supervise Helli when she's getting changed. I open her bedroom door and she looks up and smiles. She's sitting on the bed and does indeed have headphones over her ears—and a magazine in front of her, which she's reading as she paints her nails. I make clicking noises with my tongue, bobbing up and down and raising my hands as if I were holding reins. It works: Helli gets up and takes off her headphones. She leaves the little bottle of nail polish on her bedside table with the lid off, and the magazine slides to the floor—right in the middle of the clear path between bed and door, so that she can't help but tread on it on her way out.

We go down the stairs together and I hand Helli her jodhpurs and boots. She chatters on incessantly, telling me about singers I've never heard of and film-star couples who've split up or got back together again, using words I'd rather not hear from the mouth of an eleven-year-old. I've got used to it, though—dragging other women down and calling them obscene names seems to be the done thing these days.

She pulls off her jeans one leg at a time as she talks. Then she breaks off because she's just noticed an umbrella she doesn't recognise in the umbrella stand. She pulls it out, puts it up and walks up and down with it.

'Where's this from?' she asks. 'Is it new?'

'Jodhpurs,' I say.

Helli sighs and discards the umbrella. I fold it up and put it away while she obediently attends to her jodhpurs. Her thighs are soft and white and pudgy, but the jodhpurs are so tight that they transform her legs into sturdy, shapely columns. Helli doesn't notice—she's not self-conscious about her body yet. I live in fear of the day when she starts seeing herself through the critical eyes of others. Almost all children think themselves beautiful. They love their round tummies and soft skin and are proud of the charming functionality of their design. Their legs can run and jump, their hands can wave and hold scissors and paintbrushes—how could you suggest they're not beautiful?

As if Helli has read my mind, she goes to the mirror and begins to gather her hair into a ponytail. She fiddles around with it, tugs a few strands over her forehead and examines herself through narrowed eyes.

'Do you think I should grow my hair longer?'

'Zip!' I say.

She does up her jodhpurs and begins to get into her boots. She manages the first without help. Then she discovers a hole in her left sock, flops down on her bum and begins to poke about avidly in the hole with her index finger.

'Boots!' I say.

Now Alex saunters onto the scene. He comes down the stairs, languid as a big cat, grins at me and vanishes into the bathroom. With one boot on and the other off, Helli struggles to her feet and goes after him.

'No, Helli, we have to hurry,' I say.

'I have to go to the loo because of you know what,' she calls back to me.

'Is my blue shirt in the dryer?' Alex calls through the closed door.

'No,' I call back.

'Shit. Can you iron it dry or something?'

'No.'

They clatter about in the bathroom and I use the time to gather my own things together. Coat, notebook, phone, bag. I look for a scarf in the hall, but all I find is a tiny bandana Alex used to wear when he was a toddler. I'll have to turn up my coat collar—I always feel the cold around my neck more than anywhere.

From the bathroom I hear Alex declaiming: 'Is this a tampon which I see before me?'

'What else would it be?'

The toilet is flushed, the tap turned on. In a powerful voice, Alex sings: 'Here's the smell of the blood still. All the perfumes of Arabia will not sweeten this little hand.'

'Idiot,' says Helli.

Sometimes I think brothers and sisters are more important than parents. Parents love you no matter what, but brothers and sisters see you the way you really are.

When at last the two of them are finished with their toilet antics and emerge from the bathroom, I hand Helli her second riding boot. 'Is there a musical of *Macbeth*?' I ask Alex, who's slinking, big-cat-like, back upstairs.

'Nope,' he says. 'Not yet. Be great though, wouldn't it?'

BY THE TIME we're in the car at last, it's quarter past two and I still haven't got the spare room ready.

Our street is about as quiet as a parent could wish for. There are old trees in the front gardens and lovely old-fashioned street lamps that light the pavements on both sides of the road at night. On a day like today, the smell of log fires hangs in the otherwise clear, frosty air, giving everything a cosy, nostalgic feel. Cindi lives in a family-friendly neigh-bourhood of a different kind. Her house is in what was once a new development—one of the ones with a map at the entrance because it's all too easy to get lost, if you don't know your way around. Four out of five roads end in turning bays. I know exactly where Cindi lives, but even so, I twice flick the indica-tor on at the wrong turning because they all look the same.

The house itself, though, is different from the others. The garden is big and full of toys, garden tools, rain barrels, crates and heaps of gravel, wood and sand. Cindi's father is always about to embark on some building project or other—improving the house, either inside or out—but unlike Costas, who tends to go about these things with the perfectionism of a professional architect, aiming to make the house as elegant and pleasant to live in as possible, Cindi's father seems to be looking for an excuse to get away from his family while giving others the impression that he's doing a great job of taking care of them.

Cindi is waiting—she comes out to the car and opens the door before I've even finished parking. Without saying hello to me, she drops onto the back seat beside Helli: 'That was some show you put on today, Helli. Everyone was talking about it. There was a trail of blood all the way to the staffroom.'

My daughter is too tall and heavy now to need a booster seat, and so is Cindi, but I still haven't got used to seeing them sitting in the back with so little protection. The seatbelts look as if they'd strangle them if I happened to brake too sharply. Alex could get his learner's permit this year and start taking lessons, but he claims not to have the time. His singing teacher says these are critical years for his voice training. If he wants to get into the academy of performing arts, he'll have to be impeccably prepared.

◊

Sissi got ready for her entrance exam without a word to anyone. Our father hadn't shown any interest in her for a long time—except when she shouted and started smashing things. Sissi must have spoken to her cello teacher, and perhaps to others at the music school or to her one friend, a girl she knew from the regional young musicians' championship and often talked to on the phone for hours. I was halfway through university myself and knew nothing about it—until Sissi turned up on my doorstep one day with her cello, to play to me and see what I thought. She played Haydn, the second Bach suite, the Chopin sonata (I had to imagine the piano accompaniment), and it was like having music injected straight into my soul. It was so beautiful it made me want to weep—I'd never heard her play like that—but there was pain in that beauty, and bitterness. I had the disconcerting thought that our mother's death had given Sissi something other musicians her age didn't have. I felt frightened listening to her—frightened for her, because she looked so fragile behind her cello and because her playing laid bare every nerve—a sensitivity so great that she could never be happy, or healthy. Her decision to devote herself to music was a decision to spend the rest of her life confronting her grief, stirring it up, so that it would never fade, never retreat into the background. Dedicating yourself to classical music meant taking yourself to the edge over and over again.

Of course Sissi got a place at the academy, and because all her concerts were in Lübeck we saw each other often during those years. She threw herself into being a musician, if not quite in the way I'd expected. Over time, Sissi developed a deep disdain for permanent appointments and the life of an orchestra musician, but she played out all her traumas constantly, endlessly, by throwing herself at the most egocentric men she could find.

◊

The road to the stables is narrow and winding. Country lanes in this part of the world have laws all their own, and one of these stipulates that no road must be straight for longer than it takes to perform a quick overtaking manoeuvre. The hedgerows to the right and left were cut right back not long ago, and the brutally lopped branches are still lying in the fields, now romantically covered in hoarfrost. Every twenty metres or so is a 'field tree', a small tree that has been left unlopped so that the rest of the hedgerow can get its bearings when it begins to grow back—all those eager bushes and trees and shrubs that shoot back up every spring without fail, year after year, though they're regularly shorn bare by slow-moving machines. Nothing here is left to grow the way it wants. And yet few landscapes are as soothing to the human soul.

Seeing Helli alone with her phone, you'd imagine that young people today must have trouble talking face to face. But the two girls on the back seat are clear proof that girls are just as capable of talking and giggling nonstop these days as they've always been. They shuffle up as close together as the seatbelts will allow, their heads bowed over Cindi's phone. They don't look out of the window. They miss the hoarfrost and the powdered furrows, the frozen ditches and the low winter sun shining as if through milk glass.

Cindi's real name is Cinderella—excellent camouflage for someone who is highly gifted and prefers to pretend she isn't. No one would dream that a girl called Cinderella might be intelligent. On her very first day at school, her solicitous teachers put her in a pigeonhole labelled *disadvantaged*. That is, in fact, far from the truth. Her parents are university-educated people with full-time jobs and irreproachable environmental credentials. (Cindi is the youngest of four, so almost everything she owns is much handed-down.) But because Cindi is a good girl as well as being highly gifted, she swiftly conformed to expectations and made herself at home in that pigeonhole. Her fate was sealed when she took up with Helli, two years her junior in the grade below her. She even re-sat Year Six for Helli, so that the two of them could at last be disruptive in class as well as out of it.

The pair of them have a hilarious time looking at some photos or other they've been sent, then they shriek in unison and take a photo of themselves, leaning in towards each other and holding the phone at arm's length. I suppose the selfie is immediately sent to all the girls in their class—or almost all, for there are bound to be one or two whose parents are stricter than I am and haven't bought their daughters smartphones. Then there will be a couple more (who might or might not change from week to week) who aren't part of the group and whose 'friend requests' go ignored, and you can bet there's some dreamy girl too who doesn't even want a phone because she thinks she's someone out of *Harry Potter* and is so absorbed in lying as low as possible in this Muggle world that she can't begin to understand how anyone could be interested in photos of builder's bums and puke-covered pizza, unconfirmed reports about the sexual orientation of their history teacher or selfies shot on the back seat of a VW on the way to a riding lesson.

If I were young today, I'd probably be the *Harry Potter* girl. Until my mother's death I lived in a fantasy world and never had any idea what was going on around me. At Helli's age I fell madly in love for the first time. It was an exquisite, confusing feeling that kept me awake at night. The boy was called Dirk—he was quite a bit older than me and very good- looking. Once a week we sang together in the school choir, standing next to each other where the second sopranos flanked the tenors. I sang especially nicely for him and always put on some of my mother's perfume before cycling to choir practice. I left my hair loose for him too—it was incredibly long at the time, which meant that it was also incredibly impractical—more or less unmanageable unless it was in a plait. It would never have crossed my mind to reveal my feelings to Dirk, let alone that he might reciprocate them. He shared his carton of apple juice with me, letting me suck through the same straw, and hung around next to my bike after choir practice to talk to me. When he dropped out of choir because our rehearsals overlapped with his basketball games, he tried to persuade me to take up basketball. I just didn't get it. It was only later, when I'd stopped living in my fantasy world and learnt to do laundry and fry fish fingers, that I realised he might have been in love with me too. I didn't take up basketball, though—I stayed on in choir, silently grieving. I hardly saw him after that—our school had two playgrounds, so the younger children didn't often bump into the sixth-formers. Much later, in the age of the internet, I googled him and found out he'd gone on to be a chimneysweep.

On the back seat Cindi is saying: 'Actually, Pluto isn't a planet. It's been downgraded. Hasn't it, Katha?'

Sometimes it seems as if I grew up in another world when I remember that I used to call my friends' parents Mr and Mrs as a matter of course. First names weren't so important back then—they were for close friends and official forms, and that was it. You had the same surname as your husband, no matter how ridiculous it might be, and if your children had the same names as everyone else's, that was proof that you'd chosen well. Wacky spellings were seen as pretentious, and no adult ever had to listen carefully as a child spelt out its name, after asking (in a nannyish voice and with no attempt, of course, to crouch down to the child's level): 'And what's your name, dear?'

'Some years ago, I believe,' I say, referring to Pluto and its downgrading.

'What?' says Helli.

Cindi says: 'Pluto is now Mickey Mouse's dog.'

'Oh, I see,' says Helli.

That's Cindi's strategy: if she accidentally betrays the fact that she knows more than the person she's speaking to, she says something to confuse everyone and throw them off the track. Besides knowing that Pluto is no longer a planet, I'm sure she's also aware he's the god of the underworld—and would be quite capable of citing a few details about his marital status and living arrangements. But she disguises her intelligence by turning everything into a joke.

We arrive at the riding school and stop in the car park. The girls set off alone—they know the way. Sometimes I go as far as the stables with them, share in their frustration or delight at the horses allocated to them, breathe in straw dust and saunter about for a while. Occasionally I even watch a riding lesson, but only very rarely, so as not to put pressure on Helli. Usually I wait in the car until the two girls return, filthy, sweaty and smelly—ready to be driven home.

Today I'm tired—I don't feel like getting out, although I know that the cold will soon be creeping in regardless. I always keep a blanket in the boot once winter has set in, in case the car gives up the ghost in an unexpected snowdrift and I have to wait for help cuddled up on the back seat with the children. I also have two muesli bars in the glove box and a small plastic bag with a change of underwear and socks for Helli. She used to kick off her shoes and socks in the back of the car and then forget to put them on again before getting out. And it's not so very long ago that she'd get distracted on the way to the toilet and wouldn't remember where she'd been heading until her pants were wet. I have bandaids in my handbag—coloured and plain—along with a small bottle of hand disinfectant, a whole load of tissues, rescue remedy, cough lozenges and a Swiss Army knife. In the glove box, fastened to the registration documents with a paperclip, is a piece of paper saying in nice clear writing: *Please ring the following number in an emergency.* Written beneath it is Costas's mobile number. I don't know whether other mothers drive about similarly equipped or whether you have to be semi-orphaned at the age of seventeen to be like this.

It will soon be time for my telephone conference with Sissi. I'm not particularly interested in her problems today, but I put my phone ready on the passenger seat, alongside the ice-scraper beaver, the shorn-off wing mirror, the blood-smeared tissue and my handbag. While I'm waiting I put this morning's CD on again.

Protschka sings: 'One radiant summer's morning...' so exquisitely softly that you'd think the flowers he's singing about really were whispering sweet, tender, idyllic things. But the piano, with its clear, rolling motifs, tells of the insatiable anguish the poet has to bear—anguish that knows no relief and will from now on be the ground bass of his life. Even the flowers in the garden will no longer talk of anything but lovesickness. The poet has been cheated and betrayed and abandoned, but his love is so great that such a paltry emotion as anger doesn't stand a chance. There's no curing such a man—he may be wounded, but it doesn't stop him loving. That kind of love can be the end of you.

My eyes closed, my head against the headrest, I hear Protschka sing: 'Don't be angry with our sister, you sad, pale man.' Some lines, I'm afraid, make me weepy in spite of myself—bring me out in gooseflesh, too. It's embarrassing, but it's the way I am—even experience, which hardens us against all kinds of sentimentality, hasn't changed me. I used to cry in movies when the heroine was disappointed in love. Since I've had children, this no longer affects me much, but I howl like a banshee when film families say goodbye on train stations. I can tolerate shootings and muster a certain scientific interest in mutilated corpses, but the mere mention of cruelty to children makes me feel sick. But the gooseflesh strikes without fail when I hear certain passages of music—always the same ones—and each time I'm surprised and ashamed and ever so slightly pleased, because at least some things in my life never change. The gooseflesh is a visible reminder of an earlier self, an essential self, that still lives on inside me, even if no one can see it.

Once, when we were rehearsing Dvořák's Mass at school, I came out in gooseflesh during the *Agnus Dei*, right in the middle of summer. It was so noticeable that Ann-Britt nudged me, pointed at my bare arms and whispered: 'You love this, don't you?' I always wore long-sleeved tops to choir practice after that.

I open my eyes, dig my notebook out of my coat pocket and leaf through it until I find the page where it says:

> *Pieces guaranteed to bring the gooseflesh out on me:*
> * *Schubert's string quartet, 1st movement, violin passage*
> * *Mozart's Kleine Nachtmusik, 2nd movement, in spite of all those long evenings when I hummed it over and over to Helli to get her to sleep*
> * *2nd Bach suite, Sarabande, preferably played in our sitting room by Sissi, and listened to with closed eyes*
> * *Così fan tutte, trio*
> * *Chopin's cello sonata, doesn't matter what recording—even an amateur concert would do the trick.*

The list is long. It goes on like this until halfway down the second page.

I add:
> * *One Radiant Summer's Morning, last passage, probably best in the Pears/Britten recording*

And:
> * *Dvořák's Mass, Agnus Dei*

Looking up from my notebook, I see Helli and Cindi coming out of the stables, their horses saddled and bridled. Both lead their horses by the reins, their riding helmets tucked casually under their arms. They won't put the helmets on until the very last minute, just before swinging themselves into the saddles. Now that the girls are eleven and thirteen, helmets are starting to be uncool. When they were nine, they could hardly wait to put them on—like real riders, but now they think being safe and following the rules is boring. I'll just have to hope they begin to see sense by their eighteenth birthdays, when it will be up to them what they do with their heads and what dangers they expose themselves to.

Helli is leading Aladdin, and Cindi has Scheherazade, whose name is a struggle for any child to read or pronounce. The kids call her 'Sherri', so there go Helli, Cindi, Sherri and Aladdin. Aladdin is a stubborn old thing—he and Helli always seem to me a particularly explosive mix, but the riding teacher likes to match horses and riders according to the birds-of-a-feather principle. The two girls lead their horses to the riding ring, and now more girls are coming out of the stable, all with their helmets under their arms.

I wave, but Helli and Cindi aren't looking. They're deep in conversation and I can tell from Helli's jerky movements that there's trouble brewing. Without thinking twice, I open the car door and go after them. It's possible that everything will sort itself out, but it's also possible that Helli will erupt at any moment, and I feel it best to be on stand-by. Maybe I can stop things from getting out of hand. But how? I'm too far away and too late—same as always, same as all mothers, the world over. It isn't enough to notice the danger when it's upon you—you have to anticipate it. You can't let your attention slip for a second—it's no good listening to music or trying to snatch time for yourself.

I stride out towards the girls and their horses, calling Helli's name, trying to distract her and make her look at me. Instead I hear her burst out at Cindi: 'Fucking cow! I'll kick your fucking head in.'

She puts her foot in the stirrup and swings herself onto Aladdin's back. Before I realise what she's doing, she yells, 'I hate you all,' and Aladdin whinnies and rears up, his front hooves pawing the ground like a horse in a western. Then he tears off. Cindi has her hands full trying to calm Scheherazade; the other girls gape as a cat slinks across Aladdin's path and he shies away, arching his back, then gallops towards the woods at breakneck speed. My daughter is bouncing up and down in the saddle, the stirrups dangling free. She's let go of the reins and is clinging to the pommel. Her helmet is on the ground at Cindi's feet.

I run after her, but it's pointless, of course. Even a horse going at a leisurely trot would be faster—so I turn back, tear the reins out of Cindi's hands and mount Scheherazade. I give her a stronger kick than I mean to and she streaks off, head held high—after Helli, into the woods.

◊

In tarot, which Ann-Britt and I dabbled in as teenagers, there's a card called the Knight of Swords which shows a rider charging along on a horse, brandishing a sword. He wears an expression of furious determination, and scraps of cloud are scudding along behind him—clearly the weather is as frenzied as he is. At the same time, though, there's something pointless about his frenzy because there's no enemy on the card. I came to hate the Knight of Swords because I never drew any other card. Ann-Britt would laugh every time, and every time she would read to me from a tarot manual written by the disciple of some Indian guru: the Knight of Swords, she would tell me, tried to resolve things rationally, and so never achieved any good. His sword stood for analytical thinking, which destroyed everything in the world that was beautiful or full of feeling. I began to dread the card and ended up sneaking it out of the pack. Ann-Britt never noticed.

Chasing after Helli, I'm filled with panic and anger. I know galloping after her like this is pointless, but somewhere beneath my rage and panic I'm enjoying this. The icy wind lashes my face, the stables no more than a blur as I fly past. The only thing I can make out clearly is the horse's head in front of me, and instead of yelling, 'Helli, stop!' which would be the appropriate thing to do, I want to let out an ox's bellow, a primal scream like the roar that broke out of me when I pushed my children's fat heads through my narrow pelvis.

As I'm carried through the woods at full gallop, I realise that the Indian mystic got it wrong. The Knight of Swords isn't charging into battle. He's running away. He knows he doesn't stand a chance but, like a cornered animal, he's decided to make a lunge for it and is hurling himself forward in a desperate attempt to save himself. He should be pitied, not feared.

Helli is sitting in the middle of the forest path watching me approach. Aladdin is a few metres further on, drenched in sweat, his flanks quivering. My horse slows of her own accord, allowing me to focus and regain control over myself, the reins, the situation. As soon as Scheherazade has dropped back to a walk, I slip out of the saddle and rush to Helli. She's crying softly, quite unlike her usual self.

'Are you hurt?' I ask breathlessly.

'Don't think so. Not much,' she says. She shows me a few scrapes on her arms and hands. There's a graze on her face too and leaf mould on her jacket.

I'm hot—my cheeks are burning. Here among the trees there's no cold wind and the ground is muddy, not frozen. The horses amble over to us. Aladdin sniffs Helli's hood and sprays a small shower of horse snot down her neck. She looks up at him, strokes him between the nostrils and murmurs: 'It's all right. Wasn't your fault.'

I've never seen her like this. Both the soft, distraught weeping and the implicit admission of guilt are completely out of character. She usually wails like a fire-engine, throwing her head back and opening her mouth so wide that you can see her molars, and it's often hard to tell whether she's angry or sad. She sometimes curls up on the floor, or even tears her hair or punches the wall. She can't calm down on her own—I have to wrap her in my arms and hold her tight until she stops squirming and goes all limp. She ends up conked out over my shoulder or on my lap, giving the occasional hiccup as the sobbing gradually subsides.

If she's angry or gets into trouble, it is, of course, always someone else's fault. Often it's objects that rebel or get in her way or play up, and sometimes it's fate that's unkind to her, but most of the time I'm the one to blame for her tantrums. I give her the wrong glass, fill it with the wrong drink, distract her so that she doesn't watch out and runs into the open door, give her reproachful looks to make her feel guilty about some incident in the school cafeteria that I can't possibly know about, nag her to do her homework, brush her hair or thank Grandad for a Christmas present, or freak out her friends with embarrassing small talk, asking them how old they are or what they're called or where they live. In the end, what it comes down to is that she needn't have got angry at all, if only I'd been able to read her mind.

◊

One day, many years ago, when Helli was still in kindergarten, I rang Costas to get him to come home. Helli had got up at five that morning, pushed a chair over to the kitchen counter, climbed onto the benchtop and taken a kind of inventory of the crockery cupboard. Apparently her plan was to sort out all the cups and plates she didn't like, and I was woken by loud smashing sounds coming from the kitchen. While I was dealing with the broken china, Helli decided to have a bath and turned on all the taps in the bathroom. She'd already emptied the shampoo into the bath to get a good foam going and was about to add a second bottle when I caught her. She thought it most unreasonable of me to deny her this early-morning bubble bath, and kicked me and pulled my hair while I threw up in the toilet. I was twelve weeks pregnant with Berenike and this start to the day was more than my stomach could take. By the time our alarm clock went off later that morning, Helli had gone back to sleep between Costas and me, and we slipped out of bed carefully so as not to wake her. She slept so long and so deeply that I rang the kindergarten to let them know I wouldn't be bringing her in. I told myself she should get all the sleep she needed, but to be honest I was too scared to wake her.

I don't remember all the details of that day. As soon as Helli was up and about again, one tantrum followed another. She scrawled secret messages all over the furniture with a marker and climbed on the kitchen counter whenever I wasn't looking. She tore up books and made a sort of papier-mâché out of the scraps in the toilet bowl. She experimented with her pee, aiming into various-sized containers and then pouring it all in together and mixing it up with oats into a soup that she wanted to take to the homeless people outside the super-market down the road. I must have forgotten to lock the front door on the inside after fetching the post—at any rate, Helli had reached the first set of traffic lights with her soup by the time I found her. She hit me and bit me and spat at me and scratched my cheek bloody, and when I tried to cart her back home she poured her oats-and-pee over my trousers, then ran onto the road while I was busy puking at the bottom of a lamppost.

By the end I was contemplating suicide. The easy method—stepping out in front of a truck, with no time wasted over plans or preparations. I can't remember now what it felt like, but I can see myself sitting on the edge of the bed while Helli writhed on the floor, screaming with fury. I see my face, stunned and vacant, my tense, desperate posture, and I wonder at myself. What kind of a person contemplates suicide in such circumstances? We hear so many stories of parents who shake their children to death or throw them against walls—but how many mothers step out in front of trucks each year, so terrified that they'll shake or throw their children that they turn their murderous rage on themselves?

I rang Costas and told him to come straight home. And he did. I'd never done that before. I usually asked other people for help—Heinz, for instance, or one of the kindergarten mothers I was friendly with. When I'd hung up, I let Helli watch television and eat ice-cream, and lay down on the sofa for half an hour until I felt slightly better. When Costas saw me, he understood. I didn't need to explain. I've never told him about my thoughts that day—I've never told anyone. But I see myself sitting on the edge of the bed, my body tense, my eyes vacant, and I know that it really could have been the end—that there's a dark, tragic side to me that was prepared to do anything.

◊

The horses are steaming—I can smell their coats and the trees and a whiff of the waterproofing on Helli's jacket. For a moment I can't remember how I got here. The winter woods are very quiet. I try to put an arm around Helli but she pushes me away. It's a gentle push, not a shove, and the forlorn, lonely feeling leaves me, just for a moment.

'Mum,' she says, and there's something in the way she says it that makes my heart swell. Alex doesn't need me anymore, not really, but Helli's still my little girl, at least for now. Sometimes I wish she'd stay my little girl forever, so I could always take care of her.

'Yes?'

'Can I get that medicine?'

For a moment, I don't know what she's talking about. I rummage frantically through my brain trying to figure out what she's talking about. *Medicine?*

'You mean painkillers? Does anything hurt? Move your legs,' I say.

She moves her legs, watching them intently. At the edge of the path, Aláddin and Scheherazade begin to crop stray blades of grass left over from summer. Greenish froth gathers on their lips.

'No, they're all right,' says Helli.

'Tummy ache?' I ask, suddenly remembering what torture riding lessons were for me when I had my period. Jolting along on a trotting horse was agony, and as soon as the lesson was over I had to make a dash for the toilets before the blood started to run down my legs. The already shapeless sanitary pad in my pants was a bloody, twisted sausage by the time I got out of the saddle.

'Why?' asks Helli.

'You wanted medicine.'

'Oh, yeah. I meant the one the woman talked about where I do the tests.'

'Why are you asking about that now?'

Tears gush out of Helli's eyes. 'I don't know what happened just now.' She starts to sob again. 'All I remember is that I was really angry with Cindi for talking such shit and the next thing I know I'm in the woods, falling off some stupid horse. I'm always in trouble at school too and I don't know why. What am I doing wrong? What should I do differently? What should I be like?'

'You should just be Helli,' I say. But that makes her cry even more. She's so choked up now she can hardly speak.

'I don't want to be Helli anymore. Being Helli is shit!'

'And you think taking the medicine might help?'

'No idea. But if it'd make my head shut up for once, I'd be happy.'

I take a deep breath. Even here among the trees, the chill of the frost is palpable—a freshness, as if the air were particularly rich in oxygen. I feel the warmth of the horses and hear them cropping the grass. I'd like to stay here with Helli and never return to civilisation. Here I could be me and Helli could be Helli. There are no medicines here, no chemo.

Helli says: 'The medicine makes you thin too.'

'Where on earth did you get that?' I ask, but I already know the answer: even a child can find anorexics and bulimics exchanging weight-loss tips on the internet.

◊

When we come out of the woods, leading the horses by their reins, the riding teacher hurries up to us. Heike is about my age, and sturdy, with short hair and a carrying voice. When it gets cold she sits in the riding ring with a cat on her lap to keep her warm during the lesson. She's never sick, never loses her voice, never gets annoyed—but she's never friendly either. The girls worship her.

'There you are,' she calls out to us. 'Everything all right?'

I wave and nod vigorously so that she can see even from a distance. To Helli I say: 'Do you still want to ride or do you need some time to catch your breath?'

'Ride,' she says. But when we get to Heike and she takes Scheherazade, Helli changes her mind. She lets go of Aladdin and throws herself into my arms, burying her face in my shoulder. She's nearly as tall as me now—it won't be long before I'm looking up at her. Maybe in some strange way it's a blessing if you die before your children are taller than you. That way Helli would be my little girl forever—she'd remember me as someone she could turn to for comfort, a shoulder to cry on.

'I think we'll call it a day, Heike,' I say. 'We'll see to Aladdin, then we'll wait for Cindi in the riders' room. Will you let her know, please?'

THE RIDERS' ROOM is a common room fitted out with a counter and bar stools. It's ugly and musty-smelling, but at least it's warm. Right now we have it to ourselves. I've brought Helli the two muesli bars from the glove box.

'Are you managing with the tampons?' I ask. I want to signal to her that I'm willing to talk and I can't think of any other words that'll do the job.

'Why isn't Dad coming home?' she asks with her mouth full. I'll never cure her of the habit now, I realise bitterly. Any common courtesies I haven't yet managed to instil in Helli will have to go by the board now. The days when she regarded me as an authority are over. Maybe some day she'll work out for herself that it isn't nice for others to have to look at her chewed-up food or listen to her mumbling through a full mouth—or maybe some kind person will get through to her where I've failed. Maybe it will take a broken relationship to persuade her to mend her ways. Or maybe she'll never mend them, but forever more forget to flush the toilet and borrow other people's clothes without their permission.

'Why do you ask?'

'Well, he usually comes home for the weekend, doesn't he?' she says.

'You know all this. It's his office party this evening and he has to go—it's more or less part of the job.'

'Did you ever go out with Kilian?'

'No, we were just flatmates.'

'Alex has a girlfriend—did you know that?'

'Of course,' I say. 'Do you know her?'

'She's such a typical girl. Really, she could so win a dumb girl contest. Have you got anything else to eat?'

I hesitate. Of course I have more emergency rations—there are fruit bars, dried apricots and chocolate in my handbag— but I'd rather not throw them down the bottomless pit that is Helli's throat. They're things I've bought for myself, things to revive me and help me through faint spells, fits of the blues and occasional moments of anxiety. On the other hand, I can't deprive a hungry child of food, especially since it would mean risking a tantrum. No dried fruit on earth is worth that.

'I'll fetch you something,' I say. 'Wait here.'

As I get up and go to the door, she says to my back: 'Mum? If I didn't have you, I don't think I'd know what to do.'

◊

Next to the gearstick is my notebook, which I'd put down at the start of the Helli crisis. I pick it up and find my phone underneath.

You have 8 missed calls, the screen tells me. There's also a text from Sissi, which I read guiltily: *If you don't want to talk, just say so.*

I put the notebook on the dashboard and push the rest of the stuff aside so that I can sit in the passenger seat and reply to Sissi. My fingers are strangely numb—maybe because I was gripping the reins so hard when I was riding. It's hard to type on tiny keys with numb fingers, but I wouldn't dream of admitting it to all those people who think it's time I got myself a smartphone. No, I shall cling to my tiny old-fashioned black phone for what little is left of my life—you won't catch me swiping around on one of those things as if I were mentally deranged.

Hello Sissi, I'm sorry. An emergency. I'll explain later and ring when I get home, promise. Love K.

I usually get a reply from her within seconds, especially if I say there's been an emergency, but this time there's silence. Maybe she's sulking. But it's more likely that her message bank is full—full of ambiguous messages from her composer that she doesn't want to delete until she's teased out every possible nuance.

Sissi's full name is Elisabeth—Elisabeth Maria, even— and my middle name is Victoria. This fondness for aristocratic names must have been a quirk of our mother's. Unlike me, with my clown's face, always ready to break into a laugh, Sissi has truly aristocratic looks to match her name. She wears her straight dark-brown hair long and loose, but somehow manages to keep it off her face and out of her cello strings. Of the two of us, she's the real musician—and not only because she plays an instrument professionally. It would never enter her head to have children or do up a house or commit to voluntary work—why would she ever do anything that didn't advance her musically? The only problem is her composer. She would have realised this ages ago if he were a builder or a dentist, but a composer, in Sissi's eyes, is always beyond reproach.

She gave up a permanent position with a Nuremberg orchestra to join him in Hamburg. Now she's a stand-in cellist in various orchestras, plays in ensemble projects and spends most of her time admiring her boyfriend, who earns even less than she does and thinks it's proof that he's a genius.

Sissi's playing was a source of great happiness to my parents, but it was also a burden. Her talent and passion for the cello were evident very early on—as a ten-year-old she coaxed such exquisite sounds from the cheap instrument she rented from the music school that our mother would put her head on one side and listen with closed eyes, and even our father would sit there with a dreamy smile on his face that made him look strangely young. But when Sissi was twelve, she refused to stick to the agreed hour of practice a day. For as long as I can remember, Sissi and I were told that if we didn't show consideration for the neighbours, they'd be knocking on the door to complain. In fact, this never happened, but my parents preferred not to inflict more than an hour's cello practice a day on the neighbours. At first Sissi argued and begged, then she changed tactics and began to practise at the music school, where she was given the key to a small room next to the bike racks in the basement.

I'd gone for a quieter instrument from the start and

could have practised the flute for more than an hour if I'd wanted to, though I rarely did. The idea of being a musician had been mine—I was the one who got Sissi started on the whole thing. I played in the school orchestra and put on concerts at home, and my favourite part was the applause at the end. Although I had a lot of hobbies, none of the others had such an immediate effect on an audience or elicited such an audible response.

After a while, though, I had the feeling that Sissi's louder instrument was more versatile and expressive than the flute. And it suited her so well. I too wanted an instrument that suited me—that would seem like an extension of myself when I took it in my hands. At the age of sixteen I decided to switch to the oboe. Of all the woodwind family, it was the loveliest. Whereas the flute was hissy, breathy, warbly and sometimes squeakily shrill, the oboe lamented and rejoiced in a power-ful voice that made people stop and listen. When I told my mother what I'd decided, she brought up the neighbours again: what if I wanted to practise for more than an hour? But I had provided for all eventualities—no one was going to banish me to a basement. I produced a sheet of paper—a declaration of consent signed by both sets of neighbours, confirming that they had no objection to my playing the oboe during the day, even if I practised for hours on end.

I had gone round to ask whether our music bothered them. It was a solution that would never have occurred to Sissi—or to our parents, for that matter. I discovered that our neighbours to the left—a childless couple called Mr and Mrs Winter—were practically never at home in the daytime, while Mrs Hansen, to the right, said that she liked hearing us because she was glad of any sign of life. It was indeed strikingly quiet at the Hansens' since her husband had moved out. Mr Hansen now lived somewhere else, 'where he'd be happier', as our mother had told Sissi and me. I had seen Mr Hansen one last time, on the morning he left. It was our father's habit to put his shoes out to air on the patio overnight if the weather was fine. He said it helped keep athlete's foot at bay. That day he asked me to bring them in, a job I was always glad to do because I loved breathing in the brisk early-morning air. When I stood up with the shoes in my hand, I caught sight of Mr Hansen urinating against a gooseberry bush in the next-door garden, with nothing on but a ribbed vest. I said good morning, but he didn't respond. Instead, he turned and strode purposefully to the back gate, opened it and vanished onto the street. I took the shoes in and told my father what I'd just seen. I was worried because Mr Hansen was more or less naked and rush hour was approaching, and I grew even more anxious when I heard Mrs Hansen calling for him from next door. But my father drank his coffee unperturbed and said, 'Don't worry yourself—it's none of our business.'

He was a great believer in minding your own business, especially if you happened to live in a terrace house.

As I triumphantly presented the signed consent forms to my mother, I felt something new stir inside me. For the first time, I realised I could take care of myself—and I didn't have to step on anyone's toes or be banished to a basement. I had my own way of dealing with things. So that was what growing up felt like.

Soon afterwards, our mother fell sick. I'm sure there's no connection. But thinking about it now, I do wonder whether it's possible that a mother only finds a something—only *allows herself* to find a something—when she senses that she's no longer needed.

◊

Someone is knocking at the window of the driver's door. I glance up, realising as I raise my head that I must have been staring at my feet for a very long time. I didn't hear footsteps or any other sound. I'm clearly not quite with it today—I keep getting caught off guard.

The face at the window is familiar. I have it filed under 'kindergarten parents', but I can't place it more precisely. I get out, walk around the car and dutifully hold out my hand.

'Hello, I'm Yonna's mother,' says the woman. 'I once sat in on one of your classes.'

'I remember,' I say, because I do remember now. 'Yonna always joins in very enthusiastically. We're doing Christmas stuff at the moment, but I'm planning to start a rhythm project in the new year and I'm sure she's going to love it.'

Yonna's mother is dressed for an expedition to the North Pole: woolly hat, mittens, scarf, a silver quilted coat reaching to her knees, knitted leg warmers, lined boots. Her cheeks are flushed pink and she looks so healthy and happy that anyone would envy her—not just me. I remember her well—remember her pink-cheeked healthy glow when she sat in on my music class, crocheting in the corner and jiggling her foot as I sang with the children. She wanted to be sure that her money would be well invested before enrolling her daughter with me. At least she's not about to tell me my classes aren't at all what she'd imagined and would I please set homework.

'Do your children ride here?' she asks.

I think she's called Anja.

'Yes, my daughter.'

'Are you happy with it? Good lessons and all that?'

'Very happy.'

'I'm thinking of enrolling Yonna in the preschool riding class, but I didn't bring her along. I wanted to check it out for myself first, before she had a chance to fall in love with the horses.'

Maybe Anja's approach is wise. Some people say you shouldn't let children make too many decisions themselves because they find it overwhelming. Not that I've ever come across a child this theory applies to—not even Helli.

'The stables certainly get great reviews on the website,' says Anja. 'But there's nothing like seeing things with your own eyes.'

'That's right,' I say.

'And what are the teaching methods like? Any good?'

'Heike's pretty no-nonsense, but you get used to it. I'm not sure she follows any particular methodology, but then teaching methodologies aren't really my area.'

'Aren't they? What is your area, then?'

'I'm a musicologist,' I say.

I wish people were more impressed by my professional title. Anja smiles, but she looks doubtful.

'Oh, so you need a degree to teach the kindergarten group?

I hadn't realised. A friend of mine offers craft courses for children—she just taught herself somehow or other.'

'Yes, it's possible that I'm a little overqualified,' I say.

Anja's face falls as it dawns on her that my career may not have gone quite to plan.

'I did freelance PR before I had Yonna,' she says, touching my shoulder lightly. 'By the way, did you know you've lost your wing mirror?'

I nod and sigh dramatically, making a show of it, just for her. She sighs too and laughs, probably imagining that the mirror was knocked off by some reckless hoon.

'Do you have much longer to wait? You look cold. Don't you have a scarf?' She points at my turned-up collar. 'Take this—you can leave it in Yonna's cubbyhole in kindergarten next week, okay?' She extricates herself laboriously from her long scarf and winds it loosely around my neck. 'There,' she says. 'And now I'll go and have a look at the riding ring.'

◊

The scarf is warm and slightly scratchy. It smells unfamiliar. I wonder if you can tell that I have a transitional Monday looming. Some people start all over again at my age—learn new professions, split up from their partners, move to a new country. Do I look like someone whose chances have run out?

While Anja trudges across the yard in her North Pole gear minus the scarf, not stopping to look back, and while I try to work out what I'm doing here next to my car, where my daughter is and why I'm feeling guilty, I suddenly recall something that someone once told me. My mother was dying and I was sitting at her bedside in the hospital when a doctor stopped by on his rounds, an old, white-haired man who did little more than glance through his papers muttering to himself. Then, on his way out—without actually looking at me—he said, 'Sometimes this kind of thing is in the family. Take good care of yourself, young lady.' I suppose the horror I felt was as much at the casual way he delivered such bad news as at the realisation that the disease might also hit Sissi and me. But for a few seconds I felt a peculiar energy, a burning determination to grab life by the horns—what a hackneyed phrase—because you never knew when your time was up. Then the feeling vanished, and I stashed the doctor's information in some dark corner of my subconscious, together with his take-good-care-young-lady advice. Now something must have brought it back out into the light—maybe Anja's scarf.

Theo, who had a very religious upbringing, once told me that as a child he hadn't believed in dinosaurs. He was still a little girl in those days, and everyone dear to that little girl, everyone to whom that little girl turned for advice, believed that the world was only six thousand years old and had been made in six days. In his teens, he earned a bit of pocket money babysitting for small children, and one day he came across a five-year-old boy who was crazy about dinosaurs. He patiently read the boy book after book, doing his best with all the difficult names and helping him to sort the species into the correct periods: Triassic, Jurassic, Cretaceous. But all the time he was thinking: *Poor little thing, he really believes all this.*

He was almost thirty, he told me, by the time he learnt that he was the one who'd been told a fairytale. How had it happened? Looking back, he said he'd realised that as soon as there was any mention of primeval creatures, Neanderthals or dinosaurs, he'd just switched off. He called this an 'automatic thought block' and was unsettled by the notion but also extremely curious to find out whether there were other such blocks in his head.

When it comes to genetic illnesses, I too have an automatic thought block. If it were a topic Costas was at all interested in, he'd probably call me irresponsible for switching off the way I do. He doesn't believe our minds can play tricks on us, that we can fool ourselves—at least not to that extent—but then he never asked the right questions either, about my mother or about me. Like most men, he probably doesn't even know that most women go for regular check-ups. Every six months a cervical smear and breast scans, every six months the same humiliating, unpleasant, ridiculous examinations, every six months the hoping and fearing and crossing your fingers that everything's all right. I can't believe any man would voluntarily step onto this treadmill. I have yet to meet a man who made a dentist's appointment before he got toothache. I book a biannual check-up for Costas along with the rest of us, and he dutifully joins us if he can, to set a good example for the children. So far he doesn't have a single filling.

◊

My cousin Erika told me about her treatment plan in a group email. After several months of chemotherapy and with a great deal of staying power and optimism, she managed, as she put it, to 'bounce back'. When, a year later, she discovered that the cancer had returned and threw herself in front of a train, my automatic thought block was still in perfect working order. Now that it's gone, I'd like it back.

My own favourite suicide fantasy goes like this: one frosty night when Costas and the children are asleep, I steal out of the house. I have no need to leave a note—in this version of things I die a relatively palatable death and don't have to warn anyone about my appearance. I've always thought highly of people who leave a note to save others the shock of finding a corpse. I'm sure there are plenty who kill themselves for the shock effect, but I'm not one of them and would try to arrange things with as much consideration for others as possible.

I steal out of the house, then, and keep walking straight until I come to the sea, which is frozen over along the shore-line. I take a bottle of water from my handbag and swallow a few sleeping pills. Then I find a place where the ice is thick enough to withstand my body heat for a while and lie down—on my back so that I can look up into the sky, which on this cold, clear night is full of stars. Of course, I'll feel the cold creeping into me—I'll feel the ice on the back of my head, on my fingers and thighs—but you can't have everything. The pills will help. After a few hours I'll have frozen to death. Passers-by will find me when it gets light—probably someone out walking a dog. Whoever it is will see me from a distance, so I won't give anyone a shock.

It's just the right weather at the moment, but the cold snaps that freeze the Baltic are rare, so I might, if it came to it, have to resort to the Virginia Woolf method—less roman-tic, but quicker—and wade into the sea with stones in my coat pockets. Once it was deep enough, I'd drop down into the water. I'd have to fight my panic for a while, but here, too, the sleeping pills would be handy. I'm afraid, though, that this alternative is rather less considerate towards the poor dog walker, who, instead of a wan blue ice queen, would find a drowned body rolling in the surf. In this scenario, a brief note on the hallstand might be in order, so that Costas and the children wouldn't have to spend days hoping and fearing if the surf took a long time to wash me up with all those stones in my pockets.

◊

I see Helli coming across the yard. I'm glad she's come to find me rather than trashing the riders' room out of sheer boredom—it would have been entirely my own fault for leaving her alone for so long with nothing to occupy her.

'I'm hungry,' she calls. The passenger door is still open and before I can stop her she's reached in, grabbed my notebook and begun to flick through it, as if it were the most natural thing in the world.

'Give that back at once.' I lunge at her, but she skips to one side and I find myself grasping thin air. She runs a little way, giving herself a head start, and as I run after her, cursing, she reads aloud:

'Books in my bookcase that I really ought to get round to reading: *Treasure Island, The Handmaid's Tale, Revolutionary Road, Madame Bovary*, anything by Dostoyevsky...'

I can't believe she can read 'Dostoyevsky' running along and I can't believe I'm chasing my daughter over a muddy stable yard, waving my arms about. If this were a scene in a film, I'd be laughing. When at last I catch Helli—reading as you run slows you down—it's all I can do not to slap her.

I've never hit my children, but I'm all too familiar with the impulse. It doesn't surface when you might think—it isn't a show of authority, designed to put an unruly subject in her place. It's not anger that makes me want to lash out, but a sense that my inner self is under existential threat—triggered not by exhaustion or stress, but by the blatant transgression of a boundary I wasn't even aware of until it was crossed. I sometimes have the feeling that being a mother has turned me into a sort of flexible, amoeba-like creature with no form of its own, which can contract whenever someone else needs space, and mould itself around any obstacles. I'm so used to being a shapeless mass that it's always a terrible surprise to me when I feel the urge to push back. By stealing my notebook—and worse still, reading it—Helli has entered dangerous territory. My immediate reaction is to defend myself. But I don't slap her. With this something in my breast, it looks as if I'm in with a good chance of soon being able to say I never hit anyone in my life.

Since I don't believe I'll be going to heaven, I can't expect to be given a posthumous pat on the back for my self-control. Any back-patting has to be done by me, and the more persistent my praise, the more patient and controlled I'm able to be. It is with this in mind that part of my notebook is given over to lists of my achievements, however trivial they may be—which Helli, thank God, did not discover when she ran amok. A typical list of my good deeds might look something like this:

- *Listened to Sissi for over an hour without interrupting her, leaving her happy (and myself exhausted).*
- *Persuaded Joelina to join in the sea snake song (with the help of a rattle).*
- *Got hold of some fresh basil at the garden centre so that Costas can cook a proper meal. (He's been going on about Italian herbs for weeks.)*
- *Bought a birthday present for Alex's unspeakable singing teacher. Hope she likes kitsch. (Rubbish—she adores kitsch, of course!)*
- *Ordered cookie cutters shaped like musical notes for kindergarten. Actually remembered the pre-Christmas baking ahead of time. Well done me.*
- *Replied to Dad's email, even managing to be fairly friendly. Promised to send him photos of us, though, which won't be quite so easy—I don't seem capable of keeping us all in one room for five minutes at a time these days.*

I'll have to be more careful with my notebook. Now that Helli's discovered it, she won't give me a minute's rest. I mustn't let her get hold of it again—it contains some delicate subject matter. Maybe later today I'll have time to make a new list: *Things I ought to burn before I drown myself in the Baltic.*

MY PHONE'S RINGING in the car. It's probably Sissi trying to get hold of me for the ninth time. I'm too far away to take the call unless I run like a deer.

The ringing distracts Helli's attention and she suddenly turns and heads for the stables, leaving me panting in the mud with my notebook, trying to control my violent impulses. The girls—there really isn't a single boy among them—are coming out of the riding ring one by one with their horses. They lead them by the reins across the forecourt and into the stables, where they'll unsaddle them and give them a pat on the neck before climbing into their parents' cars to be chauffeured home, stinking to high heaven. The first cars are already turning into the car park. It's a mystery to me what the other parents get up to in the hour and a half or so while their daughters are riding. It's not quite enough time to go shopping—the drive to the next supermarket, petrol station or even convenience store is too far. Maybe they all drive down one of the many dirt tracks, park behind a hedge and pair off for car sex.

Helli vanishes into the stables and I get in the car, put my notebook deep in my coat pocket and take out a bag of dried apricots. I'm feeling dizzy, probably from hunger, and polish off the entire bag without anyone interrupting me. Even my phone is silent, and a wonderful feeling spreads through me, that deep sense of peace that only comes after a violent upheaval. I can almost feel my blood sugar rising. Then I see Helli and Cindi coming across the yard, and there's something about the way they're trudging through the mud that makes me nervous. Their expressions are dark, and they drag their bags of grooming brushes, hoof picks and curry combs behind them. They climb into the back seat without even bothering to knock the mud and straw off their filthy boots, and Helli drops herself down so heavily that the car shakes.

'Is something the matter? Haven't you made it up yet?' I ask.

'Made it up?' says Helli.

'We're okay,' says Cindi.

'What were you fighting about?' I ask.

In the rear-view mirror I see Helli looking puzzled. She doesn't seem to have a clue what I'm talking about.

Cindi translates for her: 'Earlier on, when you freaked out at me and went galloping into the woods.'

'What?' Helli says. She's utterly incapable of bearing a grudge—no matter what happens, good or bad, she's forgotten it twenty minutes later, and never thinks of it again. It usually drives me up the wall, but every now and again it comes in handy.

'You and Cindi had a fight, or at least some kind of disagreement. You started shouting and said you hated everyone. Don't you remember?' I ask.

'Oh, that.'

Glancing in the mirror again, I see her frown.

'It was about Berlin,' Cindi offers helpfully.

'Mum,' says Helli, leaning forward, 'you've got to go to Berlin. You've got to go to this rave tonight.'

'First of all, it isn't a rave. Secondly, I can't just drop everything and go to Berlin because I feel like it. And thirdly, I don't feel like it.'

'But you've got to be seen there.' There's a shrill undertone to Helli's voice that tells me I should listen carefully.

'Why?'

She doesn't answer me. It's hard to show her that she has my full attention when she's in the back and I'm half swivelled round in the driver's seat—which is presumably why therapists tend to sit opposite their patients.

I try some good old active listening, the technique recommended by all modern parenting books. Rather than come up with questions of your own, you simply repeat the child's last words in the form of a question.

'You think I need to be seen? Show people I exist?'

'Yes.'

'Why?'

She's silent again. The techniques suggested in self-help books are never much help in real life. What would the authors tell me to do next, I wonder. Then I see the look on Helli's face, distraught and helpless and oddly panic-stricken all at once, and I realise she doesn't know how to express her fears—can't find the right words. Cindi says nothing. I suspect she could help if she wanted, but she seems to enjoy a good family fight and is always on the lookout for a bit of drama. I suppose that's what comes of having a lot of older brothers and sisters.

I try to put Helli's feelings into words. 'You want people to see that Dad's married, is that it?'

'Something like that.'

'Because you think maybe they don't know?'

'Hmm.'

'Or because maybe they think he's married, but not properly married? Not married enough, you might say?'

'Yeah, not married enough.'

'Not enough to keep other women away? Is that what you were arguing about—that Dad might be having an affair with some woman in Berlin?'

'Cindi said that, not me,' says Helli. 'And the others said it must be true, because he's there by himself all week and all that.'

'I'm by myself all week too, and I'm not having an affair.'

'But you're not a man,' says Cindi.

'Oh yes, how silly of me. I was forgetting that it's different for men. They can't go for five days without sex—and this week Dad's not coming home at all. You only have to put two and two together, don't you? Do you really believe such sexist nonsense?'

'It's different for you, Katha, isn't it, because you've been married for such a long time?' says Cindi.

'What the…?' says Helli.

I laugh, start the car and let it roll slowly across the yard. Time to get home. As we crunch through the ridges and ruts of frozen mud, I hear Cindi say to Helli, 'My dad had an affair with our cleaning lady.'

Helli: 'You have a cleaning lady?'

Cindi: 'Not anymore.'

I'm passing the riding ring at a crawl when Heike comes out and throws herself in front of the car. I brake, but she's shunted along a little way before the car comes to a standstill. The girls let loose a string of obscenities. I get out and call, 'Heike, are you all right?'

She dusts down her jodhpurs and comes towards me with a smile, as if being hit by a car is an everyday occurrence. And who knows, maybe some people think nothing of stopping vehicles by lunging in front of them rather than standing at the side of the road and waving. Maybe humankind is divided into those who lunge and those who wave. I know which category I'm in.

'I wanted a quick word with you,' says Heike. 'What you did earlier—what both of you did earlier—was a bad idea.'

'I know,' I say. 'I don't know what got into us.'

'Would you make sure Helena understands that this is her last warning?'

'Yes, of course,' I say. 'I'll make sure she realises how serious the situation is.' The words come out of my mouth as if I'd learnt them by heart. It isn't the first time I've had this conversation.

'Same goes for you,' says Heike, turning to go. She pats

the bonnet with the flat of her hand by way of goodbye. 'Last warning for you too, okay?'

◊

I know what Heike's final warning means, and it's only a matter of time. Helli's never given up an activity or a sport because she wanted to—she's always asked to go. At mums-and-kids gym we were advised to leave when Helli bit another child—twice—and the other mothers closed ranks and complained about her. At judo Helli was thrown out after only six weeks, having defended herself a little too keenly from the other kids when they were only supposed to be practising simple moves. At dance, she sabotaged all attempts to organise the children into any kind of formation, because it was too much for her to remember the steps and keep up with the other kids at the same time. In the end, the teacher lost it and shouted at her, so I took her out of the class before anything worse happened. At unicycling there was a mysterious accident that no one ever got to the bottom of, but because Helli—the chief suspect—refused to apologise to one of the other girls, there was a last and then a very last warning and finally a letter to me explaining that they had only one teacher proficient in unicycling and Helena was undermining her authority by refusing to say she was sorry. At tennis she broke the net with her racquet and then kicked her coach in the shins. At Scouts she got lost hiking more than once and behaved so abominably on camp that when I went to pick her up early, she begged me to drive her home without asking any questions, saying only that they never wanted to see her there again. At football the tactics were slightly subtler—after a few minor incidents, the coach simply left Helli sitting on the bench in the changing room whenever they played, until she worked out for herself that they didn't want her on the team anymore. But the riding lessons had been going well for such a long time that I had inwardly breathed a sigh of relief.

◊

Back at the wheel, I smile bravely at no one and give myself a nod of encouragement, then manoeuvre the car out onto the road.

'Can I stay the night at Cindi's?' asks Helli and gives a loud belch. Cindi laughs.

'That's up to Cindi's parents,' I say. The car is growing warm and smells of horse manure. My phone beeps and vibrates.

'It's fine by them,' says Cindi and then belches too. Helli laughs so hard that she gets hiccups, making Cindi laugh even harder.

'We'll have to ask them all the same,' I say when the hiccupping and laughing finally stop.

'Really, it's okay,' says Cindi. 'My mum says once you've got four children it doesn't matter how many more you have in the house. It makes no difference to her.'

I wish I was that relaxed. Far too many things make a difference to me.

'If I'm at Cindi's, you'll be free to go to Berlin tonight,' says Helli.

She is worrying pointlessly if she has doubts about her

father's fidelity—it went out the window years ago. He's been unfaithful to himself by taking on the job he hates in Berlin and he's been unfaithful to me by refusing to talk about how he's feeling. Our unspoken agreement never to keep things from each other was always the bedrock of our relationship, but he hasn't honoured it. What difference would it make now if he slept with other women? It couldn't make things between us any worse. The real threat to our marriage—the thing I worry about—is the distance between us. The only time we're honest with one another now is when we fight.

We've been married seventeen years, which is pretty good going. We married just before Alex was born—it had never been important to me until then. We didn't need a marriage certificate to bring up a child together—our relationship was no one's business but our own. We didn't need to make vows or sign pieces of paper or change our names—trivial gestures that had nothing to do with the commitment we'd already made. But I had underestimated the effect of my hormones during the last months of pregnancy. The nesting instinct set in with such a vengeance that not only did I tip out every last drawer in the flat and rearrange the contents, but I was also gripped by a massive sense of unease whenever I contemplated my ringless future. In the end I bullied Costas into accompanying me to the registry office. Dressed in the only maternity trousers that still fitted me and one of his white shirts, I popped a ring on his finger—and as I did so, my ears sang for sheer relief, my knees buckled and I keeled over, pulling Costas down with me. I came to even before he'd disentangled himself from me, saw his face close to mine—the stubble on his chin and the furrow in his lower lip—and as I breathed in his aftershave and the smell of warm bread that always hung about him, I hoped at that moment that I'd be the one to die first.

He was already working for an architecture firm at that point—at the local branch of a Hamburg company where he'd once done an internship during the summer holidays. He had worked through all his holidays, doing one internship after another—partly because it was expected of architecture students and partly because he wanted to improve his prospects of landing a job that really suited him. He was determined not to end up doing any old work in any old place. He didn't like leaving things to chance. Driven, forward-looking and idealistic in the extreme—that was my husband.

Three years later he became a full partner in a practice that an old university mate had set up in Lübeck. For twelve years things went well. Then the financial crisis hit, leaving a lot of smaller businesses reeling. Costas's office merged with an architectural giant in a bid to stay afloat, and as part of the so-called necessary restructuring, Costas lost his job. He'd been a partner and worked hard, so he wasn't expecting that.

It turned out he wasn't so good at coping with change. Over the years, I've proved myself the more flexible of the two of us, and I no longer harbour the naive wish to die before him.

◊

'Ew, look, is that a mummy?' asks Helli on the back seat.

'Look, Katha, a mummy,' says Cindi, waving her phone in

my direction. I glance at it obediently and give a nod to show that I've seen what she wanted to show me. In fact, I barely saw a thing.

'The other day someone sent me a photo of a drowned body,' says Cindi. 'That was really disgusting.'

'Have you still got it?' asks Helli, excited.

'I'll find it for you,' says Cindi.

'Mum, do you know what? Yesterday on TV there was this thing about this man who didn't answer the door anymore because he was really old, so the neighbours called the fire brigade to break the door down. And they found his wife in his bed, and she'd been dead for two years. Isn't that so gross? That's completely sick.'

'No,' says Cindi, 'that's not sick. He just really loved her.'

'But not, like, decomposed.'

'Yeah, always, whatever she looked like. Ah, here's the drowned body. Are you ready?' Cindi holds out her phone to Helli, and I glance in the rear-view mirror so I won't miss her reaction. She makes a face like the one she made as a baby when she crammed a sprout in her mouth for the first time, all eager anticipation.

The day Costas was made redundant, he seemed no different from usual, but then, during his last weeks at work, he behaved increasingly out of character. He came home early without putting in his usual overtime and on weekends he sat around at a loose end, although the patio steps creaked and the garden furniture had been left only half-sanded. He stopped cooking for us and spent the evenings watching television. When he'd officially finished at work, he dutifully registered at the job centre so he could apply for unemployment benefits, but it was pretty much the last time he left the house without a compelling reason. From then on, he passed his days in his study.

This went on for a year. It was the same year Helli was almost expelled from her new school after conducting an experiment to find out whether curtains burnt better when dipped in chemicals borrowed from the school darkroom. It was the year Alex took part in a youth musical project and had to be driven to the back of beyond twice a week for rehearsals; he'd somehow convinced me that he was doomed to a life of misery if he didn't go. It was the year the rats died and were replaced. It was the year the local kindergartens discovered that offering preschool music classes was a way of making parents happy with little trouble or expense and were suddenly keen to find teachers. There wasn't much competition in our part of the world, and before long I had two full groups at the music school and was driving back and forth between various kindergartens three mornings a week—I didn't dare turn down any opportunity to earn money. It was the year I had been hoping to take up my PhD again. After Berenike was born, I'd written off the lecturer's job in Lübeck once and for all, but I told myself that at least I could get my thesis out of the drawer now—and I did manage to write a little more and draw up a decent work plan before admitting defeat. It was the year I completed my transformation into 'the music lady' and stopped lying to myself about my chances of ever achieving anything beyond clapping rhythms and banging bongo drums.

What did Costas do in his study? For a whole year, he didn't once go to the door when the doorbell rang, or answer the phone. He turned up for meals but ate little. When we talked, he smiled a horrible absent smile that caused me deep pain in the first weeks, then began to get on my nerves and eventually had me fuming.

When this hideous year was drawing to an end, Costas came out of his study to talk to me. He told me he'd decided to do the right thing and provide for his family, so he was going to accept a job offer in Berlin. The job wasn't quite his cup of tea, but it would be all right.

I was so glad he was talking to me again that there was no way I was going to argue with him. My fear that he might relapse into silence was greater than any misgivings I had about the new job. A short time before his unemployment benefits were due to run out, he packed his bags and disappeared to Berlin for five days. That was over a year ago, and he hasn't really been straight with me since. The only thing that keeps me hanging on is the fact that we argue with each other more than ever before—because when Costas gets angry, he's as fierce and driven and feisty as the old Costas. As long as he can still get angry about it all, there's hope. Recently, though, he's begun to speak better of his job. Last year it would never have occurred to him that being seen at an office party was important enough to stay away over the weekend. Maybe it really is because of some pretty colleague. Or maybe it's because he's moving away from the person he used to be.

It wasn't until he was safe in Berlin that I dared enter his study. I was afraid of what I might find. An army of plasticine figures, perhaps; confused notes; a hopeless—or even brilliant—attempt at starting a novel; scribbled song lyrics; newspaper clippings that he'd examined for coded messages. Maybe only scraps of paper or mountains of origami cranes—or even nothing at all. That would have been particularly hard to bear, because it would have meant that he'd just been sitting at his desk staring into space, day after day.

At first I just stood there in the middle of those twelve square metres that had been a kind of junk room before we bought the house and declared it a study. You could hardly tell that no one had cleaned the place for months. There was nothing strange on the desk—only untidy piles of drawing paper that looked as if each sheet had been picked up and put down again several times over. I sat in Costas's chair and tried to imagine what it would be like to sit there every day. Then I reached out for one of the piles of paper and examined the sheets one at a time.

No, Costas had not been idle. It was clear that he'd not only submitted applications all over the country, he'd also been drawing like a man possessed. He was old school, preferring to draw by hand and use the computer only when he had to. Building after building filled the sheets, and it took me a while to realise that they weren't designed from scratch—they were old buildings transformed, a kind of architectural upcycling. I recognised a primary school where I'd once taught for a week—an asbestos-riddled seventies building with a flat roof. A public swimming pool, an office building, a department store and a bank, tower blocks and silo towers—they'd all been given a face lift. Costas had planned and designed their conversion, so they were no longer bleak and shabby but sleek and serviceable.

I didn't know whether to laugh or cry—laugh, because throughout those awful months behind his study door, Costas had still been Costas—or cry, because it was clear that he had given up and reconciled himself to the job in Berlin for our sake. Cry because we were stopping him from being what he wanted to be—because there was so much that he wouldn't or couldn't tell me. I settled for laughter, and sitting there in Costas's desk chair, I gave a hoarse laugh. I seem to recall that it sounded like a barking cough.

◊

Despite Cindi's mother's enviably laissez-faire attitude, I insist that Helli ask an adult whether she can stay the night. Waiting in the car, I fish my notebook out of my pocket as soon as she's out of sight so I can draw up a new to-do list for what's left of the day: vacuuming, laundry, Kilian, Sissi. The bookmark slipped out when Helli absconded with it, and as I leaf through the book looking for the next clean page I read:

Topics that keep me awake at night:
- *human trafficking*
- *child soldiers*
- *contaminants in food*
- *paedophile rings*
- *nuclear power*
- *climate change*
- *the NATO mutual defence pact*

Immediately below, it says:

Topics that should keep me awake at night but don't:
* *unemployment*
* *old-age poverty*
* *serious diseases*

I hastily add:

* *divorce*

Helli is standing at Cindi's front door waving at me when I look up. I don't know how long she's been standing there. It's just like her not to walk the few metres to the car and knock on the window. I'm suddenly not sure that this whole staying-the-night plan is a good one. She's just had one of her nosebleeds, after all, which still haven't been looked into by a doctor and might not be entirely harmless. And this afternoon she fell off her horse after having a total meltdown. A better mother wouldn't let Helli out of her sight for the next twenty-four hours.

I wind down the window—that's how old my car is, but at least turning the handle provides an old lady with exercise—and she calls out: 'Can you bring my things round later?'

I'm suffering pangs of maternal guilt and am glad of any opportunity to assuage them.

'Sure,' I call back. I have to take the car out again anyway when I collect Kilian from the station along with his amp and bass. I might as well make a little detour and drop off Helli's pyjamas and a handful of tampons.

She turns and goes into the house. She's still wearing

her jodhpurs and filthy riding boots, and even from the car I can see that the hair at the back of her head is sweaty and matted, although it's already so dark that the street lamps have come on. It gets dark so early here in winter. I hope someone can persuade Helli to have a shower or a bath this evening. I picture her and Cindi in the bath together. (Do girls their age still do that kind of thing—have baths with each other?) I see them splashing and laughing, Helli with the rolls of puppy fat on her belly and Cindi with her small but noticeable breasts: two children whose bodies have decided that it's time for a change—and nothing anyone can do will stop it.

The front garden looks neglected. I'm reluctant to drive off and leave Helli in this house where one child more or less doesn't make a difference. It occurs to me that I don't even know whether or not she actually found a parent and asked permission. But at the same time, I'm desperate to get away.

I wind up the window, start the engine and press play on the stereo. Protschka sings of dreams and fairytale worlds as I glance at my phone and see that I have a new text message, this one from Heinz: *When will you be back? There's a Barbie doll in your living room drinking chamomile tea.*

IT WASN'T A LIE. Sitting on our sofa, gazing at my son in admiration as he pours out tea, is something that looks more like a doll than a human. I know this kind of girl from mail-order clothes catalogues and had always assumed they owed their existence to Photoshop, but here's one that walks and talks.

Heinz and Theo have settled down in the two armchairs—they know which of our chairs are comfortable and have no qualms about appropriating them. Our sofa looks nice, but you can't sit at ease on it. Costas calls it the sex sofa. Not that we've ever put it to the test. Whatever the time of day or night, the danger of one of the children catching us at it on their way to the fridge would be too great. Heinz and Theo have a bottle of beer each—they must have brought them from home, because we only have juice, and the vermouth I bought for tonight. As Alex sets the teapot down I realise I don't recognise the tag of the teabag hanging from it. Is it possible that Barbie has brought her own tea?

I've often noticed that beautiful people have dreadful voices. They speak like Miss Piggy, or a cartoon character—strained or squeaky, throaty or shrill. Maybe it's the price they have to pay for their good looks. I gird myself before greeting Barbie, so that no one will notice if I wince.

'Hello,' I say, holding out my hand. 'I'm Katharina, Alex's mum.'

Barbie takes my hand with an agreeably gentle grip and says: 'Nice to meet you. I'm Leonie.'

Her voice is pleasant and melodious—a mezzo with deeper resonances, a voice you can sink into, a voice made for reading erotic audio books, a voice that promises you solace in your despair. I don't know what kind of a face I make, but I can't hide my surprise.

She seems relieved that I'm back. So does Alex. He gives me a nod and sits down next to his Barbie, putting an arm firmly around her shoulder.

I understand why they're so pleased to see me when Heinz says: 'We only wanted to drop in and thank you for the rescue operation this morning—and to show you Theo's bandage.' He leans over Theo, grabs his arm and holds it up. 'We rang the bell, but you were out. Alex let us in and we had a bit of a chat while we started in on the beers we'd brought along. When Leonie came to pick him up they were too polite to chuck us out, and they've been keeping us company and drinking chamomile tea while they wait for the beer to run out or for you to take over as hostess.'

'You're going out?' I ask Alex.

'It's Friday,' says Barbie, as if that explained everything. And maybe it does. Maybe everything in her world follows such simple rules. On Friday you go out. Every other evening of the week you go to bed early, because you need your beauty sleep, and it's school the next day. My life must have been like that once, but trying to remember it is like trying to remember life in the womb, like yearning after something we can't have, something so frustratingly unattainable that the desire for it spoils even our most peaceful moments at some subconscious level.

I sit on the floor, on one of the meditation cushions left over from a time when Costas and I had a lot of guests and never enough chairs. Leonie sips her tea, blowing on it to cool it and smiling shyly at me. I'm the adult here—it's up to me to start the conversation. I glance at Heinz and Theo, who are sitting in their armchairs, grinning and drinking beer, watching us as if we were an early-evening soap opera.

Leonie's hair is long and an indisputably genuine honey-ish blond. Her skin is flawless, her make-up immaculate and discreet. Her fingernails—like those of almost all girls these days—are obviously manicured, each nail smooth, shiny and trimmed to the same length. I glance at my own hands, in spite of myself: my knuckles are chapped and my nails flecked with white—presumably a symptom of some vitamin deficiency I don't have time to deal with. A couple of nails even look as if I've taken a chisel to them—they're just starting to grow back after large pieces flaked off following a bout of the infamous hand, foot and mouth disease, which I managed to catch at kindergarten back in October. I've kept my nails short since having children, but they're edged with grime even so, and when I paint my toenails in the summer, I never manage to sit still long enough to let the varnish dry, so it's either embossed with sock pattern or has bits of grass stuck in it. I ask myself where girls like Leonie find the time to take care of their nails on top of everything else. Hair and skin demand quite enough attention as it is: there are eyebrows to be plucked, callouses to be rubbed away, elbows to be moisturised—and then, of course, you have to shave yourself in all kinds of places or coat yourself with sugar paste that you rip off with a jerk, leaving yourself with a little girl's private parts for evermore. I suppose it won't be long before Cindi's teaching Helli all that. One way or another it seems to me incredibly time-consuming, being young today.

I realise that I probably smell of manure. I'd love to tell everyone that I rode a horse today, grasped the meaning of a tarot card and noticed that it's warmer in the woods than out of them. But no one here wants to listen to my stories. My mother's stories never interested me either, and now that I'd like to hear them, she's not around to tell them.

'Do you and Alex know each other from school?' I ask.

It's probably a good idea not to let on that Alex has told me about her.

'From choir. I'm in the year above him.'

That gives me a pang—but I can't expect exclusive rights to school choir romance.

'Do you sing alto?' I ask.

Alex frowns. I'm not asking the right questions.

'Usually. But if there's a second soprano, I sing that.'

'I always sang alto,' says Heinz dreamily. 'A low alto. My voice broke quite dramatically when I was fourteen. How about you, Theo? I bet you were a soprano—a nice girl like you.'

'I didn't sing at all if I could help it,' says Theo, peering into his beer bottle. 'But I did ballet. In a tutu, with my hair in a bun.'

Barbie looks confused. You can see the cogs whirring. Not that I think she's stupid—Heinz and Theo would confuse anyone who's led a normal, sheltered life.

'So you'll be doing your exams next year?' I ask.

'Yes, that's right,' she says, putting down her cup. She turns her head a little, just enough to catch Alex's reaction without being impolite to me.

'What do you want to do afterwards?' I ask.

'Medicine,' she says.

Heinz and Theo make a noise halfway between an exasperated sigh and a forced laugh.

'Sounds good,' I say, giving Heinz in particular a stern look.

Now Alex chimes in at last. 'Yes,' he says. 'Anyway, I'm sure it was interesting for Leonie to hear about your work, Heinz. And about Theo's accident. But now we really have to go. Drink up, Leonie.'

They've probably been sitting here far too long, politely listening to one case history after another—each apparently more hopeless than the next, but all with some prospect of recovery, thanks to Heinz and his healing globules, perfectly attuned to the songs his patients sing. Of course Alex is in a hurry to get away. All the same, the way he's just spoken to his girlfriend disturbs me. I'd thought boys his age were different, that their generation would finally put an end to the tired old nonsense of men giving orders and women doing as they're told.

Watching Leonie throw back her tea, I see I'm not mistaken—and when she gets up and goes to stand next to Alex, slender and blond and almost as tall as him, they really do, for a moment, look like Barbie and Ken.

◊

When I was in my early twenties, Costas once told me I looked sweet when I woke up in the morning—tousled and crumpled and adorable—and because I wanted him to like me, I began to make an effort to look as tousled as possible. It wasn't conscious—there was no calculation behind it—but one day I noticed, for instance, that I had got into the habit of rubbing my eyes with my fists in the morning like a small child. That was something I'd never done before. Another thing I'd do was to sit up in bed and blink dazedly for a few seconds, then yawn and stretch, mussing up my hair in the process. Part of me had evidently decided to put on a good show for Costas, if sweet was what he liked.

As soon as I realised, I stopped, not just because I felt silly, but also because I knew I'd never be able to keep up this sweet-and-tousled act. What looked adorable when I was in my early twenties would be ridiculous by the time I was in my early forties. Of all the qualities Costas valued in me, sweetness would probably be the first to go.

I never aspired to beauty—it seemed too complicated. Sissi

is beautiful, especially when she plays her cello, absorbed in the music, her eyes closed, her long, slender fingers on the fingerboard, the broad instrument between her thighs drawing your eyes to her ankles—and Sissi's ankles are the stuff of poetry. Maybe her beauty has been of benefit in certain situations—that's something I can only speculate about. What I do know is that she's had to contend with envy because of it. It has made no difference that the first round of auditions for orchestra positions are now held behind a curtain, or that juries are made up of an equal number of men and women—there has been talk whenever Sissi has won a competition, or landed herself a post. I know too that a lot of people don't take her seriously. No one expects her to be clever, or profound. She has the most incredible stories of sexual harassment and inappropriate come-ons, but the worst thing, she once confided in me, is that when she does come across someone who genuinely cares for her, she can't trust him. Beautiful people are like rich people in that respect—they can never be sure that they are loved for their own sake. My sister is an ornament and a status symbol—an objet d'art to admire and display. She divides her boyfriends into hunters and gatherers: the hunters want to exhibit her like a trophy, the gatherers to keep her to themselves and look at her all the time. Her composer, to whom she's been faithful for so long, is a gatherer—anyone can see that.

And like sweetness, beauty is fleeting. It isn't a quality you want to be loved for, because you can never be sure if you'll still be loved once it has gone. That leaves me, with my clown's face and dirty blond hair, in the better position. I'm not saying I'm wholly unattractive, but I hope Costas had other reasons for falling in love with me, and I've always been certain that my marriage would last even if I did have a minor but disfiguring accident with the gas barbecue.

I can, at any rate, imagine that it would be quite a strain to be a doctor who looks like a Barbie doll. For a career in musical theatre, on the other hand, a certain doll-like quality can only be an advantage.

Alex was a wonderful child, mischievous and clever, open and friendly. He could talk to anyone and everyone, and always joined in, no matter what the plan. You could take him on holiday or leave him with his grandparents—you could even, with a clear conscience, let him stay the night at a friend's. He reached all his developmental milestones right on schedule: he cut his teeth in the correct order and at the expected time, learnt to walk and talk and go to the toilet just when the experts said he should. He was extremely polite, even as a little boy, and quickly made friends with other children his age. Everything he did, he did well and with ease. He sailed through school, exactly as we had expected. Looking back, I probably smooth over a lot, and of course he sulked every now and again, and had the occasional tantrum—but generally speaking, Alex was the perfect child.

In his early teens, he went through an awkward-looking phase. His arms were too long, his nose too big for his face, and he got pimples on his forehead. From a distance there was even something gibbon-like about his movements. But soon after his sixteenth birthday everything sorted itself out, and the results of his metamorphosis from little boy to young man are more than satisfactory.

Costas and I were proud of our perfect son. It was a pleasure to give him advice, because he always followed it. He stuck to the rules—we leant back and relaxed. He didn't seem inclined to rebel, not seeing the point in it, and cheerfully accepted our authority without question. He's still like that today. I really ought to be glad about it. He'll go his own way eventually, making a career for himself in musical theatre, with some adoring blond or other at his side who drinks up her tea when he tells her to. He'll stick to the rules, never stopping to question life as it unrolls before him like a carpet. He probably won't even feel bored.

But looking at this Ken doll standing before me, I wonder whether I haven't spent the last seventeen years encouraging him in the wrong direction—whether doing all the right things isn't perhaps less important than developing a personality.

Where are you going? I want to ask. *What are you doing? How late will you be?* But I stop myself, and like a good mother I say: 'Have fun.'

'I might stay the night at Leonie's place,' says Alex, my irreproachable son.

I want to say: *Then you'll miss Kilian.* I want to say: *Use a condom.* Instead I say: 'That's fine. Kilian will still be here in the morning. You could come back in time to talk to him if you liked—one musician to another.'

I don't count as a musician in this family.

'Yeah, Mum. Kilian. I know. Sounds like I should be the one saying have fun.'

Alex pats me on the shoulder, gives Heinz and Theo a

nod, takes Leonie's hand and vanishes into the hall with her. She calls out a goodbye—she knows how to behave—but her attention is already on Alex, like a dog who tires of whatever game it's been playing as soon as its master moves.

I follow them out into the hall and to the front door. Leonie must be eighteen—there's a brand-new black Nissan Micra parked in the drive.

'Have you fed the rats?' I call out after Alex.

'Of course.'

I go back to the living room. We are quiet until we hear the car doors shut and the engine start up. Then Theo says, 'She's quite the accessory. The other boys must be envious.'

'Hard coral,' says Heinz. 'Just a hunch, but I'm pretty sure I'm on the right track with hard coral. Beautiful stuff when it's polished, but it can give you a nasty cut if you're not careful. I once had a patient who sent me a piece from the Galápagos. Well, actually, he wasn't the patient—his dog was. The poor creature was on its last legs. He'd tried everything: vets, animal psychologists, dog trainers, you name it—but the dog kept having these funny turns, lay in the corner panting, as if it was having a heart attack, although physically everything seemed fine. Post-traumatic stress disorder probably, but no one ever seems to think of that right off the bat. I prescribed belladonna. A run-of-the-mill cure, I know, but the dog's symptoms were just the same as if it'd been poisoned. The man couldn't tell me what triggered the attacks, but I'm sure I'd have found a more effective treatment if I'd had longer to observe things. Animals sing songs too, after all. Anyway, I wrote him a prescription, and at first the dog got a great deal worse. It looked as if it was going to kick the bucket—for three days it just crawled around, drinking water like a rabid thing—then suddenly it was all over and the attacks never came back. The man was one of those scruffy backpackers who sell homemade jewellery, and wear it too. He was halfway round the world by this point, but he wrote to me to let me know the dog had been cured. He was completely broke—at his first appointment he'd produced twenty euros, hoping it would pay for the entire treatment, so I said why didn't he pay me in kind and send me some nice thing he found on his travels. And one day I got this parcel from the Galápagos with a big piece of coral inside, and a letter. Theo knows the story.'

Theo nods. That Heinz keeps coming up with such stories—new ones every time—never ceases to amaze me. I sometimes suspect that he and I have rather different views on what is commonly known as the truth.

'I'd love to go to the Galápagos,' I say. I wonder whether to add it to my list of things I'd like to see and do, but it seems too arbitrary. The Galápagos or Lanzarote? Namibia or Mongolia? How do you decide?

'I wouldn't,' says Heinz. Theo smiles quietly. He's heard this spiel before too. 'Wild horses couldn't drag me onto a plane or ship. The furthest I've been in my life was the Black Forest, and the climate there didn't agree with me at all. It sounds ridiculous, but I suffered symptoms of altitude sickness. I'm a coastal plant and always will be—this is where my roots are, and where I'll stay. If I can't smell salt in the air, I shrivel up and die.'

'Saltwort,' I say. 'You sing the saltwort song.'

'Not bad,' says Heinz, pointing his finger at me like a game show host.

I have trouble understanding people who don't long to be somewhere else at least some of the time, but I suppose the journey from one sex to another is long and arduous enough for one life.

◊

The way things are looking, I'll have to throw them out—they aren't going to leave of their own accord. Of course I pause to admire Theo's bandage—so fat and knobbly that it's impossible to imagine what his hand is going to look like without a thumb. Dizzy from mixing painkillers and alcohol, Theo has progressed to the sofa. I can't send him home as long as he's feeling unwell. But time is short. I'm supposed to meet Kilian at the station in half an hour, but first I have to ring Sissi, maybe packing Helli's things with my free hand while I'm on the phone. I could do with shedding these smelly clothes too and getting into something else. Kilian may not set much store by personal hygiene—unless he's changed dramatically—but I still feel the need to make a decent impression. We haven't seen each other for years, after all, and I don't have much else to impress him with. When you've fallen as far short of your dreams as I have, the only way to save yourself awkward questions and pseudo-sympathetic enquiries about how you're 'dealing with it' is to make damn sure you look as if you're satisfied with your lot. I have some clothes in my wardrobe that might do the trick.

I'd never have dreamed that I would one day spend that

period of life so crucial to a career—or even just to getting a foot in the door of your chosen line of work—as a housewife and mother. I was always aware, though, that my line of work wasn't really a line of work at all—that anyone who ventured into the jungle of the job market with a background like mine was going to struggle. I planned to find a fulfilling and challenging job, and to work on something more enduring on the side. To me the be-all and end-all of life was to produce something for posterity.

My first foray into professional life was an internship in musical dramaturgy at a theatre in Lübeck, a surprisingly dull job that involved a lot of coffee-making and photocopying. My mentor, a woman in her late thirties who had a new job in a new town every other year, always knocked off late for lunch. Since I was only the intern, I had no choice but to go late to lunch too. By the time we got to the canteen, they'd have stopped serving regular food, and she would call out: 'Harald, is the deep-fryer still on?' I ate badly and got too little sleep, working all day only to spend my evenings at concerts or the opera—but I liked the atmosphere of the theatre and added it to my mental list of places I could imagine working.

During my student years, I also did a stint on the till at the Thomas Mann museum, which was in an old eighteenth-century house. One of my duties was to walk through the rooms turning out the lights after I'd totted up the day's takings. I felt like an angel of death, trailing darkness in my wake. Then I hung up coats at a theatre cloakroom for a while, and for a few weeks I cleaned deserted offices. That was so boring that I began to shuffle around the ornaments on the desks, rearranging the Kinder Egg figurines and Smurfs and pot plants and family photos, and hoping the employees would be pleased when they saw my handiwork the next morning. In fact, the things were invariably back in their places when I returned the following evening. This frustrated me so much that I quit. I embarked on a second internship on the music team at a regional broadcaster, hoping that it would open up another area of work to me, but I never felt comfortable there. I was surrounded by men who never missed a chance to point out that I shouldn't, whatever I did, expect to land a permanent job there, because no one in human resources was stupid enough to employ a woman under thirty, who would immediately get pregnant and go on indefinite leave. Women over thirty, mind you, were even riskier—they really did say 'riskier'—because either they hadn't had children yet and their biological clock was furiously ticking away, or else they already had a family, which made them more or less completely unreliable.

When I graduated, I decided to focus on my thesis for a while and not worry about finding the perfect job. For one thing, I hoped I'd be taken more seriously with a PhD—a 'Dr' in front of my name would, I thought, show my male colleagues I was in their league. It was completely ridiculous, of course—no one on the music team had a doctorate. But at the time it seemed to me perfectly logical that I needed to be better qualified than them if I wanted to compete.

By the time Alex was three, I felt ready to return to my career—but I hadn't finished my thesis and had no job experience at all apart from those lousy internships. I was going to have to start from scratch—and now, of course, I was one of those unreliable women with a child. It was true that I could no longer cope with the kind of hours I had worked at the theatre.

When Alex's music-school teacher was off for an extended period of time, I stepped into the breach at short notice, managing to sidestep the usual bureaucratic procedures. After a time I even had a class of my own. But it was never supposed to be anything but temporary—a favour to the music school as much as anything else. I certainly didn't regard it as a proper job.

Then Helli started kindergarten, and I realised I was caught in a trap. She would have torpedoed any regular nine-to-five job. Every few days I got a call telling me she'd fallen off the climbing frame, pushed a green bean up her nose, or almost torn her ear off trying to wriggle beneath the partition from one toilet cubicle to the next.

After a while things seemed to calm down a bit, and I determined to make a fresh attempt as soon as she started school. I began to make plans, contacting former friends at the university, having photos taken for my CV and applying on spec to my old school because I could imagine teaching there. I was anxious to prove to myself that the old Katharina still existed—that motivated, flexible, competent woman I thought I had once been. But then came Berenike. By the time I'd mustered enough energy to get going again after that, Costas had lost his job—and rather than being in a position to take over and provide for the family, I was condemned for evermore to play the 'music lady', offering an integrated child chauffeur service on the side.

I'm reconciled to it now, glad that I'm at least doing something related to my degree. As well as the kindergarten and music-school work, I teach occasional week-long courses at the local primary school. It's not fulfilling, or intellectually stimulating—I leave no mark, and barely scrape together enough hours to be able to call it a job. But it's fun, and it's better than nothing. On good days I manage to convince myself that I'm doing important groundwork—that I'm contributing more to society by singing 'Old MacDonald Had a Farm' with small children and bashing wooden instruments than if I were writing academic articles and trying to cram information into the brains of apathetic university students. On bad days I feel sick at the thought of what a meagre life I'll have to look back on from my deathbed.

'THEO CAN STAY HERE on the sofa till he feels better,' I say. 'But I'm going to have to be a bad hostess now and leave you on your own. I've got to be at the station in less than half an hour.'

Heinz is sitting in his armchair watching Theo act the indisposed young lady, eyes closed, upturned hand on his forehead. I drink a quick gulp of tea from Barbie's cup and go up to the bedroom. As I'm getting undressed, I wonder whether I might manage to make up the spare bed after all. But that would mean disappointing Sissi again, and she'd be deeply wounded if she found out she'd been stood up because of a bedspread. It's only half past five. The evening is young—the bed can wait.

Singing the trio from *Così fan tutte*, I hurry to the bathroom in my underwear. I spray on plenty of deodorant and take my perfume down from the shelf. I rarely use it these days—it's called Zen and is made by a Japanese company, but

I've had it so long they probably stopped selling it years ago. Not that it matters to me—I don't suppose I'll be needing another bottle in this life. I dab perfume on my neck and spray a little on my knickers, where prickly pubic hair is sticking out through the fabric. This is a habit from times gone by and nothing to do with Kilian. I examine my face in the mirror, run my hands through my hair and bare my teeth to make sure there's nothing stuck between them.

I haven't seen Kilian for years. He was my flatmate when we were students, but more than anything he was a friend—only I wouldn't have called him that at the time because I didn't have enough experience to recognise friendship when I saw it. Our little era came to an end when I met Costas, and for a long time we were out of touch. Then, six years ago, Kilian sent me an email out of the blue, when he was going through a sentimental phase and spending a lot of time googling old friends. (I'm easy to find online—my name and photo are on the music-school homepage.) Since then we've written to each other from time to time. All our emails begin with a long ritual apology, explaining why we haven't been in touch for so long. Two years ago we planned to meet in Hamburg when he was giving a concert there, but Helli ran away from school that day after an argument with her teacher and didn't turn up for four hours, so I had to cancel. Now another concert has at last brought him to Lübeck, and he's stopping over to see us. I suppose it means he saves on hotel costs too. I'm suddenly embarrassed about having bought the vermouth.

◊

I've always found it hard to distinguish between the pragmatic and the romantic. Sharing a drink carton with someone can, after all, be either, and I fear that more often than not I've misread the signs and failed to recognise friendship or love when they've come my way. Costas, however, courted me in a strange, methodical fashion. We met at a party. He made one glass of red wine last all evening, while I—like all the others—drank as much and as indiscriminately as I could. I drank a lot during my student years. I also went to a lot of parties. Studying and partying seemed to fill my life and satisfy all my needs: education, friendship, eating and drinking—what more could you want? I wasn't even aware that I was living in one of the most beautiful cities in Germany, where the air smelt of salt when the wind was in the east and the sky flaunted extraordinary cloudscapes.

My last years at home had been marked by the insistent absence of my mother and an atmosphere heavy with the sadness and loneliness of my sister and father—a thick fog I had to navigate daily. The minute I moved into my room in a shared flat in Lübeck, I was struck by how intense the colours were, how easy it was to breathe, how clear my voice sounded. I liked that clear sound so much that I got into the habit of laughing louder than the others when I found something funny. I discovered that I had a loud, ringing laugh and I began to laugh all the time, everywhere, simply opening my mouth and letting it bubble out. At parties it hung over the music and the buzz of conversation like a flare.

Costas later told me it was my laugh that attracted him. He heard it and followed it, and we talked until I had to dash to the loo to throw up. When I got back he'd disappeared and it seemed unlikely we'd meet again any time soon, because architects and musicians didn't overlap much. But Costas took things in hand in his usual way—purposeful but restrained, and all the more effective for that. He had seen through me from the beginning.

One Tuesday morning he was sitting on a bench that I passed on my way to the academy. We said hello and I was pleased to see him again, but I was in a hurry and didn't know how to start a conversation after our last encounter had ended in so abrupt and unsavoury a fashion. But the following Tuesday he was there again—and the Tuesday after that. The second time he was reading a book and holding an umbrella to keep the rain off. We said hello, smiled and exchanged a few words. On the fourth Tuesday I sat down beside him so we could talk a little longer. But I didn't want to be pushy. Maybe he wasn't sitting there because of me. Maybe he spent every morning of the week on a different bench because his flat was smelly. Maybe he was waiting for another woman who turned up as soon as I left. Maybe he simply had his habits.

I began to look forward to these encounters more and more, and to become more and more afraid he might not be sitting there. But Costas took his time. Even back then he understood what I'm clearly never going to learn—that good things come to those who wait. Of course, he'd never had time slip away from him and lost someone who had promised to hang on until Christmas.

◊

I get dressed as quickly as I can. The temptation to feel for the something is too great otherwise. I'd only confirm what I already know—that it is there, the same size, insensitive, immovable—all bad characteristics, if you're hoping for a favourable diagnosis. I have no idea how I know that—read it in a magazine from the chemist's, I suppose. My automatic thought block must have faltered now and again these last years. I decide on a black T-shirt under a black wool jacket, my uniform for situations that require a certain degree of self-confidence—it doesn't show sweat marks, makes me look slim and can be worn on any occasion. No woman in Germany in her early forties can go wrong in a black wool jacket.

I pause for a moment in front of the wardrobe mirror, leaning forward and examining my face, my good old clown's face that looks just the same as ever, with the arched eyebrows that give me a look of permanent surprise, and the rather too soft, puffy lips that pucker up and go blue at the edges in the cold. I smile and sniff and it strikes me that my nose is crooked. I make my face serious, then smile again—and again, my nose is crooked. As I turn my head this way and that to examine my nose from different angles, a terrible mixture of delight and despair wells up in me. There's no denying it—my nose is asymmetrical. *Wonderful*, I think—it's really rather distinctive—but was it always like that or is this a recent development? What does it mean? I must confess, I've never felt any particular longing for a distinctive, asymmetrical nose, but now that I've noticed it, I'm thrilled. It's always the crooked and contorted and irregular that appeals to me in other people. Costas, who still looks like something out of a men's fashion catalogue, hides his imperfections well, but I've ferreted them all out over the course of the years and carry the knowledge of them around with me like a secret. A crooked nose gives my affable, innocuous face something rakish. I'm pleased, but I'm screaming inside too. I don't want to hear the screaming, but it's like tinnitus—there's no blocking it out. *Too late*, it screams. *Too late*. If only you'd noticed it earlier—now it's too late. Soon that rakish nose of yours will be nothing but food for worms.

◊

On my way to the phone I check on Heinz and Theo in the living room. They've invited themselves round and brought their own drinks with them; no one is expecting me to play the perfect hostess, but I can't stop myself—it's a kind of compulsion. Theo is sitting up again, talking to Heinz, and they're each holding a cup of tea. The pot was almost full and Heinz must have fetched cups, because Barbie's cup is sitting unused on the table. I give them a wave and spread my thumb and little finger by the side of my face to mime a telephone receiver. Then I pass the living room again, phone in hand, waving and pointing ahead to show them the way I'm going. It's as if I were part of some comedy act: *woman passes open door, gesticulating*. Meanwhile I dial my sister's number, glance at the rat cage under the stairs where all is calm, and go into the bathroom to pack Helli's things. I needn't go in her room—I can take the things straight from the tumble dryer.

'At last,' says Sissi.

I don't have the heart to start the conversation by telling her we only have about ten minutes to speak. Out in the hall I hear my mobile beep on the hallstand. Sissi talks and I go back and forth, gathering up Helli's things. In my head I go through the typical morning routine of a not-quite teenager, so as not to forget anything: toothbrush, toothpaste, shampoo, shower gel, deodorant, mousse, hairbrush, acne cream, concealer, perfume. Helli uses vile-smelling stuff that gives me a headache, but it's cheap and easy to get hold of. When I was her age I only ever filched the odd drop of Old Lavender from my mother.

Sissi is saying: 'I don't know how much longer I can take it with Richard, I really don't. I think I'm going to break up with him. Could I come and stay for a few weeks if that happened? Until I'd found a place of my own?'

Her composer isn't really called Richard. He changed his name when he was eighteen, in homage to Richard Wagner. In her rare moments of spite, Sissi says he called himself after Richard Clayderman, but only when he isn't around—she would never deliberately provoke him. She'd never break up with him either—or at least that's what I'd always thought, but today things sound more serious than usual. She's asking for somewhere to stay, after all. What if she isn't just saying it this time? What if, on top of everything else, my sister ended up moving in with us? She actually has a place of her own, a studio flat in Hamburg, but for years a friend and her married lover have been using it for their trysts, so it isn't free twenty-four seven. In fact, if I understand correctly, this friend spends most of her time there, so I suppose Sissi would have to throw her out before she could move in. She keeps a few things in the flat and drops in to wash or change now and then, but she doesn't practise there—she has a special deal with some caretaker or other who lets her practise in the catacombs of the opera house. Officially, though, she doesn't live with Richard—he needs his freedom, even if it's only symbolic.

'You're always welcome here,' I say, deciding I'd better pack two pairs of knickers, because who knows how well the tampons will do their job, whether Helli will remember to change them in time and how heavy the bleeding is at night. The washing machine has come to the end of its cycle—the tumble dryer too. With one hand I pull the dry laundry onto the floor, stuff the wet laundry into the dryer without sorting it, and turn the dial to *cupboard dry*, because I like the sound of it. The words have a comforting ring—you can't, I feel, go wrong with *cupboard dry*. I rarely use any other program.

'He's an egocentric,' says Sissi as I rummage around the pile on the floor for Helli's knickers. 'He calls the shots and I have to fit in around him. I don't think he even cares anymore whether I'm there or not. As far as he's concerned, I'm just like a coat hanging in the wardrobe or something.'

That's a good simile, I think—*a coat is pretty useful, but it's by no means essential.* But then I wonder whether anyone's essential to anyone else.

'Last Saturday we were standing outside the cinema,' says Sissi, 'Sabine, Frank, Michaela—the whole gang—and there was a bit of a queue because, my God, it was Saturday night, and what do you expect if you go to the cinema on the weekend? But we were all in a good mood, and Sabine and Frank were showing us photos of the kids on their phones—and then out of the blue Richard blurts out: "I'm going home. You have a nice evening." We all tried to talk him out of it, but he was adamant. He didn't make a scene or anything—he'd just changed his mind and wanted to go home. He'd rather sit and read a score than watch Tarantino—something like that. And that was it for me too—I wouldn't have enjoyed the film for a minute if I'd stayed. But of course that wouldn't occur to him—after all these years, he still doesn't know how I tick. On the way home, I asked him what had got into him to make him go off and leave everyone like that when they're our friends and whatever, and he said, deadly serious, he's decided to put himself first more often. He's been thinking lately that he's too accommodating—that he does too much stuff he doesn't actually want to do, just because people expect it of him. From now on he's going to listen to himself more and not give a fuck about social norms, and if that means going off and leaving his friends standing there on the footpath when he realises he doesn't actually want to spend the evening with them, then so be it. I say: "What about common courtesy? What about keeping appointments and being reliable and all that? Do you want us to only ever make provisional plans from now on, just in case you change your mind and decide you'd rather go home?" And he said: "Yes." He just said yes. I was completely gobsmacked, although I do see where he's coming from, and he's right that it's important to know what you want and all that. So I asked: "And what about me?" And he said: "You could have stayed at the cinema. This isn't about you." Can you believe it, Katy? He actually said: *This isn't about you.*'

'Mhm,' I say, doing up the zip of Helli's wash bag with my teeth.

'I mean, I know what his problem is. He's always done what he was supposed to do—he's always done the right thing, always accommodated other people and done what was expected of him. This is a kind of belated adolescence. He's suddenly decided to find out what he wants, what he likes and doesn't like, what suits him and what doesn't. And when you're going through that, you overdo things slightly to begin with—we were just the same when we were younger. He's come to it a bit late, that's all. But I don't know whether I can go through this with him. What if he has to wait a minute or two for his vegetable curry at that Indian place near the station and he gets thinking and decides he's fed up with me and is only sticking around because it's what everyone does, or because I forced myself on him, or because he's been too lazy to break up with me until now?'

That's her true fear. Always was. This has nothing to do with Richard's late adolescent whims.

'Sissi,' I say, taking a deep breath. Helli's things are gathered up in a small heap on the floor. All I have to do is throw them in a bag, chuck Heinz and Theo out and whizz up to the station—although I'm too late now to be smiling and waving on the platform when the train draws in. 'I have to go. Kilian's at the station.'

'Oh, okay, fine,' she says.

Then there's silence. I don't hang up—I can't.

149

Richard has been Sissi's composer for almost six years. She was unlucky enough to fall in love with him just when her biological clock was starting its famous ticking, because although he seemed to like children, he made it clear to Sissi that he thought them too much hard work. Hoping to soften him, I once explained that there's a difference between other people's children and your own. When other people's children visit, you want to spoil them and make sure they have everything they want—so you soon get sick of them. With your own children, you get into the swing of things and can give them all the attention they need without being on permanent high alert.

It's like learning a foreign language. You start out translating everything word for word in your head, painstakingly assembling each individual sentence and struggling with the grammar—but gradually, over the months and years, it gets easier. You become fluent. You have stock phrases ready and eventually an entire fund of language to fall back on, because you stop thinking in your own language. But if you don't have children of your own or don't spend much time with children, you remain at the arduous building-block stage and putting up with their funny ways is exhausting.

Richard prefers to devote his energy to composing—his whole life is geared towards conserving or increasing his powers. Every day he practises the piano and reads scores for hours on end. He does yoga, goes for walks and eats unimaginative, dull, but healthy meals. He tries to get enough sleep and spends a lot of time fussing over his hair. It isn't so easy to be a composer—commissions are few and far between, so it's a good thing that his dreary way of life is so cheap. He's somehow or other managed to keep himself afloat over the years, and things have certainly been easier since Sissi moved in with him and felt a responsibility to help fill the fridge.

Sissi worships him. When I picture the two of them together, I see her languishing at his feet on a silk cushion. She's the type to go in for such arrangements—she can assume an expression of such devotion, you could be forgiven for being sceptical. Richard, meanwhile, I envisage seated at the piano, eyes closed, hands poised to sink into an exquisite chord. On the wall behind him, a photograph of the elderly Liszt looking like a wise Sioux chieftain completes the tableau.

Sissi will never leave Richard. I needn't worry that she's about to move in with us. No matter how often she's announced it, my sister has never left a single one of her artists. She doesn't do break-ups. I expect she sings the song of the barnacle.

She's on the phone still, but silent.

'Sissi,' I say, 'don't sulk. Shall I ring again later?'

'It's all right,' she says. 'Don't worry about it.'

'There's a funny smell in here,' I say.

'Where are you?'

'In the bathroom. It smells of burning.'

'Burning? In the bathroom?'

'I think it's the tumble dryer.' I lean over to sniff it.

'Have you left the dinner in the tumble dryer?' asks Sissi, beginning to enjoy herself.

I lean over a little further. Then I say, 'I'm going to have to go. The tumble dryer's on fire.'

As I run around the bathroom, unplugging the dryer and filling the only vessel I can find with water—an old-fashioned inhaler stamped with the logo of a pharmaceutical company— I call out for Heinz and Theo. I pour water over the small flames flickering out of the back of the dryer, run back to the basin and pour on more water. There's a dramatic hiss and a cloud of smoke. Heinz and Theo appear at the door and watch the scene, fascinated.

They offer me assistance in the form of advice. A wet towel seems to them a good idea, and an irate call to the manufacturing company imperative. They make fun of the inhaler and praise me, not entirely convincingly, for having the presence of mind to unplug the dryer. They lay their hands on the doused dryer and announce that it's still very hot and may burst into flames again—they once heard a talk on the subject given by the fire brigade. Heinz and I join forces to lift the dryer, and Theo, who looks astonishingly perky, considering that a moment ago he was lying on the sofa looking like a wounded deer, directs us along the hall with his disturbingly large bandage. Panting, Heinz and I carry the tumble dryer out into the garden, where we drop it on the frosty grass and press our palms to the smalls of our backs. Kilian will be at the station by now, scanning the faces of all the women hurrying in his direction.

'We should open up the back,' says Theo. 'Do you have a jemmy?'

I have to laugh. It's not that I want to laugh—this isn't the moment. Really I'd like to cry—to howl into the dark like a wolf, to wail and thrash about. I'd like to lay into the tumble dryer with a baseball bat and give these two useless men in my garden a good hard kick in the shins. Instead I laugh so hard I double up because I can't get my breath. Tears spring to my eyes—I grunt like a pig and then screech and hiccup alternately until, unable to stand any longer, I flop down on my bum like a sack of potatoes. Theo and Heinz join in my laughter almost at once—they regard it as a point of honour to laugh when someone else does. If I'd managed to make myself cry, they would, as a matter of course, have cried instead. They know how to behave.

Eventually, I'm sitting on the crisp grass with my legs drawn up to my body—Heinz is draped over the dryer and Theo is crouched down with his back against it, his face buried in his hands, his bandage glowing with unnatural brightness in the deep dark of winter.

'I don't know if we have a jemmy,' I say, forcing out the words. 'I'll go and have a look.'

In the house I hunt through all the drawers I think might yield something. There are real tools in the shed, but I hope to find something suitable without having to brave the shed because that's Costas's territory and I avoid rummaging around in there if I can help it. Maybe I'm afraid of what I might find. Armed with a screwdriver, barbecue tongs, a meat mallet, a small spanner and a cake slice, I return to the garden. On the way I stop in the hall for a moment to glance at my phone. No worried text from Kilian yet. The message I heard from the bathroom when I was talking to Sissi is from Costas. For a second my belly seizes up and I silently vow to read the text as soon as this potential fire has been put out. Costas's presence at this moment wouldn't have helped in the slightest, but it would have made all the difference. I should never have let him take on that whore's job in Berlin.

Heinz is more enthusiastic about the screwdriver than anything else, but the cake slice also comes in handy when the back of the tumble dryer doesn't immediately come away. It's pitch black in the garden. What little light we have comes from the windows of the house. The three of us lean over the back of the dryer and peer into its entrails. None of us has any idea what we're looking for. Heinz tips the tumble dryer forward a little way to get a better look. He hammers around inside with the meat mallet, giving us glimpses of secret passages and hidey holes where the insidious fire might be lurking. But there's nothing there. To be on the safe side, I lug a ten-litre bucket of water out from the kitchen and Heinz takes it upon himself to empty it into the disembowelled machine.

He and Theo are in high spirits. They toddle off home happily and I'm glad that I've somehow managed to brighten up their day, even if it did entail sacrificing an expensive household appliance. I pack Helli's things, shovel the wet washing on the bathroom floor into a basket, fetch my coat and get in the car to go and pick up Kilian—at last. At long last.

THE STREET LAMPS light up the frosty bushes on both sides of the road. It's icy—I can't drive as fast as I'd like. In the labyrinth of the housing development where Cindi lives, I suddenly remember Costas's text message and pull over to read it. He writes: *Downtime. Too tired to work, too hungry to wait for the buffet. If you got the train you could be here in three hours—think about it. Heinz could keep an eye on the kids. I'll die of boredom without you tonight. C*

I feel drained and at the same time terribly harassed. What shall I reply? He's clearly forgotten I've got someone coming to stay this evening. I type: *If YOU got the train, YOU could be HERE in three hours. Your secretary could keep an eye on the buffet. K*

Deep down, I'm touched that he bothers to write such meticulous texts. I'm glad, for instance, that I am 'you' rather than 'u'—it gives me the impression that he takes me seriously and makes me feel tender towards him. My Costas, who takes as much trouble over the little things as over the big ones. I put the CD on and go on my way to take Helli her bag.

Kilian will be waiting at the station. Josef Protschka is singing 'The Old Bad Songs' and I notice too late that my eyes are shut, and mount the kerb with my right wheel. It's the last song of the cycle and the words are sad without making me weepy, which I appreciate. The closing bars on the piano are different, creeping straight into my soul and filling it with an icy chill. Heine knew exactly what he was doing—so did Schumann. I wait for the singing to stop and then turn off the CD before the devious piano begins its solo, pitting despair against the singer's defiant resolve to overcome his pain. Maybe, rather than have anything to do with me, my epitaph should be addressed to Costas: *Don't be angry with our sister, you sad, pale man.*

Outside Cindi's house a solitary street lamp flickers erratically. I park the car directly underneath and walk to the door in the flickering light, Helli's bag in hand. At first there's no response to the doorbell, but at the second ring the door opens and I find myself looking at a young man I don't know from Adam. I see my own surprise reflected on his face.

'Well, well, well,' he says, 'and who do we have here?'

I realise that he isn't sober. He's clutching the doorframe and looking at me very seriously and intently, as if making an immense effort not to appear unfocused. The muffled bass thump of music turned up to full blast comes from somewhere inside the house.

'Here we have Helli's mother,' I say. 'With Helli's toothbrush.' I hold up the bag so that he can see it without making an effort, and Helli comes into view behind him. She pushes him aside in an almost motherly fashion—firm without being rough, allowing him to retain his dignity as well as his balance. She's out of breath and red-cheeked. Before she closes the door behind her, leaving it slightly ajar, I catch a glimpse of the room off the hall. It looks well-populated. Helli knows at once what I'm thinking. I'm often left speechless by her ability to read me like an open book. Shouldn't a girl who has something with the words 'attention deficit' in its name have trouble guessing people's feelings? But mothers aren't normal people—the rules that apply to others don't necessarily apply to them. Maybe all mothers are open books to their children, and it's just that most children are too polite to let on. Was I able to read my mother like that? I wouldn't have said so. I think I was completely blind when it came to my mother.

Helli, at any rate, launches straight into a rant designed to reassure me, not without effect: 'It's just a little party, that's all. Roland's passed some test or other and asked a few people over. They won't be staying long. It was a spur-of-the-moment thing. Me and Cindi are allowed to hang out there a bit, but it's Roland's party and we're going up to Cindi's room anyway soon to watch a film. We're just ordering pizza for everyone and then that's it. Me and Cindi won't hang around after that. The guy at the door just now, Hauke, he's a bit crazy—you can't take him too seriously. He's harmless, really—he's always completely out of it.'

'He seemed pretty drunk to me,' I say.

'Yeah, maybe. He probably started drinking before he got here. The rest of us are just listening to music and stuff and having a bit of a party because Roland's passed this test.'

'What test?'

'No idea. The sixth-formers are always having tests. Ask Alex. Or no, hang on, I think it was karate. Purple belt. Or brown. Whatever, as long as we get to order pizza.'

'How many people are in there?'

'A few.'

'And where are Cindi's parents? Are they around?'

'Dunno,' says Helli. She opens the door a crack and turns and yells into the house: 'Cindi! Are your mum and dad home?'

Cindi's voice comes from inside the house—it sounds as if she has her mouth full. 'Not right now. But they'll be back later. Tell your mum they're definitely coming back later.'

'Not right now,' says Helli, almost closing the door again. 'But they're definitely coming back later.'

My phone's ringing in my coat pocket—it will be Kilian, wondering why he's having to stand around on a dark, deserted station in the freezing cold. I thrust the bag into Helli's hand and try to catch her for a kiss, but only manage to brush her ear. She's already on her way back in and has forgotten me the second she's turned away.

I take my mobile from my pocket, press the little green button and say: 'Katharina Theodoroulakis.' But the caller has already given up. I dash back to the car. From force of habit, I wave in the direction of the front door as I start the engine, but nobody sees me.

Helli is only eleven, I tell myself. She's still a child. Of course she's interested in parties. Maybe even in older boys.

Possibly even in alcohol. It's too early for anything that goes beyond mere interest. But I know that's not true. I know I'm lying to myself. It might be what I thought until this morning, but it should be pretty obvious to me by now that I'm not very well up on what Helli does or doesn't get up to and what stage of life she's at. The big change must have set in recently without my noticing—a line was crossed when I wasn't looking. It's possible that Helli is still wandering between worlds, that she's in that confusing no man's land between childhood and adolescence. But isn't that a particularly dangerous place to be? Isn't this a particularly dangerous time? The child that Helli still is can be hurt, maybe even permanently damaged or traumatised, by seeing and hearing things that are meant for teenagers—and the worst of it is that it will be Helli who gets herself into these inappropriate situations, because the adolescent part of her will rush into things. I strain to remember how it was with me, but all I can recall feeling at that time—apart from my school-choir crush—is my fear of vomiting attacks and the horror of dying a solitary death in the girls' toilets. There were no parties for me in those years of transition between childhood and adolescence.

The day I knew I'd crossed the boundary to the adult world was by no means horrific. It was more like putting on a pair of glasses after years of seeing things blurred. One autumn day, I stayed longer than usual in the stables after my riding lesson because it was cold and windy and I didn't feel like cycling home. I wandered around the tack room, trying to coax the stable cats out. I roamed up and down the aisles between the stalls, stroking the horses. I did a bit of sweeping, daydreaming and wondering which of the horses I'd buy if I had the money. In one of the aisles a mare was being prepared for a show. Her owner was braiding her tail and polishing her hooves, and I stood and watched for a while.

Then the stable door opened and one of the stud horses was led in. His name was Paris—all the studs in that stable were called after cities; it didn't occur to me to find that strange at the time. Paris was walked right through the stable. He was a big horse, but nervous and jumpy, and the young man holding his rope talked to him soothingly. Paris was usually in another stable, separate from the riding-school horses and the private horses and the lower-ranking studs—it must have been the unaccustomed surroundings that unsettled him. But then he caught sight of the mare standing in the aisle. He stopped dead and began to snort like a steam engine. The man tried to pull him away, but it was useless—Paris stood there, snorting, his legs peculiarly far apart, his flanks quivering and, as if in slow motion, he let out the gigantic penis that hung under his belly like a tube.

I stared at it.

'Hurry up and take that mare away,' the man said peevishly.

The mare's owner hastily untied her horse and led it to a stall while Paris quivered and snorted and pawed the ground with his hoof as if preparing for a bullfight. The polish on the mare's hooves wasn't dry—the straw in the stall would stick to it. Her tail would probably have to be plaited all over again too—with every move she made, the elaborate braid unravelled a little further. The man pulled at Paris's rope, patted his hindquarters and tugged and pushed and shoved until, at last, he had got the stud past the stall where the mare was standing.

Then he turned briefly and called back to the woman: 'Mares in heat belong in the stall, you know that.'

'I wasn't to know there'd be two randy blokes wanting to get through,' the woman called back.

And it was then that I understood. I saw that everything was quite different from what I had previously thought. Grown-ups' conversations, ads on TV, nature, animals, plants, the whole of evolution—it was all sex.

I cycled home and rang Ann-Britt to talk it over with her, but soon realised that she didn't understand. For her everything was still perfectly normal and straightforward and one-dimensional. Things were things—there was no ambiguity, no hidden meaning. It was over a year before she changed her way of looking at the world and could laugh with me at the new meaning of words. It really was hilarious. Sausages, bananas, umbrellas, branches and woodwind instruments were suddenly so obtrusive that you had to laugh. Handbags, wet wipes, screwdrivers, rabbits, petrol stations, eggnog, stables—why hadn't I noticed earlier? And then there were the grown-ups' conversations, the glances and smiles they exchanged over the heads of the uncomprehending children. Now I was part of the club—I too could giggle knowingly. I understood the point of clothes and fashion, and realised that the words I had previously sorted according to the violence of reaction they provoked from the grown-ups were actually governed by a quite different hierarchy. It wasn't that 'wanker' was a worse word than 'pig' because it was worse to be a wanker than a pig. It was more straightforward than that: the more a word had to do with sex, the more reprehensible it was.

I felt the way I'd felt in primary school when I suddenly learnt to read. Until then I'd been spelling everything out laboriously, putting the sounds together letter by letter—and then all at once, as if by magic, as if someone had flicked a switch, the letters came together into words that I knew and the things I read made sense. From then on I read everything in sight, but in spite of the satisfaction it gave me and the myriad possibilities it opened up, there were moments of exhaustion and frustration when I'd curse my new skill. I wished I could once again sit at the breakfast table without having to read the words *Oats*, *Whole Milk* and *Muesli*. It sometimes even frightened me that there was no returning to a world in which writing was nothing but meaningless symbols.

I hadn't noticed Helli giving the knowing looks and giggles of the initiate, but I was wrong to wait for those signs. Times have changed. The taboos have been broken, and all that mystery-mongering is a thing of the past. The internet can tell everyone everything at any time—it no longer takes a real live horse's penis to get you out of no man's land. The adult world has been insinuating itself into childhood for some time now, making it porous and unsafe. Helli has been in that uncertain territory for a while and I've been too blinkered to notice.

Just now, knowing that there's some kind of teenage party

underway at Cindi's house, I'm almost glad that my daughter looks like a lump of raw dough. With any luck it will protect her for a while to come.

◊

The station is deserted at this time of day. The commuters from Lübeck were tipped out onto the platform a little while ago—they will have poured out of the building and distributed themselves into cars and taxis and onto bikes to scatter in all directions and melt into town, into the surrounding countryside, into the evening. As I skirt the side of the station building, an icy wind hits me, bringing the smell of cold and train brakes, and perhaps a hint of kelp and salt, a smell my nose is so used to that I only notice it in contrast with others. In the car it smells of car. Outside it smells of the sea.

The paving stones of the station forecourt are laid in regular but staggered rows so that, looked at the right way, they form a long stretch of hopscotch squares. My legs want to hop—the urge is overpowering. I could fight it—so far, I've always managed—but today there's almost no one here to see. What do I have to lose? Apart from anything else, I feel that my legs are right—*hop, Katharina, hop while you can.* And I do. I hop and jump, hop and jump towards the station, on and on, until I'm hot—until a sense of exuberance floods over me. It is in this state that I meet Kilian.

Like me, he has grown older. Unlike me, he looks better for it. He was always on the short side—too small and delicate to look manly and mature, his big eyes those of a child. He evidently had to turn forty before his childlike demeanour would become boyish charm. I find him inside the station, beside him a squishy sports bag, an instrument case and a medium-sized amp. He's studying the arrival and departure times in the display case on the wall—there isn't much else you can do here to pass the time. His long coat doesn't look particularly warm—a kind of trench coat you wouldn't usually recommend to anyone under five foot eleven. When he turns to face me—of course he heard me coming, but he deliberately waits in front of the dull display case, pretending to be absorbed in reading the train times, because he's a jazz musician, isn't he, and there's nothing they despise more than overeagerness and impatience—when he turns to face me, I immediately see the lines at his eyes. He smiles at me and they run from the corners of his eyes almost to his ears, broken only by the thick frames of his glasses. They make him look kind and worldly-wise, and along with the joy at seeing him again after all these years, I feel a pang of jealousy. Looking the way he does, a lot of women must fancy him, and all this time I'd somehow imagined he was all mine. Every woman with limited self-confidence should find herself a male friend who's incapable of relationships.

'Goodness, Katinka,' he says, and his voice is deeper than I remember. Can he have deliberately changed it, in line with his new image?

'Well,' I say and shrug.

He spreads his arms and puts his head on one side and I smile indulgently before letting him hug me.

◊

The minute I fell in love with Costas—the minute my head or heart or whatever is responsible for these things decided that he was the one, I became blind. Everything I saw from then on was somehow connected to him, because if it wasn't, it failed to hold my interest and I instantly forgot all about it, didn't see it, didn't hear it. I was so taken up with Costas and everything to do with him that the other people I knew became mere shadowy forms on the edge of my field of vision. Kilian was one of these. But it hadn't always been that way. Before Costas, Kilian had occupied an important place in my life. He was my flatmate, a slight but energetic boy, blessed with a natural wit that not everyone understood. He looked as if he were still at school and he had little luck with women, but because he didn't seem bothered by this, I felt infinitely at ease with him.

Today Kilian is a jazz double-bass player—a studio musician most of the time, though he occasionally works as a sound technician and gives the odd lesson. But when I knew him in Lübeck, he was studying classical double bass, his face pulled into an unconscious grimace at every pluck and bow on his enormous instrument. His mother is Japanese—at that time he had jet-black curls and almost no facial hair. He was untidy and a little bit slovenly—sometimes the dirty dishes would gather in his room until there were too many to fit in the kitchen sink and he would rinse them off in the bath. When we were both at home, I'd hear him practising in the next room—scales, more often than not, because it was clean playing that gave him the most trouble. As soon as he stopped for a cigarette break, I'd drop whatever I was doing and join him in the kitchen. The two girls we shared with were seldom there during the day—they practised at the academy and went to seminars, or sat in libraries and cafes—hardworking students who went on, I'm told, to get married, and ended up just like me.

Kilian and I spent most of our breaks together. I'd drink tea while he smoked, or rolled endless cigarettes, and we would talk about everything that came into our heads. We talked about music theory and why jazz was better than classical—a question very much on Kilian's mind at the time—about women and men and our ideas of a good life. Almost everything revolved around the future—the present was only a springboard—somewhere to start from, somewhere to rehearse—while the future held everything that was good and right and worthwhile. Kilian didn't want much: a family, music, a little house in a part of the country where it was warm in summer and snowy in winter. He wanted freedom—he wanted to be able to express himself, to make his own rules, be his own boss, and accountable to no one. He wanted a leisurely, peaceful life. Upheaval and movement and experiences would come automatically as a result of all the travelling he'd have to do as the member of a popular jazz combo. Money wasn't important to him. He was more interested in style. You could, after all, live stylishly even without money—at the end of the day, all you had to do was make scruffy clothes your trademark. Kilian talked a lot about styles of glasses frames.

When I was low, he would take my hand. If I complained about my workload, he would get up and massage my shoulders. Since leaving school, I had lost my casual attitude towards exams. Late one night, Kilian found me sitting shivery and exhausted over a cup of warm milk because thoughts of an approaching exam were keeping me awake. He led me back to bed and lay down behind me, his belly against my back. With his breath on my neck, I was asleep within minutes.

I'd ask Kilian for advice when I was dressing for a date because he seemed interested in underwear and had sensible views. I confided in him that I had trouble relaxing during sex, and he recommended techniques to me and nodded wisely at all I said on the subject. I never locked the door when I had a shower, let Kilian rub cream on my back, and hugged and kissed him if I happened to be in the mood, more often than not swept away by my feelings for something quite different.

I recall one morning in particular, the day after an exam. I was in a bad way because I'd slept fitfully all week and felt overworked and burnt out. It was early—I didn't have to be anywhere—and I sat shattered and brooding at the kitchen table in front of a cup of unsweetened black coffee because I was too lazy to fetch milk and sugar. Kilian came into the kitchen. He was taciturn in the mornings, but energetic, and he made himself a substantial breakfast of fruit, yoghurt and an enormous pile of oats dusted with cocoa powder because, as he said, it was the weekend.

Since my mother's death, I had forgotten what it meant to eat healthily and I was impressed by the effort Kilian put into making his breakfast. He joined me at the table and began to tuck in. There was some relatively warm coffee left in the pot and he poured himself a cup without asking.

Looking up from his bowl, he mumbled: 'My mouth's full. You'll have to do the talking.'

I didn't feel like talking. I was uneasy about the previous day's exam because I was always unsure about harmony. Everything seemed perfectly logical until someone made an alternative suggestion and suddenly my theories looked simplistic and over-obvious.

'All right, then,' I said. 'I'll talk. First of all, I can't believe how much you're planning to eat. You're small and skinny and I don't suppose your stomach's much bigger than a grapefruit, even at maximum capacity. If you want to get the entire contents of that bowl into your body, you're going to have to eat so slowly that your stomach can pass something onto your gut before the next lot comes.'

Kilian grunted contentedly and nodded, but didn't stop shovelling oats into his mouth.

'I suppose you need a lot of energy to play the double bass,' I said. 'Maybe I should eat more oats. I might be able to think better then and wouldn't have to waste time wondering whether the first song of *Dichterliebe* is in F sharp minor or A major. I'm inclined to go for F sharp minor, but that would be like a black hole—all around it, everything is moving, so you know it's there, or was there, but you can't see it. Whatever would induce someone to begin a song cycle in a key that's nothing but empty space? It's madness.'

Kilian opened his mouth to pour in coffee and wash down the oats. That gave him the opportunity to say something: 'Schumann *was* mad.'

'But not at that point,' I said. 'You can't interpret someone's life and work from back to front like that, starting at the end. That's a bad habit of academics. Someone dies young and everyone decides that must be the reason why he produced so much so quickly. As if he'd known in advance. That's as ridiculous as saying it's going to be a harsh winter because there are such a lot of beechnuts. How are the beeches to know what the weather will be like in two months' time?'

Kilian laughed and wiped his mouth.

'What exactly are you talking about? Trees?'

'No,' I cried. 'About life. About an artist's work. About everything an artist does and creates and all the nonsense people talk when they try to give meaning to the overall picture.'

'But death is a part of life,' said Kilian. He stopped eating and pushed his bowl away. 'If you want to consider life in its entirety, then the way someone dies is part of that—it can be present as a latent motif throughout their life so that it comes to seem inevitable. If someone smokes nonstop, they'll get lung cancer. If someone's always taking risks, they'll end up falling off a cliff. And if someone is cautious and modest, they'll live to a ripe old age and die a dull death in their bed. It's so simple—why shouldn't it be possible to come up with similar explanations in more complex cases? Why shouldn't it be possible to find indications of Schumann's insanity in his work if that's the way he was going to go? His death has to be consistent with his life.'

'But I could be crossing the road and just happen to get run over,' I said. 'I can be as modest and sedate as I like, but some drunken moron can still come round the corner and mow me down. In what way is my death consistent with the overall picture then?'

'Academics will still be able to take that as the starting point for your life story. Instead of studying your work or behaviour for signs of your death, they'll interpret everything in the light of your tragic accident. It's impossible to tell the story of someone's life without being constantly aware of their death.'

'I don't trust double-bass players who start philosophising. Your brains aren't made for it.' I was awake now and feeling strangely exhilarated. The kitchen, which earlier that morning had seemed small and smoky and filthy, suddenly seemed cosy and rather laid-back. Good conversation was more important than clean dishes, and a truly wise person knew that. You could say that the mess and lack of hygiene in our shared kitchen were proof of how intellectual we were, how focused on the essential. I got up to fetch milk and sugar.

We sat there drinking coffee until the afternoon. Kilian fetched me books from his room, which I looked at and stacked beside my cup. He smoked cigarette after cigarette and we talked and laughed, and time disappeared, leaving us in the kitchen without letting us know where it was going. Later, when all the ground coffee was gone, we put on our jackets and went for a long walk to a supermarket that was still open. We bought coffee and vermouth and a single frozen lasagne that we later warmed up and shared in the kitchen. We hadn't had enough money to buy two.

◊

Not long ago, in a magazine in the paediatrician's waiting room, I came across a questionnaire designed to help you work out which of five different 'happiness types' you were. I answered the questions in my head without giving them much thought. One of them was: *Think of a day in your life you'd like to relive because you felt so happy—what elements did it contain? A) Friends and family, B) Exotic places and nature, C) Adventure and excitement.*

I closed my eyes for a moment to recall a day in my life when I had felt really good, and although I hadn't thought of it for years, I remembered that day in the kitchen when Kilian and I talked about deep-and-meaningful things and shared a frozen lasagne.

Later, in a quiet moment, I'll try to make a list. It will be headed: *Days I'd like to relive.* I deposit the day with Kilian in the hall of my childhood house, ready to pick up later. One thing, of course, that will have to go on the list is a day from the time when there was only Costas and me—no house, no children, no rats. Probably one of those completely normal days when we watched television and went for a walk and then fell asleep together.

'Do you remember the time we sat in the kitchen all day long?' I ask Kilian, who is strapping himself in beside me, having removed the broken-off wing mirror from the seat with enviable aplomb.

'Of course. We talked about children's books and I ended up massaging your feet.'

'About children's books?'

'We discovered we'd liked the same books when we were children. Don't you remember?'

'Children's books? Are you sure?'

He laughs. 'As long as you remember the foot massage. I tried so hard—I was hoping to show you I was the right man for you.'

I laugh too, but say nothing. I don't remember any foot massage—in fact, I'm rather taken aback by his words.

The temperature display on the dashboard flashes and beeps to warn me of frost. Stars made of artificial fir branches hang from the lampposts, twinkling distractingly. Over the course of my life these Christmas lights have grown smaller and smaller and more and more glaring. I think wistfully of the dingy yellow glow of the imitation candles of my childhood. We drive along roads where brick houses are set out in rows behind evergreen hedges, each front garden decorated with precisely one string of lights draped over precisely one bush. It's the same in hundreds of north German towns and villages coming up to Christmas. I wonder what Kilian makes of it—this restraint, this moderation so characteristic of the local style.

'How was your concert?' I ask.

'Amusing,' he says. 'We played Christmas carols but hadn't had time to practise. I think we all had slightly different ideas of how they went. The audience didn't notice. They just thought that's what jazz sounds like.'

'Are you hungry?'

'Not specially. They gave us a few biscuits and I ate mine on the train. They must have been feeling guilty about how little they were paying us.'

'I still have to make up your bed.'

I'd like to make a short list now—there's so much I must

remember to do this evening. I step into my childhood house to deposit a few items, but the hall is already taken up with our student kitchen, and I give up because I need to concentrate on driving and Kilian is chattering away beside me. I'll just have to hope I remember the important things when I'm standing right in front of them.

'It was so funny this afternoon. Clemens tried to sing "Ring, Little Bells", but he'd forgotten the words. I tried to help and started to sing too but I couldn't...'

Kilian talks and talks and I test the brakes at the traffic lights and discover that the temperature display was right to warn me—it's icy. But I know the roads around here—every bend, every bridge, every stretch of shade where the cold lingers. I've lived here so long I could drive it blindfolded. And I'd know the words to 'Ring, Little Bells' if you woke me from a deep sleep in the middle of the night. I can sing it, whistle it and play it on various instruments—I can teach it to children and tell them what it's about and perform it with them. If we do organise a Christmas party for the music-school class, that carol is guaranteed to feature in one form or another. The music-school parents aren't afraid of Christian content, unlike the kindergarten parents, who would go on the warpath at a line like 'meek child, how blessed'. I'd like to make Costas sit in on one of my classes sometime to show him what I can never manage to explain to him—that if you work with children, you inevitably find yourself having to contend with society as a whole.

It suddenly seems irresponsible to have left Helli at Cindi's. The threat of a tantrum, Kilian's visit, the lure of a quarter of an hour to myself—none of that can justify my failure to bundle her straight into the car when a spaced-out sixth-former I'd never seen in my life opened the door to me. What kind of a mother am I to offer my eleven-year-old child so little protection? A child who probably has ADHD, and is equipped with almost no impulse control or sense of consequences—a child who lives entirely in the present and cares only about what she feels like doing at any given moment. I break out in a sweat. Kilian goes on and on but I can't listen— the images in my head are overwhelming me.

I pull over to the side of the road, switch on the warning lights and get out my phone without cutting the engine. Kilian looks perplexed and falls silent.

'Won't be a moment,' I say, holding the phone to my ear. 'I'm afraid I might just go mad if I don't make this call.'

After four rings, Cindi's dad picks up.

'You're at home,' I say.

'Of course I am,' he says. 'Where else would I be?'

At the cleaning lady's, I think. 'You were out when I dropped off Helli's things.'

'Mhm,' he says.

I'm suddenly embarrassed. 'Just wanted to make sure everything's all right.'

'Everything's fine,' he says.

'Great. Thanks so much for having Helli to stay. She was thrilled.'

'No worries.'

'Well, then,' I say, 'have a nice evening. And a peaceful night, I hope.'

'You too,' he says, and hangs up.

All this time Kilian has been looking at me. In the light of the lamppost decorations, I can see that he's amused.

I flick on the indicator and drive off. 'Don't ask,' I say. 'You wouldn't understand.'

I sometimes think I could be free if it weren't for the children. As long as they're around, I'm bound and chained to them, plagued by worries, consumed by doubts and unable to make the slightest decision for myself without considering their feelings.

But I know it's not true. If they weren't around, it would mean they were dead—that I'd lost them. And no one is less free than parents who have lost children. I know that. Costas knows that. Berenike shackles us together in a way that Alex and Helli do not—we can never be single again now, no matter what happens. If I really am dead and buried soon, Costas can fall in love again as often as he likes—he can marry ten new wives—but in his will he has asked to be buried alongside me, because I'm Berenike's mother, and through her we are bound to one another for evermore.

THE HOUSE IS EMPTY at last, apart from the rats. Theo and Heinz are back next door, Barbie and Ken are enjoying the freedom of an early Friday evening together, and Helli is safe with a family where her presence is neither here nor there. Soon Costas will write me an evening text message and I'll send a good-natured reply, because evening texts should never be waspish or ambiguous—we both need our sleep. Nasty remarks late at night count as war crimes in our marriage and violate the unwritten Theodoroulakis conventions.

Kilian puts his amp down in the hall, leans his double-bass case against the hallstand and disappears into the toilet without taking his coat off. When he's back, he asks: 'Is it far to the sea from here?'

'Quarter of an hour's walk,' I say. 'But it's freezing out there.'

'Let's go anyway,' he says, taking my hand. His is still a little wet, but I don't mind. At least I know he washes his hands after going to the toilet—that's more important to me than fastidiously dry skin.

He's the guest, so he gets to choose. I'm horribly tired—the last hours were rather too stressful, even for me. I haven't vacuumed upstairs or made up the spare bed and I didn't get a chance to check my email again. The little light on the answering machine will be flashing and I'm desperately hungry because I haven't had anything but tea and dried apricots since lunchtime, in spite of riding horses, comforting children and lugging burning whitegoods all over the place. Still, the prospect of going down to the beach is beguiling. I haven't seen the sea for weeks. I always go the other way in the car, and although it really is only a quarter of an hour's walk from our house, I never get round to going. When do I ever have a spare quarter of an hour in my life to see the sea?

I put all my winter things back on. I feel a bit ridiculous wearing my woolly hat in front of Kilian. I look good in proper hats—broad-brimmed summer hats, for instance, the sort no one wears anymore, except the insecure and the attention-seeking. Hats like that never worked in a windy place like this anyway—they don't stay on for a second. But woolly hats make my already small head look even smaller—add a thick winter coat, and it looks like a pinhead on top of a dumpling, and my hair sticks out at the bottom like straw escaping from a scarecrow's hat. I suppose I should be thankful that I have hair at all. I'm definitely the kind who would need a wig during chemo.

I keep the hat on all the same. Never mind what Kilian

thinks—it's too cold to be vain. My fingers are still frozen and drained of blood from clutching the steering wheel, and we've only been out of the house a few minutes when my toes announce that they'll soon be going the same way. Kilian's in a good mood, though, striding out along the pavement.

◊

But the sea—oh my goodness, the sea. In my imagination it grows dirtier and more disgusting by the day—I think of seaweed and jellyfish, of stony beaches full of rusty Coke cans. I remember it as flat or choppy, grey or vaguely green—and with every day away from the sea, it becomes smaller and less sublime, an almost disagreeable body of water with a penetrating odour, always there, just around the corner. I sit in the weekend traffic jam surrounded by cars from all over Germany and wonder what the fuss is about. I sometimes go months without setting eyes on it, although I see a lot of the river, with its fat passenger ships inching along like icebergs. But leave our house and head through the streets straight to the beach, and there's a moment when a gap opens up between the buildings on the promenade and you're looking out over the open sea. It always makes me catch my breath.

For the sea is never dirty, dull or grey—it's the only thing worth seeing in this world, and puts everything and everyone into perspective. The land we are standing on is no more than an island—the living creatures that we know, nothing but a handful of textbook species adapted to life on land. We think we are big and important, but down there in the deep are leviathans who would laugh at us if they could.

Everything that makes our planet special has some connection with water. But sometimes—now, say, standing by the frozen Baltic, looking sidelong at Kilian, who seems pleased but unimpressed—I think that men maybe aren't capable of truly understanding such things. Their bodies aren't subject to a rhythm—they can do research into a phenomenon like tides, but they have no personal experience of it. I used to dismiss such thoughts as arrogant and unhelpful to the great cause of equal rights, but I'm increasingly dogged by the suspicion that there's an important correlation between the exploitation and destruction of our planet and the fact that for centuries it has been men who have made all the decisions. They know nothing of cycles and rhythms.

'Walkers don't have to pay resort tax,' I say. 'We can walk here for free. Isn't that great?'

'There can never be enough free things for a jazz musician,' says Kilian. 'Are they icefloes?'

The sea is frozen at the edge and the tide is pushing the ice further and further up the beach. Lapped by the waves, the sea wall is covered in ice—beneath our boots, the sand crunches like the crust of a crème brûlée. I hadn't guessed that it would look like this, although the recent cold snap has been more severe than for a long time. The ice is achingly beautiful, and as if that weren't enough, a large rip in the clouds reveals a clear night sky. You can even see the moon, in a somewhat gnawed-at form. I quickly work out what phase it's in—waning. And at that moment it hits me: I'm going to die. All this will continue to exist. Sometimes the sea will be frozen at the edge—sometimes it will lie smooth and glistening in the sunlight—sometimes autumn gales will whip up the surface—and I won't be here.

'Gosh, it's amazing,' says Kilian, and he runs down the beach to the water's edge, the mosaic of icefloes creaking and breaking beneath his feet. I follow him, also crushing as much ice as I can—it helps me to fight the feeling rising in my chest.

We crush ice underfoot for a while, and then walk along the beach, revelling in the fact that it's not costing us a thing. Or rather Kilian revels—he can't stop talking about it.

'Resort tax,' he says. 'Who came up with that crap? When I have money, I certainly don't spend it on going to the beach. I buy myself something to eat first—but without taking a trolley, because you have to put money in them too. Did I really use to say money wasn't important as long as you could do what you cared about? To be honest, I'm afraid I envy you. I want a house like yours and an account with an overdraft and a pension. When I think that we were basically paid in biscuits for our performance this afternoon, I don't know whether to laugh or cry.'

I say nothing, least of all that my pension too is practically non-existent—not that it matters, in my situation—or that I too have basically been paid in biscuits for everything I've done these last years. I don't tell him how much I envy him for bringing something into the world with his music, something that wasn't there before—for creating something and leaving a mark that will survive him. I don't tell him I envy him so much I could burst.

◊

The wind is bitingly cold. It's blowing inland from the sea, from the horizon, from Scandinavia. I feel its chill in my lungs—my eyes are watering. My anger at the something is still there, but has shifted to my legs and is pumping them with the energy I need to walk at a brisk pace, on and on, without stopping.

'I'm going to be a father,' says Kilian when we come to the cliffs.

'Congratulations,' I say. 'That's wonderful news.'

I'm honestly delighted, even if it does confirm what I sensed earlier—that he's no longer all mine. At the same time, though, my delight is little more than a reflex. As soon as you have children, you can't understand how anyone could possibly manage without.

'Not really,' he says. 'I hardly know the woman and I have no desire to get to know her. We saw each other in Berlin a few times when I was playing there, and now she's pregnant and wants child support from me, of course. I don't have a choice about it. She gets to do a test, go to the doctor, make a decision: child or no child. But I receive formal notification that I'm to be a father and have to pay money for the rest of my life. I only hope for the poor child's sake that it's not a boy.'

'Why?'

'Wrong sex.'

'Aha.'

'I don't just mean that a man can suddenly find himself up the creek financially with no say in the matter, all because of a dud condom—which, by the way, came from *her* bedside table, not mine. That's only part of the story. Seriously, I was reading about this the other day—it's a major problem in the western world—so many kindergarten and primary-school teachers think boys shouldn't behave like boys. Did you know that's why boys perform much worse at school? All the good grades are nabbed by the well-adapted girls, and anyone horsing around or causing trouble gets chucked out. Apparently the majority of school dropouts are boys. The list of disadvantages goes on and on. Men die earlier and are more at risk of addiction. Even children's books these days are full of tough, savvy girls, and every low-budget crime series has its female detective. Girls are given encouragement and support on all sides, and the boys just have to get by as best they can without getting in anyone's way. It's appalling. Don't you think?'

'Yes,' I say. 'Appalling.'

I breathe the cold air and feel as if I were inhaling the sea and the sand and the starry sky. I smile to myself at Kilian and his children's books, which clearly mean a lot to him, and I take his arm and slip mine through it. He's confused—who wouldn't be? He sees the world as a morass of injustice and interprets all the statistics to his disadvantage. It must seem to him a cruel trick of fate that the average man has so many fewer years to live than his female counterpart. To make up for my mother and cousin and me and to keep the statistics in order, I suppose there must be a few women out there who live to be as old as the hills. And if, against the odds, Kilian does live to a ripe old age, he might be surprised at first, but then it will occur to him that the average is dragged down considerably by the higher mortality rate among male infants.

There are plenty of other things, though, that won't occur to him, things he won't see because they don't affect him, or interest him. That girls aren't breastfed as long as boys, for instance. That most school support programs are aimed at boys. That even at an early age boys are allowed to be more aggressive, more disobedient and freer than girls. That they are given more encouragement in almost every kind of sport. As for children's books, I don't suppose he'll stop to wonder why Joanne Rowling kept her first name quiet when she was starting out, and he'd probably dismiss it as ridiculous if I told him that publishers are afraid boys won't read books if they're written by women. The curious fact that it's the poor disadvantaged boys who end up getting all the executive positions and gold medals, while the women with their top grades are left waving from the sidelines, is something he will regard as a complex problem involving too many factors to allow for generalisations. He might wonder at the number of studies showing that women who specify their gender are rated worse in all areas, while in anonymous tests their performance is indistinguishable from that of men. But I say nothing and deem it wiser not to get started on such trifles as the pay gap, tougher career conditions, higher health insurance rates, increased chances of poverty in old age or the disproportionate number of single mothers receiving benefits, with no prospect of independence.

Instead, I squeeze Kilian's arm and stop walking. A scrap of cloud drifts across the moon. It's beautiful here. Then, about fifty metres ahead of us on the frozen moonlit beach, I see a fox trotting along at the foot of the cliffs. It's not in a hurry and doesn't look our way—it doesn't give a damn about us.

◊

I've managed not to spend too much time thinking about Berenike today, but my thoughts are defiant—they come when it suits them, like tunes that stick in your head, and if you aren't firm with them, they do as they please. The soundtrack to Berenike's story is Fauré's *Élégie* for cello and orchestra—that initial sadness when the sounds merge, thick as syrup, then the steady, unhurried advance, the attempt to assert normality by evoking an old familiar rhythm before anger flares up—passionate revolt—the orchestra rumbling like a storm and the cello shooting out flashes of lightning until exhaustion wins out, leaving nothing but the perpetual, impossible longing in which cello and orchestra are as one.

When Berenike was born, our bedroom was ready for her. We had bought a changing table and squeezed it into the gap next to the wardrobe. Costas had converted an old cot, taking off one side and attaching it to the frame of our bed with clamps so that I'd be able to reach out half-asleep and stroke the baby, pull her over to me when I wanted to breastfeed her, hear her breathe as she slept.

Helli had painted a picture saying *Welcome Gummy Bear.* On the first scan, the baby had looked like a gummy bear and the name stuck for the rest of the pregnancy. Perhaps the only reason Costas and I were so quick to agree on a name was that we had got used to 'Gummy Bear' and it was only a small step from 'Bear' to 'Bear-enike'. There was something rather psychedelic about Helli's painting—it wasn't quite the thing for a baby's room. But Helli couldn't paint any other way. It was rare that she finished a picture at all, and if she had a good day and managed for once, it looked like a child's LSD trip. We hung the picture over the cot all the same and Costas pinned a mobile of shells—a gift from Alex—to the sloping ceiling. Alex had bought it with his pocket money in a souvenir shop near the beach where he sometimes met his friends.

The big age gap between the new baby and the others was planned. The six years or so between Alex and Helli had proved very useful, and it was possible that the third child would turn out to be as high-maintenance as Helli. Experience had taught us that it was better to have both hands free and the siblings out of the house, at least in the mornings. But even early in the pregnancy I realised that Gummy Bear was a quiet customer. While Helli had kicked and thrashed about nonstop, Berenike slept a lot and moved cautiously and dreamily in the waters. I imagined her as self-sufficient, wrapped up in her own world, unmoved by external events and not particularly bothered by the reactions of those around her. She communicated with Costas and me by responding to pressure, but never more than once in a row. She wasn't up for playing and never demanded attention. Costas would lay his cheek on my belly in the evenings and commune with her, and I knew that he thought she was like him and that it made him happy.

Everything about the pregnancy and birth was thought-out

and planned. We knew this would be our last child—I didn't feel young enough to put myself through the physical ordeal of pregnancy, birth and breastfeeding more than this once more. There would be a lectureship coming up at the Academy of Music in six months and a woman I'd known as a student who now worked there had said she'd support my application if I wanted to give it a go. Costas had promised to take paternity leave and we'd found a place in a crèche where our daughter could start on her first birthday. We felt up to the task as never before. This time everything was different: two mature and experienced adults were taking this on. We were no longer the students in love who had gigglingly given up contraception and then somehow muddled their way through, terrified and anxious and confused. Nor were we the enthusiastic young parents who had thought they had it sussed, naively confident that the familiar patterns would repeat themselves. We had survived the first years with Helli without going mad or getting a divorce—we were seasoned parents and wise enough to regard a third child as an adventure. In the time leading up to Berenike's birth, we didn't argue—we moved in a world of hormone-soaked contentment and productive activity. Costas designed a solid-wood highchair, child-proofed the garden pond with wire mesh and patiently fetched box after box of babies' clothes from the attic.

The night I went into labour, Sissi drove down from Hamburg to be with Alex and Helli. We rang her at three in the morning and she arrived in under an hour. My waters had broken and I already had painful contractions so we set off for the hospital straight away. On the way there we listened to the *Davidsbündler Dances* and I felt so strong and uncertain, so terrified and happy, that it was as if the music had been written especially for me. When Costas changed gear I laid my hand on his and took comfort in its warmth.

The birth was straightforward and undramatic. The midwives told us that the way things were going, we'd be home in time for lunch the next day. We had brought a little baby seat for the car, a tiny warm jacket and a hat with an aeroplane on it that had been worn by Alex and Helli on their drives back from the hospital.

No one knows why things suddenly stopped. There was no warning—no slowing heartbeat or problems with contractions. An emergency caesarean could have been performed within minutes, but it didn't occur to anyone that it might be necessary. Somewhere on her way out, Berenike must have decided to stay in her own world. She must have decided it was enough for her to give us a little nudge and then return to her amniotic cocoon. I always tell myself that it was her decision, that there was nothing preventing her from being born and having a look at us—at Costas and me, her parents. Maybe it would have been too much for her. Maybe she realised, as the pressure on her grew stronger and more insistent, that she couldn't cope.

During the last contractions I had the feeling that she was no longer doing her bit. She kept slipping back and I did my best to manage the job alone. At twelve minutes past eight Berenike was born, but at some point in the last minutes she had died without our noticing.

Driving home with the empty car seat and the little hat

wasn't as bad as it might have been. Explaining to the children what had happened when they came charging out to meet me, noisy and excited, proved doable. The funeral in the local cemetery came and went—I got through it. Taking care of my body as it gradually readjusted after the pointless birth—because there was no baby needing its milk or smell or warmth or soft skin—that was pretty much bearable. But I couldn't go into our bedroom. I couldn't face Helli's psychedelic picture and Alex's shell mobile, the bedside cot and the changing table. I slept on the living-room sofa. Costas, meanwhile, couldn't bring himself to clear the baby things away and lived surrounded by them. I shouted at him to take down the cot so I could go back into the bedroom, but he refused. Everything was to stay the way it was.

Six weeks passed before anything changed. Then, at last, Costas took the things down and put them in the attic, and I went back to sleeping in our bed. But now I had to resist what were, to me, his absurd advances. The only moments when we were both all right were when we lay there quite still, clinging to one another. Only then was life bearable.

Kilian is going to be a father. Whatever the circumstances, that is a kind of state of emergency. No one has to think logically or fairly when faced with the prospect of parenthood. Kilian is only afraid because his life as he knows it is coming to an end. He doesn't know how lucky he is.

BACK AT HOME we drink tea with rum. Kilian brought the rum, one of those miniature bottles from the supermarket check-out. He carries it in his coat pocket, where I keep my notebook. The tea isn't chamomile, but a dark, malty Assam that I buy loose and keep in a well-sealed tin for moments like this. I usually drink it by myself, because visitors always want coffee and none of the rest of the family likes tea. I drink it when I feel that the ground is slipping from under my feet and I'm not sure I haven't walked off the edge of a cliff without realising, like some stupid cartoon character. The rum makes the tea sweeter and I'm warmed twice over: the heat of the tea is redoubled by the burning of the alcohol in my belly. I'm soon so hot that I'm sweating under my arms, and after only a few sips I feel dizzy and dull in the head.

Kilian goes to the toilet again and I fetch my notebook out of the hall and make a new list.

Drinks that do me good (on a psychological level, at least)
- *Tea with rum (on cold days, in the dark)*
- *Coffee (in the morning, strictly alone)*
- *Becherovka (soothes the throat like the cough sweets of my childhood)*
- *Whisky (cowboy taste, confidence-boosting)*
- *Hot milk and honey (comment superfluous)*

I don't get any further because Kilian appears behind me. I slip the notebook under this morning's paper.

'Do you have pets?' he asks.

'Why?'

'It smells of animals in the hall.'

'That's the rats. They have a cage under the stairs that opens onto an outdoor run.'

The rats. I hit my forehead, a gesture I only make when I've had something to drink. It's as if I have to counteract the effect of the alcohol by jolting my thoughts into action. Hitting my forehead means I've had a sudden thought. And if I've had a sudden thought, I must stick with it before it disappears into the rum-induced fog in my brain. In this case the thought is: *I forgot to shut the rat flap.* An hour ago I was mentally together enough to remember to check with Alex that he'd fed the rats—now I've gone and forgotten my own daily duty of shutting them in when it gets dark. During the day I trust the rats to make up their own minds whether it's warm enough for them to go out, but at night I put a plank in front of the flap.

'I have to shut the rats in,' I say, getting up. From my little trip to the hall just now, I know that the lovely effect of the rum only really kicks in when I get up, and this time I'm prepared. I steady myself on the back of the chair before setting off. Kilian follows me to the cage under the stairs—and indeed, neither of the rats is there. Who can blame them? I'm so conscientious, they practically never get a chance to see the stars. I'll have to shoo them inside before I can put the plank in place. I grab my phone and Kilian follows me out.

It's freezing cold. Overhead, the sky twinkles—the Milky Way is clearly visible. I see why the rats didn't want to miss this. In our part of town the stray light at night is minimal. People around here close their curtains—privacy is sacred to them. They all have fences and hedges around their gardens too. For a moment I feel dizzy, from the rum, the cold, the stars. Most of all from the stars. Like the sea, they put my existence in perspective. Kilian seems oblivious to such feelings. He turns to face the garden and calls out: 'Bedtime for little rats. Everybody inside.'

'Not so loud,' I say.

He laughs. 'You don't think your neighbours are asleep, do you? It's only just seven.'

Only just seven and already drunk, I think. But I say: 'You shouldn't disturb the peace. And anyway, you'll scare the rats.'

'Oh, so that's what it's all about,' says Kilian. 'You think I'm a rat scarer. That's the way you see me.' I box him on the arm and he adds: 'You don't want it too peaceful, you know. You should be grateful to me for making a bit of noise.'

I go to the outdoor run and call their names softly: 'Pink, what are you doing out here in the cold? Floyd, come into the warm. Come along, my sweets.'

But the run is empty. I shine my phone over it—my mobile does, if nothing else, have a torch function—into all the corners, under the branches and into the concrete pipes where the rats sometimes like to hide. Then I see that in one place, the earth at the bottom of the wire mesh has been loosened and the wire has come slightly adrift. It looks as if someone's given the fence a good hard kick, denting the mesh and pushing it up. The gap is so small I'd have put money on no animal bigger than a frog managing to squeeze through— no animal with a skeleton. But rats, as I've learnt, can do all sorts of amazing things. There's nothing for it—we'll have to go in search of them and hope for the best. Because even if rats can do all sorts of amazing things, they can't survive a night outside in sub-zero temperatures.

'Shit,' I say. 'Do you have your phone, Kilian? Then you can be a rat rescuer for a change, instead of a rat scarer.'

The rats don't, on the whole, come when you call their names. They're not particularly tame either, not even with me. These particular rats have been living under our stairs for a year and a half. Costas got to choose the names this time, after he was so scathing about the names of their predecessors—Ratsy and Cutesy—that Helli and Alex refused to offer so much as an opinion on the subject.

It was Costas, too, who insisted on buying new rats. I thought the children were too big to be interested anymore— and who'd end up looking after them? It wasn't going to be him, was it? But after sleeping on it for a few nights I agreed—two new rats, officially for the children, in fact for Costas. He seemed to care enough about the rats to emerge from his study. That hadn't happened for months, and by then I had worked out that his immediate reaction to loss was to attempt to undo it. Ratsy and Cutesy had died—curiously enough, within a few days of one another. I suspected Helli, although I suppose that coming from the same litter, they were probably only a few seconds apart in age. But whatever the circumstances, they were dead, and for Costas that meant replacing them as quickly as possible. I prefer not to think about those nights after Berenike's birth when Costas came crawling over to my side of the bed and I had to push him away. He seemed unaware of the state I was in. Later, he told me he couldn't explain his uncontrollable desire for me, but it was clear enough to me that it was all about making a new baby as quickly as we could.

Pink and Floyd were given to us by a boy in Alex's class who had set up a kind of rat farm. He claimed a purely scientific interest, but I could never throw off the feeling that I had saved two baby rats from a potentially cruel fate. The boy brought them round in a file box, accepting in return a pile of old Mickey Mouse comics that Alex had been hoarding for years and finally managed to part with. Costas came out of his study to see the rats being released from their box. They didn't hesitate for a second but scuttled out as soon as we put it down, apparently fearless, in spite of being so small and young. They remain little daredevils to this day and will crawl into any hole without qualms and take on every obstacle in their way, driven by a boundless curiosity for the unknown.

That makes the hunt for them particularly hard. It

wouldn't occur to them to do what I'd do if I were them—
huddle up under a bush and wait for rescue.

◊

'Pink,' I call into the darkness.

'Floyd,' says Kilian, his voice coaxing. He shines his phone torch under the currant bushes.

The frosty grass crunches underfoot. I feel an irresistible urge to giggle. There's something comic about the way Kilian says 'Floyd', his stooped silhouette ahead of me both eager and cautious—he is keen to be the hero who discovers the rats, but he's also afraid of what might be lurking beneath the bushes at this hour of night. It gives me a pang to watch him. I find it touching when humans act like humans.

'Piddy widdy widdy wit,' I say. 'Puss, puss.'

Kilian shines his torch in my face. 'You're completely nuts,' he says. 'The whole lot of you. What kind of names are they anyway?'

'English names,' I say.

He shines his torch through the lattice fence.

'And what on earth is that?' He bends over and scoops some small thing out of the grass which definitely isn't a rat, straightens himself and turns the torch onto his hand. 'Is that a finger?'

'Oh, that's Theo's thumb,' I say.

Kilian inspects it gingerly. Out of the light it looks like a half-smoked white cigar or a chipolata with a bite out of it.

'We spent ages looking for that this morning,' I say. 'Theo will be pleased.'

But then it occurs to me that it will be too late to sew the thumb back on. All Theo can do with it now is cast it in synthetic resin and display it on his desk. Or perhaps Heinz would like to crush it into a powder and make globules out of it. Who knows what they might be good for? Maybe someone out there sings the song of Theo's thumb. I seem to remember Alex expressing an interest in it too. But it's not up to me to decide the fate of Theo's severed extremities. It certainly doesn't seem right to toss his thumb in the compost bin.

'We'll take it over to Heinz and Theo's,' I say. 'But shh!' I put a finger to my lips.

Kilian is about to say something but evidently thinks better of it. Instead he nods gravely and salutes.

Quietly, quietly, I climb over the fence and he follows close behind. We keep in the shade of the trees and hedge and toolshed, so that no one can spot us from the house. We shine our torches at each other, put our fingers to our lips, gesture wildly and peer into the night. We lift our knees high as we sneak along, or jerk our heads like chickens. I hear Kilian chuckle, and once he lets out a snort, while I have to keep stopping because I'm afraid my legs might give way from so much pent-up giggling.

We creep quietly up Heinz and Theo's drive. The gravel crunches and Kilian shines his torch wildly in all directions as if scouting out the land. We deposit the thumb on the doorstep, then pick it up again—someone might tread on it by mistake—and put it on top of the letterbox. That too seems somehow callous, though. I creep over to a rhododendron, which in the darkness looks like a crouching dragon, pluck a leaf and put it on the letterbox as a kind of platter. At rest on the leaf, the thumb looks peaceful—the arrangement has dignity. Kilian raises his hand and I give him a soundless high five. Then we head back home, quickly this time and no longer caring how much noise we make because we can't hold our giggles in anymore. Like teenagers who have played a silly trick on someone, we run over to our garden and stand clutching one another, gasping with laughter.

'Can't wait to hear that story,' says Kilian, when he's got his breath back.

But before I've recovered enough to tell him about the thumb in the garden, he spots the tumble dryer on our lawn. Pointing his torch at it, he adds: 'Or that one.'

I suddenly don't feel like laughing anymore. Maybe it's a bad sign that all this seems normal to me. Perhaps my life isn't quite as ordinary as I'd supposed.

'Is that a washing machine?' asks Kilian.

'Tumble dryer. It caught fire this afternoon for some reason.'

'But it's not dangerous now?'

He approaches it, holding his phone at arm's length like a loaded gun. I don't mention the possibility of smouldering embers. Like a cop in a film examining a suspicious object, he tears open the dryer door with a flourish and shines his torch inside. There they are: Pink and Floyd—curled up and snuggled close and sleeping like babies.

◊

After Kilian and I have carried the rats carefully into the house and shut them in, I collapse on the sofa. It's only now that I realise I'm shivering and feeling a little weepy. The sight of sleeping rats or babies is too much for me if it comes without warning.

I'm not shivering with cold, but Kilian can't know that. He produces another little bottle of rum—this time from his double-bass case—and says he'll make me hot grog. He knows a traditional northern German recipe that says you can make it any way you like just as long as you don't add water.

'Put the oven on too if you're going in the kitchen,' I say. 'I have a frozen lasagne for us to share.'

'You really are sentimental, Katinka. Who'd have thought it?'

Kilian looks as if that makes him happy, and I like making people happy.

So I add: 'I have vermouth too.'

He comes over to me, bends down and kisses me on the forehead. Then he vanishes into the kitchen to try out his grog recipe.

Kilian comes from southern Germany and regards the north as something of a foreign country, whereas my family have always lived here. My father grew up on the Geest, the only part of Schleswig Holstein that can't hope to attract tourists because its landscape is so utterly without charm. My maternal grandparents lived in Flensburg for a long time, but retired to Denmark, which was where my mormor was from. They rarely came to visit us after the move, and when they did, they had such a hectic way of carrying on that I was usually relieved when they left. We never went to see them in Denmark—my father didn't want to spend his precious holiday in a country where you couldn't rely on good weather. My mother spoke Danish, but not to us children, and I never learnt it. My grandmother died in her mid-sixties of an illness that was never dwelt on in our family, although I now have my suspicions. After her death my grandfather found himself a cheerful Danish woman and stayed on in the north.

My grandparents on both sides were always strangers to me—old, eccentric folk whose way of life was so far removed from mine that they seemed to have come from a different time altogether. When my mother died, they came to the funeral, one lot with the modest air of Geest farmers, quiet and self-effacing to the point of invisibility—the other lot loud and hectic and dizzying. I never saw my mother's father again. My own father seemed to see no reason to keep him present in our lives and I hardly thought of him. Sissi must have felt similarly, but then she hardly thought of anyone at the time, with the exception of her dead composers and the occasional living musician. My father's parents died a few years later, leaving Sissi and me a substantial sum, which we put towards our studies. The farm near Leck went to an uncle, my father's only brother, whom I last saw at my confirmation. My mother had several brothers and sisters—three altogether—but we hardly mentioned them after her death, for the simple reason that we had no occasion to. They all lived outside Schleswig Holstein by then and seemed so far away. My cousins sometimes got in touch later, once we all had email.

The three of us—my father, my sister and I—shrank to a self-contained unit without my mother. It wasn't until later that I realised that families can be much more widely branching—that you can be a spider in a web, connected to a great many other people, and that this can shore you up. Maybe I'll ask Sissi to invite my mother's long-lost brothers and sisters and our remaining cousins to my funeral. The more family my children have, I think, the better.

◊

Kilian brings in a tray with two furiously steaming glasses. Even his specs mist up. He has taken tumblers, revealing his south German roots. Grog is piping hot—it needs a glass with a handle. I pull my sleeves over my hands and take a cautious sip—the alcohol rushes to my brain like a New Year's rocket. Once I've swallowed the grog, it's only a couple of seconds before my head begins to spin. Before taking the next sip, I think of Helli, who can still be quite a little girl sometimes and need her mummy at night to get to sleep. I keep drinking all the same. Before the third sip, I decide that if the worst comes to the worst I'll just have to go and pick her up in a taxi. By the fourth sip I've stopped thinking. The shivering subsides and my blood carries the alcohol to my limbs, making them feel like dead fish, a strangely agreeable sensation. I had forgotten how quickly and conclusively grog puts me out of action, but if there's one thing I want just now it's that—to be out of action—to switch off and not have to get up from this sofa for a moment or two.

Kilian has dropped down beside me—close beside

me—with the postcard of the Maoris in his hand.

'I got one of these too,' he says. 'Exactly the same. She must buy in bulk.'

I don't know what he's talking about. As if it were nothing, he turns the card over and reads what Ann-Britt has written. I'd never dream of doing such a thing. In the past, when there were often postcards in the letterbox, I'd only ever read the address, and perhaps glance at the signature, but I was never tempted, even for a moment, to read words that weren't meant for my eyes. Mind you, there was probably nothing on them of any consequence—only what the weather was like in Italy, or the comfort or otherwise of somebody's holiday accommodation. These days we hardly get any cards that aren't from Ann-Britt and addressed to me.

'What she's written is different, though,' says Kilian with satisfaction. 'That's something.'

Slowly, in spite of the grog—or perhaps because of it (alcohol sometimes helps me to think laterally)—I'm beginning to understand. 'She writes to you too?'

'Yes, has done for years.'

'She writes to you? You don't even know her.'

'True enough. Who knows Ann-Britt? The postcards certainly don't reveal much.'

'But why?'

'We were together at one point. Didn't you know? God, you really must have gone about in a daze. No eyes for anyone but Costas, eh? It was as if there were nothing else in the world for you. You'd stand your old schoolfriend up and leave her sitting in our kitchen, just because Mr Theodoroulakis happened to have half an hour to spare for you, and then, you see, your nice flatmate—who was always around, and not altogether unattractive—had to step into the breach and keep her company. We licked each other's wounds because we no longer existed for you—sometimes, the most unusual affairs grow out of situations like that. We carried on seeing each other later too, whenever she was in Germany, but it was clear that nothing was going to come of it. At the end of the day, she wasn't really interested in relationships. Then she started sending postcards. I hardly ever write back because I never have stamps in the house. The odd text is about the most I manage, but it seems enough for her. Incredible that she buys the cards in packs of two—maybe she even buys multi-packs—who knows who else she writes to? I'm going to ask her.'

Awkwardly, he fishes his phone out of his trouser pocket and starts to swipe around on it.

'Stop,' I shout.

This is all going too fast for me. The whole smartphone society is too fast for me. Somebody asks a question and instead of trying to find an answer by discussing the matter with whoever happens to be around, a phone is whipped out of a pocket and seconds later you're having to listen to what Wikipedia has to say on the subject. I like wracking my brain for someone, even if most people find it tedious. Of course it's easier to ask people what they'd like for their birthdays, whether a particular date suits them or whether they'd prefer vegetarian food, but for me the whole pleasure lies in turning the questions over in my mind. I like thinking about the people who are close to me and trying to put myself in their place. As someone who grew up before everyone was constantly plugged in, it doesn't usually occur to me that you could simply ask. In my world there are still times when you don't disturb people—it's second nature to me not to ring anyone between eight in the evening and quarter past, in case they're watching the news. My children, on the other hand, don't even know how television works. They think it odd that the programs carry on when they go to the toilet, that films start without them, that you can't watch them again the next day.

'Let me get my head round this, Kilian,' I say, because he looks alarmed, holding his phone well away from me, as if afraid I might seize it from him and dunk it in the grog to disarm it. 'You went out with Ann-Britt. And since then she's been writing you cards—probably the same ones she writes me? Only with different words? What words?'

'Well, she certainly doesn't write about orchids and jumpers.'

'What, then?'

'About her husband, for example. Or her job. Or her plans.'

'Or her cat?'

'She has a cat?'

'What kinds of plans?' I ask.

'Always something different. She's so fed up with her job, you see. She was thinking of applying for work in Germany and moving back, but I don't know what became of that. Her husband wouldn't have come with her, but I don't suppose that would have bothered her. I think she's doing psychoanalysis or something—all kinds of childhood traumas have been stirred up. My guess is that she'll end up breaking up with her husband anyway—with or without a new job in another country. It's always the same with her. She never knows what she wants—only that she doesn't want what she has.'

I collapse against the sofa back with a sigh. It's never a good feeling when you realise that the image you have of someone is way off target—that you only ever see tiny snippets of a person's life and that the picture you cobble together can be maddeningly far removed from reality.

The beep of my phone in the hall is a kind of deliverance. It's easier to forget that my oldest friend possibly isn't the person I thought she was—easier, indeed, to forget everything I've missed or neglected or overlooked in this life—when banal reality comes knocking in the form of a text, asking for a lift or advice or rescue.

I can take my time heaving myself up from the sofa and getting my balance. Texts have to be read without too much delay—there seems to be general consensus on that. It's all right to abandon a conversation, a guest or a drink because your phone has beeped somewhere. On the other hand, I needn't run because it probably isn't urgent. If the Barbiemobile had a flat and Alex wanted to ask me which of the tools in the boot might be a jack, he'd ring me. The same goes for Helli if she'd locked herself in the toilet at Cindi's and was planning to stay there until I turned up to take her away from that den of iniquity.

The text is from Costas and says: *It's a shame I can't send you photos. I need your help choosing a tie. Patterned or plain? I hate ties. Love you. C*

The last words shake me for a moment. I have to clutch the hallstand. Then I notice that none of Costas's other verbs are missing a subject and that steadies me somewhat. I write back: *I'm for no tie. K.* I can't manage more than that. Everything's a bit of a blur anyway after the grog and the tea-with-rum. I expect the grog is just the right temperature now, but it will have to wait. For the moment I have no desire either to return to the conversation with Kilian or to think about Costas in Berlin—tie or no tie.

After a glance at the rats, whose tails are sticking out of the box where they sleep, betraying their hiding place, I go into the bathroom. If there's one thing I've learnt in my adult life, it's that it never hurts to go to the toilet if you get the chance. For years now I've been going when I have the time, not when I have to, like a dog on a walk.

The gap left by the tumble dryer looks desolate. Full of dust and fluff and scrunched-up cloths sodden with fire-fighting water, it resembles an empty plot of land between the washing machine and the bath. If you remove one component from a functioning system, chaos will surface. No order is anything other than superficial—peep underneath and you'll see the grime and the crumbs. Looked at like that, there's nothing menacing about chaos—it's the most ordinary thing in the world.

WHEN I GET back, Kilian has almost finished his grog. He pats the sofa next to him, saying: 'The seat upon my right is free. I'd like it if Katinka would sit beside me.'

I couldn't stand that game as a child because everyone stumbled over my name. It's impossible to get the words to scan when you have to fit in a name of four syllables. The right rhythm must have mattered a great deal to me back then. Things improved when people began to abbreviate my name, even if they seemed unable to agree on a nickname.

I drop down next to Kilian, reach for my glass of grog and take a sip. When I lean back I notice that he has laid his arm along the top of the sofa—I feel it against my neck. We are sitting in exactly the same positions that Alex and Barbie were sitting in earlier—age-old positions.

But it feels so lovely I'm almost ashamed. Am I so desperate, so starved of intimacy, that I regard an arm on a sofa back as a kind of treat—or does everyone feel that way?

It's clear enough that I'm in withdrawal from physical contact. Costas and I have been in a weekend relationship for over a year, and my children have reached an age where, like cats, they decide for themselves when they want my affection—and, like cats, I can depend on them not to want it when I feel the need for a cuddle, but invariably when I'm holding the phone in one hand and trying to open a tin of kidney beans with the other. To think there was a time in my life when I'd have given anything to be alone and not touched by anyone. When Helli was a baby, she wanted breastfeeding every half-hour and stuck to me like chewing gum. When she was a toddler, she'd crawl into bed with me at night, climb onto my belly and snore away open-mouthed, without a thought for me. If I pushed her off gently, she would wake up and climb back onto my belly, where she'd twitch and fidget and kick and thrash about in her sleep. Costas was rarely at home at the time because he had a lot of work, but when he was around, he'd press me to him at every opportunity to show me how important I was to him. And Alex was still a cuddly little primary-school boy who wanted to sit on my lap whenever he'd hurt himself. Why can't such things be more evenly distributed over our lives?

Kilian doesn't yet have children. He's not familiar with that feeling of overkill, of too much physical contact, when everyone thinks they have a right to your body. He has no idea what it's like to have another living being literally attached to you. Who knows whether that will change when he's a father. He has no breasts, which in this respect at least is an advantage. No one will go creeping under his T-shirt in search of those two cuddly friends who are regarded as characters in their own rights and even given names: Hanni and Nanni, in my case—goodness only knows where Helli came up with that. No one will thrust an arm almost mechanically down his front and play with his nipples for minutes at a time because it's so nice and soothing. That might make him envious of the unloved mother of his child, but then again it might make him realise that he has the unbeatable advantage of having some say in how deep his physical involvement with his child is to be. He won't get to know the overkill and he won't suffer from the withdrawal that inevitably follows when it comes to an end.

Kilian drains his glass and puts it down without taking his arm from my neck. He's clearly agile, as well as holding his drink better than I do.

I wonder whether he still eats fruit and oats for breakfast, with a dusting of cocoa powder at the weekends. It doesn't fit in with my idea of a jazz musician. Isn't it a profession where you're more or less duty-bound to neglect your health?

'Don't you smoke anymore?' I ask, carefully leaning my head back to feel as much of his arm as I can without frightening him away with my greed.

'Not since we were students.'

'Do you take drugs?'

'Of course.'

'What kind?'

'Whatever's going.'

'Pretty convenient, really. I suppose you'll never get addicted because you're too lazy to get hold of your own stuff, aren't you?'

'You're sweet, Katinka. Who do you think I am? Some commitment-phobic stud who's permanently off his face? A self-obsessed jazz musician with nothing in his head but blues schemes and the next chance he'll have to indulge his hedonism? I'm going to have to disappoint you. I'm still good old Kilian from your student days who massaged your feet when you were cold and thought Schumann was over-estimated—even if I do play jazz most of the time these days and get paid in biscuits, instead of being the idiot with the monster instrument in the darkest corner of the orchestra pit.'

I feel a rush of nostalgia for the idiot with the monster instrument who used to knead my cold feet—a yearning for the old times, for long conversations and the feeling that everything is just right the way it is, a yearning so overwhelming that I think I'll go mad if I don't get instant proof that all that really exists. I put my glass down, turn to Kilian and kiss him on the mouth. He remains entirely calm, only stretching out his free hand to the table to steady his grog glass.

The dizzy feeling intensifies. Kilian's lips aren't soft at all—they're firm and thin and utterly intriguing. For almost twenty years, I haven't kissed anyone but Costas. I think of the missing personal pronoun in his text message. I think of secretaries and ties, of Maori postcards and hedonism.

It's not that I've always been meaning to betray my husband one of these days—far from it. It needn't even come to that—it would be enough just to kiss a little more thoroughly. What exactly do I stand to lose that I'm not about to lose in any case, the way things are looking? In my situation it's easy to say I'll take my secret to the grave and actually mean it. Kilian smiles at me as I draw my face back to a safe distance. He takes off his glasses.

'You know I used to be in love with you, don't you?' he says, setting his glasses down on the tray beside the empty grog tumblers. 'Back in the days when you pranced around in front of me in your skimpy stockings because you thought it meant nothing to me.'

The situation he's referring to really did seem harmless to me at the time. I was getting dressed because I had a party to go to, and I wanted company, so I went in the kitchen where Kilian was drinking a beer. We chatted and I got changed—I wouldn't have said I pranced about.

I had my first kiss worthy of the name when I was seventeen. My mother had just died and I was feeling strange—at once abandoned and liberated—and when Björn kissed me in Ann-Britt's kitchen, my only thought was: *Aha, so that's what it feels like.* It was nice, though: soft and dry. My belly tingled and the floor really did sway a little.

For a while afterwards, Björn made me mixtapes and tried to talk me into going for a walk with him or to the cinema, but I was too wrapped up in myself and my family to muster anything like enough interest. If he'd avoided me, he might have stirred my ambition. I wouldn't at all have minded trying some more kissing if it hadn't involved such a string of social commitments—making conversation, spending pocket money, turning up to dates—but my time was too precious to be spent with Björn. I listened dutifully to his tapes, but always put on Mozart afterwards to cleanse my ears. These days, I'm told, Björn is a big shot on the city council. I seem to remember that there was a lot of Chris de Burgh on his tapes.

My second serious kiss was with Costas. Nothing that came between counted. Still, perhaps in a quiet moment I might try to make a list of all the men I've kissed whose names I haven't forgotten. Then I could add Kilian's name, followed by the year.

I suppose I had my wild phase rather late, even by the standards of those days, when nobody I knew got her period at eleven or was allowed to go to her big brother's purple-belt party—but when it did start, it really was wild. I suddenly seemed to be surrounded by opportunities. I don't suppose I'll ever know what experiences Helli will have had by seventeen, unless I unexpectedly find myself on a cloud where I can sit and keep an eye on my children's lives—a real nightmare, if you think about it: able to see everything, but powerless to intervene. Alex has his Barbie and has been thoroughly briefed by Costas and me on contraception and the consequences of neglecting it. I expect they have clean and tidy and risk-free sex, which is more than could be said of me at the same age.

I have entirely romanticised that time before I met Costas, when I got off with anyone I liked and had sex with no regard for the consequences. My memories of it are marked by a curious lightness, as if they weren't mine at all, but a stranger's. Everything looked straightforward on the outside, but it must actually have been incredibly complicated. How was it done? How, for example, did you get onto the subject of contraception? And at what point? Since I had Berenike, my cycle hasn't been reliably regular. How the hell did my young self manage never to have her period when the moment came?

Had she really never eaten anything oniony or garlicky before-hand? She certainly never skipped a badly needed morning shower because she had to make two lists, scrape the ice off the windscreen and do a quick shop before her kindergarten class. Nor did she ever ruin a date by shaving herself a wacky pubic hairdo just for the hell of it five days before and then neglecting to touch it up, so that the prickles ended up poking through her approximately ten-year-old underwear in a decidedly un-wacky way.

◊

'I've forgotten the lasagne,' I say, getting up.

It would surely be a good idea to eat something. I make for the kitchen, trying to look energetic, but it can't make too good an impression that I squat in front of the freezer at a loss for what feels like forever because I can't find the lasagne. Eventually Kilian steps up behind me and taps me on the head. He's wearing his glasses again.

'What are you doing here?'

'Making us lasagne,' I say, 'for reasons of nostalgia.'

Kilian helps me as I have another good look through the freezer. We find spinach and strange packets of meat I don't recognise, but which presumably have something to do with Costas's shopping spree last weekend—he knows a farmer who sells his cows by the kilo. We find raspberries, currants, plums and sour cherries from the garden, which this year, like every year, I grudgingly picked all by myself, although Costas and the children insisted on planting the things and swore they'd deal with the fruit. I seem to recall creative descriptions of fruit tarts and visions of jams and jellies. Right at the back of the freezer, we find even more fruit from years gone by, so encrusted with ice that you can only guess what it is. We find fish fingers and salmon and frozen apple juice in moulds that must be left over from a time before Alex started to feel too old for such things, because although Helli still loves frozen juice, filling the moulds and then putting them in the freezer is one procedure too many for her—she'll decide halfway through to make pancakes instead, and before long, of course, she'll give that up to make a milkshake, and so on, until the place looks like one of those Hollywood kitchens after the men have done the cooking. But we can't find the lasagne. I almost cry because it was such a nice romantic idea and I feel unnerved without the lasagne—after all, one possible explanation for its disappearance is that I'm suffering from a form of early-onset dementia and either I forgot to buy it at all, or else I was so befuddled that I put it on some other shelf where it is now thawing away and will soon, perhaps, be rotting and won't turn up until the lid is bulging with putrefactive gases and the first maggots have made themselves at home in it.

Kilian turns the oven off and comforts me while crushing the ancient frozen juice in a plastic bowl. It only took a quick glance in the fridge for his keen eye to locate the vermouth, which he says goes particularly well with apple juice.

We end up sitting at the kitchen table where, instead of hot lasagne, we tuck into a kind of slushy made of crushed frozen juice soused in vermouth.

'Don't let anyone tell you I can't cook,' says Kilian with satisfaction.

I just manage to write the word *taxi* on a scrap of paper to remind myself that I must call a taxi if Helli wants to be picked up. The word will jog my memory, should my brain spring a leak at the critical moment and not know what to do. It's a kind of proto-list and enough to give me peace of mind. I could note down more, if I had the chance—I can feel it—but at least I've got down the most important thing. Now I can let go and forget. I know I'm irresponsible and somewhere, a long way back in my consciousness, I'm ashamed. The rest is an agreeable muzziness that has as much in common with thought as apple sauce has with an apple. We slurp down the remains of our liquid dinner straight out of the bowl, then I make a kind of decision, grab hold of Kilian's shirt and pull him close to my face.

When I feel that we've kissed enough in the kitchen, we move into the living room. We take the bottle with us and drop down into our old positions on the sofa—Barbie and Ken, old and spent and drunk, but not defeated by fate.

'Now you must tell me why I found a finger in the garden, and why Pink and Floyd were able to take refuge in a tumble dryer in the middle of the lawn,' says Kilian.

'Do you know, that's just the way things are around here,' I say. 'Calm and tranquil on the outside, but behind the hedges, severed fingers and burnt-out whitegoods lie strewn about the place and tell a very different story.' I wish we could go back to kissing—talking is such a strain.

'Really? Is it the same in your neighbours' gardens?'

'I expect so,' I say. 'You just have to drop in on the right day.'

I take Kilian's glasses off his nose and put them down on

the table—a discreet hint that the time for talking is over. But he puts them straight back on. He has more to say and I let him talk.

He wants to tell me, at length this time, that he used to be in love with me. I suppose it's his way of intimating that he is to some extent justified in throwing himself at me. He wants advance absolution. He also wants more alcohol and pours vermouth into the empty tumblers. I realise that he has seen through me and that like me he is hoping to destroy the dregs of my common sense and make me docile and biddable.

I'm so sick of being reliable. It suddenly seems to me a very long time since I last did something just because I felt like doing it—something of no benefit to my family, house, future or marriage. Even when I escape to a cafe for a quiet cappuccino, I do it at a time that doesn't inconvenience anyone and with the aim of relaxing and indulging in a low-calorie treat, as the monthly magazine from the chemist's advises me to do in every issue, if I don't want to burn out and throw the whole family into disarray as a result. It seems to me that sleeping with Kilian at a time determined by chance—and without the blessing of the chemist's magazine—is a kind of manifestation of my last shred of freedom. I'm a free person and I should act accordingly. Another few gulps of vermouth and I'll shake off the whisper of guilt trying to make itself heard in my head.

◊

I don't think I've been loved any less often or less deeply than the other girls and women I know—it's just that I've tended not to notice. Dirk and his drink carton, Björn and his mixtapes—to me, none of that had much to do with real love, and I enjoyed the interest and affection bestowed on me by Kilian all through our student years, without seeing them for what they were. Until I met Costas, I was pretty much convinced that nobody had ever been seriously in love with me.

Being in love was quite a different story. From the age of eleven, I'd fallen passionately in love with all kinds of people. What they had in common was that they were all unobtainable. No one who was able to kiss me in my best friend's kitchen was ever going to stir me to passion, but someone who cycled past me every day on the way to school without saying hello was in with a good chance of becoming the object of my wildest fantasies. I loved ardently and unconditionally—neither age nor looks played much of a role. For a time I was persuaded that a trombone teacher at the music school was the love of my life, and for one glorious summer I hankered after someone's Australian exchange partner. I wasn't unhappy, though—I enjoyed my hopeless infatuation to the full. It went with the music I was listening to at that time—with Chopin and Dvořák. I hummed my way through my teenage years, feeling that to love was great and that it was something I'd mastered better than any other girl on earth.

My mother's decline and death, and all the distress and work that followed, had strangely little effect on either my music or my infatuations. I clung to those two things when it looked as if I might fail in everything else—I was at home in them.

My response to Costas's love was pretty much like that of Shakespeare's character who says: 'Love me! Why, it must be requited!' And my years of practice at being in love helped me to turn it into something great.

Kilian looks serious as he talks. He speaks of hope and disappointment and of the feeling that eventually won out over all the others—that I should be happy, no matter how, whether with or without a double-bass player at my side. He tells me that sleeping with my best friend was not, in the end, the worst way to occupy himself—they had, after all, both been abandoned, one way or another. He talks so convincingly and movingly that before long I can hardly bear it and wish I had a little more of the jazz musician in me and a little less soft-heartedness. But at least he doesn't end his story by telling me he's been waiting for me for twenty years because he couldn't contemplate life with anyone else. That love belongs in our student years—it belongs in a shared flat in Lübeck and a phase of life when the big question was: *classical or jazz?* At last Kilian pauses, removes his glasses with a flourish and says: 'If you intend to go on kissing me, now's the moment to tell me that your marriage hasn't been a bed of roses for some time.'

Instead of replying, I pull him towards me. A new era begins in this moment: in the face of a bleak future, Katharina abandons all common sense, forgets about prickly pubic hairdos, marriage vows and long-serving underwear, leaves the realm of superficial order and gives herself up to chaos.

Kilian proceeds very professionally, or at least that's how it seems to me. Nothing he does is in any way amateurish—

nothing betrays uncertainty. That's extremely pleasant—it's like being in the hands of a good dancer who knows how to lead without being domineering. Kilian kisses me for a long time, but not too long. His movements are purposeful but unhurried. When he begins to push up my T-shirt under the black wool jacket, he does so at just the right moment, not a minute too soon or too late. At our age maybe it's no rare thing to have acquired a perfect sense of timing when it comes to sex. It is, after all, to be hoped that most of us have had plenty of practice. But I somehow doubt it's as common as it should be—not that I'm likely to have much opportunity to find out now.

I'm afraid, though, that I have to abandon my plan to keep my brain in a state of apple sauce: thoughts keep forming and distracting me. I do my best to let them drift past like clouds, one of the meditation techniques I learnt when I was trying to cope with the stress in my day-to-day life by doing mindfulness exercises and deep breathing. As I watch them drift, the *Carmina Burana* play in my head. I'm going to have to get used to the idea that every situation has its own soundtrack.

Being touched by Kilian is overwhelming. I seem to be made entirely of nerve ends. Kneeling on the carpet, he devotes himself to my belly, and it feels as if Christmas has come early. My poor old belly hasn't seen the sun for years. The only forms of touch it knows are my waistband and the occasional probing pinch, invariably followed by a sigh of resignation. Kilian is bothered neither by the far-too-soft white skin, nor by the stretch marks which you may not be able to see very well in the dim light of our living room, but which you can certainly feel. He buries his face in my broad bellybutton, which can smile or pout, depending on how I sit or stand.

I feel obliged to comment and say: 'You didn't know that, did you? That women of forty-odd have bellies like this?'

I'm about to tell him all about the menopausal paunch when he lifts his head and smiles so tenderly that I close my mouth again with a snap.

'Your belly is absolutely amazing. It's had two children in it. It's a complete miracle.'

Then he bobs down again and I try to relax. He's right about the miracle, but it wasn't two children—it was three. There aren't many people outside our immediate family who know that. Some things you don't talk about, to spare others.

The phone rings and Kilian looks up. I put a finger to my lips and wait. We keep very still. After four lots of jingling, the answering machine switches itself on. We hear my voice say: 'This is the Theodoroulakis family—we're not around at the moment, but please leave a message.'

I feel the tension in my body, the beat of my heart, the tightness in my rib cage—I've been holding my breath since the phone began to ring. My muscles are ready for the beep, ready to propel my body towards the phone, should either of my children speak. There isn't a trace of dizziness, fog or apple sauce left in my brain.

There's a shrill beep, the same sound as back in the days when answering machines recorded messages on little tapes. I remember how terrified I used to be of them—more than once I left a stuttered, incoherent message, because I was completely unnerved by the prospect of talking to a machine. After the beep we hear breathing and the sound of a throat being cleared.

'Rina? It's Kirsten. I'm ringing about the Christmas party the week after next. I'm assuming that you're practising the carols on the song sheet with your group so that it won't sound too thin. Maybe something with your instruments too? And were you planning to perform anything just with the group? I need to know soon. Can you get back to me? Hope your daughter's all right.'

It crackles and clicks—the dialling tone sounds again a few times, then there's silence. I breathe in and out, and Kilian lays his head on my belly. I can feel him laughing.

'Rina?' he says. 'Is that what they call you? Sounds like the pet name of a sweet rhinoceros.'

I clamp my legs around his body and hold him fast. I don't want him to stop doing what he's doing. I don't want him to get distracted.

'Rina,' he murmurs into my belly button. 'Rina,' he whispers at my ribs.

The kindergarten kids call me that because my name's too difficult for them. It's not a name that's used in any other part of my life, and when I assume it I become someone else. As Rina I mutate into a sort of patient pachyderm who only ever talks in a kind voice and is always in a good mood. Rina knows neither irony nor sarcasm—she always means exactly what she says and her jokes are especially designed to make four-year-olds laugh. Rina wears gaudy necklaces and flamboyant scarves to grab the kids' attention and make it easier for them to look the right way. She carries an enormous waterproof courier bag, so capacious that she sometimes forgets what's at the bottom of it. Rina never shouts at anyone and takes nothing personally. She manages to find something lovable even in a filthy, snotty-nosed little boy with a sly face and an obvious potential for violence—and can, moreover, provide a pedagogical explanation for his refusal to cooperate. Rina is perfect in a way that could make her unsympathetic. But it's a constant source of satisfaction to me to know that I'm capable of being such a person, while at home I tend to oscillate between Fury and nervous wreck.

'Rina,' Kilian gurgles, pushing my T-shirt all the way up.

◊

I forgot one thing in my list of possible deterrents from a one-night stand: *a something in your left breast*. There are people who squeeze women's breasts to give them—or indeed themselves—pleasure. I recall with horror that I once made out with Ann-Britt, who wanted me to help her find out whether she wasn't perhaps lesbian. She crushed my teenage breasts so forcefully, I was afraid they'd never be the same shape again.

Friendly but firm, I take Kilian's hand and push it away from my bra. He tries again and I remain friendly but firm—but the third time round, my friendliness is waning—Kilian, at any rate, stops everything he's doing, looks me in the face and asks: 'What's the matter? Have you got something wrong with your tits?'

I laugh so hard I can't get my breath. Something wrong

with my tits—that's one way of putting it. But my laughter gives way to sobs and I can't stop or go back to laughing, and soon tears are running down my face and my body is heaving and I give a plaintive cry that not even the drunkest of lovers could mistake for a laugh.

Kilian gets straight to his feet and takes me in his arms and I know that the seduction scene is over. No erotic encounter can recover from such an onslaught of tears, such a comforting hug. It's too far a journey from sobbing nervous wreck to passionate lover, and it would take too many intermediate steps to dispel every last suspicion of sympathy sex.

My brain produces one solitary thought and sends it tentatively to my consciousness: *Thank God.* And it's true—I'm grateful to the something. It has prevented me from acting in a way that I'd have regretted tomorrow morning at the latest. In any case, without the something, I don't suppose I'd have got myself in this alcohol-sodden situation in the first place.

Meanwhile, I'm still trying to get the sobbing under control—since it's refusing to revert to laughter. It isn't easy—Kilian's hug is working against me, almost begging me to let myself go and yield to his comfort. I dig deep for a bit of anger that might put paid to the crying—anger at the something, at Kirsten, at myself. But all I find is a deep black hole, filled to the brim with nameless horror at the situation I'm in.

'Shh,' says Kilian. 'You'll be all right. What's the matter?'

◊

There's a list in my notebook headed: *Questions I'd rather not be asked*. I wrote it two weeks ago, not long after discovering the something, and it goes like this:

- *How are you?*
- *Where do you see yourself in ten years?*
- *What are you going to do now?*
- *Do you believe in life after death?*

I free myself from Kilian's hug and heave myself up from the sofa. I must find my notebook without a second's delay. It's still in the kitchen, hidden under the newspaper. In the little loop on the spine is a biro. The lamp on the extractor hood above the stove is all the light I need. I don't know why I didn't manage to write down more than *taxi* earlier—it's so easy to put words to paper. Perhaps it's merely a matter of willing yourself to think clearly and logically, refusing chaos and confusion. Perhaps alcohol is only ever an excuse.

At the bottom of the list I write: *Shh. You'll be all right. What's the matter?*

Standing here, bent over the stove, pen in hand, I feel the tears still wet on my cheeks—that unaccustomed dampness which, until now, only the cold winter's wind on the beach and a Schumann song had managed to coax out of me today. I'm overcome by the urge to tell Kilian about the something. To tell everyone. Really everyone, from Heinz to Cindi—because don't they all have a right to know? Aren't I somebody to them? A mother, a wife, a sister, a friend—we're tied to one another, bound together—everything that concerns me concerns them too. How could I not tell them what's wrong with me? How could I believe that such a thing as a normal

222

weekend is even possible when I know something they don't know? Didn't Kilian tell me, all those years ago in our shared kitchen, that lives are read from back to front, because death casts its shadow over everything that comes before—that it's present in everything from the very beginning, steeping us all in its mystery? That means that as soon as we know how we're going to die, we can't help but see our present lives in a different light. It was foolish to believe that ordinary life was even possible under such circumstances. If it's true that I'm a spider in a web, it isn't just I who feels the others' movements along the threads—they also feel mine. One person's suffering can be enough to shake up an entire family. Can I really have forgotten that?

At this moment, Costas is standing in a function room in Berlin, flirting with a secretary, a glass of sparkling wine in his hand, unaware that everything is about to change. That isn't fair. We've always told each other everything, even at our most distant—anything else puts the one who doesn't know at a disadvantage. Wasn't that what our marriage was built on—telling each other how we're feeling, and what's going on? Perhaps the saddest thing these last months is that we have both stopped telling each other what's happening. I want it to stop at once. I'm going to put an end to this deplorable state of affairs.

◊

When I return to the living room, I steady myself against the wall and clutch the doorframe.

'Kilian,' I say, as clearly as I can, 'we have to go to Berlin.'

He has to turn his head to look at me and once again I'm struck by his agility. Maybe it's only parents who get backache at our age, while everyone else stays supple.

'What—now, this minute?' he asks. 'We were in the middle of analysing what's wrong with your tits.'

'I have to see Costas,' I say. 'I have to tell him something.'

'Are you crazy? Just give him a ring. Or wait till tomorrow. Talk to me. I'm here—I'll listen to you, whatever it is. For God's sake, let your poor husband enjoy his party in peace. There's nothing worse than wives who are desperate to tell you something.'

'And I think there's nothing worse than drunk men who think they know what they're talking about. Anyway, you don't understand the first thing about marriage. The spare bed isn't made up, but you can sleep in our room.'

'You must be mad,' says Kilian, getting up. 'No one in his right mind would stay here when he could go to Berlin and gatecrash a party.'

It's astonishing. Just like before when I refused to tell him about Theo's thumb, Kilian seems to realise instinctively that this is not the time for persistent questioning. He's more agile than most mentally as well as physically.

I glance at the clock next to the wood-burning stove that for years now we've only ever lit at Christmas. It takes me a moment to read the time: ten past eight. We could be in Berlin before midnight. I'll just have to hope the party's still going on when we get there and hasn't moved on somewhere else.

'Come on, then,' I say. 'We've no time to lose.'

I SNATCH UP coat, scarf and gloves—pocket my phone and notebook—grab my handbag. Maybe I'll manage to unearth a packet of chewing gum later. Kilian takes his glasses and the bottle of vermouth. We turn out the lights and pull the front door shut behind us—we do everything properly and responsibly. The rats are safe and sound, and have food and water—the tumble dryer is on the lawn and couldn't do any damage even if it decided to spontaneously combust at this late stage. We take the front steps carefully, one at a time, so that neither of us trips and jeopardises my plan, which so far consists of little more than determination. The car in the drive is already covered in a wafer-thin layer of ice again, but the car keys are in the house and neither of us is in a fit state to drive anyway. Concentrating all my efforts, I set out across the lawn and over the lattice fence. Kilian follows me.

We ring the doorbell at Heinz and Theo's. The light in the hall goes on, and a second later we're standing in the middle of a patch of light—Heinz has opened the door. We seem not to make a good impression on him—he backs away a couple of steps when he sees us.

'We have to go to Berlin right away,' I say. 'Can you drive us?'

For a moment there's silence as we wait for Heinz's response—then he calls into the house: 'Theo, I'm driving Katja and her friend to Berlin. Shouldn't think I'll be back till tomorrow.'

He leaves the door open and we see him pull on thick lace-up boots. Theo emerges from a back room.

'Can't she drive herself?' he asks. Then he catches sight of me and laughs. 'I see. You're going to have a headache tomorrow.'

'I'll bring some drops with me—you can take them before you go to sleep and I guarantee you won't have a hangover,' calls Heinz from down on the floor with his boots. 'Sea urchin—I mixed it myself. It's...'

'Hey, you,' says Kilian, pointing at Theo. 'We found your thumb. It's on the letterbox.'

'Oh, thank you,' says Theo, glancing somewhat confusedly at his bandage.

'Shall I give it to you?' I ask.

'No, leave it,' he says. 'I'm not quite ready to be reunited with it, somehow. And in these temperatures it'll keep nice and fresh outside.'

Heinz stands up and asks in concern: 'Theo, are you going to manage here by yourself?'

'Of course I will. You go and don't worry about me. I'll

make a nice evening of it. I've been meaning to tackle the gas boiler for donkey's years—there's something rattling in there.'

When he sees our faces, he gives a loud laugh. 'Only joking, you idiots. Off you go now. Shoo, shoo.'

◊

When Heinz has got together all he needs, he goes to the garage with Kilian. I take Theo aside and do something I've never done in my life—I entrust another person with my phone.

'You'll have to stand in for me while I'm gone,' I say. 'Helli's at a friend's and Alex is out with Barbie. If either of them rings up wanting to be picked up, just send a taxi round, okay? And if we're not back by lunchtime tomorrow, do you think you could let yourself into our house with your spare key and wait there for the children? Would you do that for me?'

Theo accepts the telephone with a grave expression and nods solemnly. We both know this is a special moment. Then I go to the garage and get in the back of Heinz's Volvo—the safest car in the world, as he always says.

◊

Out of town, the roads are somewhat less treacherous and Heinz is able to drive faster, although not fast enough for me. I have a stubborn tune stuck in my brain, the theme of Schumann's *Ghost Variations*. The fourth variation is the most beautiful, but I'd rather have something quite different in my head. I shake it a couple of times—sometimes that works, like those iPods you shake to skip to the next track on the playlist.

227

But my head skips to 'Old King Cole' and I ask Heinz to put the radio on.

Without my phone as a torch I have to use the overhead light to write myself a list. Heinz grumbles that it disturbs his driving, but lets it pass because he's halfway through a lecture he's giving Kilian, who's trapped in the passenger seat. The lecture is on jazz and homeopathy, which are apparently connected in some way, presumably because jazz musicians sing special songs of their own. My handwriting is almost illegible, but at least I manage to get the words down. I write:

The something and the world at large: aspects to bear in mind
- *Always tell people in person, never over the phone or in an email—apart from Ann-Britt, who will have to be told on a postcard (or not at all—that way I could get my revenge!)*
- *Don't frighten the children, but don't gloss things over either (let them ask questions, but don't force information on them—that seemed to work well with the facts of life)*
- *Accept all offers of help (provided the help is genuine)*
- *Probably have to give up kindergarten work in the long run because of the risk of infection (and replace it with what—sport? lacemaking?)*

The list is ridiculous. I don't add to it, mainly because it doesn't in any way contribute to my peace of mind—and what's the point of it, if it doesn't do that? It's not as if anyone actually needs lists, except perhaps for Christmas shopping. It will be awful giving up the music groups. As if it weren't bad enough losing your hair and having to grapple with nausea, it seems that you also have to do away with every last scrap of ordinary life. My music children would probably be the only ones who would treat me completely naturally. Life is a perpetual puzzle for them in any case—nothing ever stays the same, not even their shoe sizes. They just have to take things as they come and live in the moment, because for them there's no such thing as a predictable future. Some of them only notice seconds before it happens that they have to throw up—or wonder at the puddle on the floor that seems to have materialised between their feet, as if from nowhere. If their music teacher turned up without hair one day, the cleverer ones might ask a question, but the others would see nothing strange in it. After all, their teacher wears a different jumper every week, doesn't she?

My afternoon music-school group is made up almost entirely of girls. In the kindergartens, too, it tends to be the girls who are signed up for music—some of them wild and noisy, others quiet and slow. One girl called Emily is as shy as a deer, but so tall and solid, you could easily take her for an eight-year-old. She's friends with a small, wiry boy with a foxy face called Leon. His mother once explained to me that they'd wanted him to play football, but he was so much smaller than the other boys his age that they decided to sign him up for music classes for the time being. I expect that, come his next growth spurt, he'll be sent off to football, where he'll learn to behave like a proper boy. Emily, meanwhile, is going to have a hard time of it if she's made to start ballet soon. Tall, sturdy girls always have to dance in the back row.

When we're sitting in a circle on the floor, singing 'Atte Katte Nuwa' with our bongo drums in front of us, I sometimes feel a chill at the thought that these children are soon to be sorted and pigeonholed. My girls, these enthusiastic, gifted little girls with their clear high voices who take such wild pleasure in running and jumping and dancing, can expect to be systematically and surreptitiously curbed. None of them will become musicians. The future star pianists, cellists and flautists aren't in my music groups—they're having individual tuition at home, and most of them are male. It's possible that a few of my girls will follow in Sissi's footsteps—that in spite of all the difficulties, they will keep their passion alive and refuse to lose sight of their goal—but on graduation, if not before, their dreams will be dashed. None of these girls will leave behind a recording or composition. They might just about make it to the orchestra pit, but only until the first baby comes along and puts paid to working nights.

But I'm wrong at such moments—and I know I am. I'm projecting my own story onto the children. If I looked on the bright side instead, I'd see that the world has improved. I never was any good at looking on the bright side—I've only ever succeeded in mustering a kind of forced optimism, as every mother has to, to keep the ship from sinking too fast. If I don't call out a cheery 'Good morning' first thing and act as if the day ahead is worth living, nobody will. That's something I mustn't forget.

◊

When my mother was dying, Sissi was in the middle of preparing for the regional young musicians' championship. She practised with her usual dogged determination and somnambulistic detachment. It's fascinating, the way she wraps her ambition and single-mindedness in a kind of cottonwool of inevitability. When music calls, Sissi can't help herself—she drops everything and follows, as if under a spell.

Our mother didn't come home to die, nor did she go into a hospice. No one would accept what was happening to her, not even the doctors, who seemed full of bright ideas about all the different things that remained to be tested and tried out, factors that gave them cause for hope, and indications of long-term prospects. When the doors to my mother's room were closed, though, they made long faces and talked earnestly and at great length to my father. I tried to visit my mother as much as I could, but looking back, it seems to me that I didn't manage to go as often as I'd have liked. I was kept away by school and housework and other activities. When I sat with my mother she smiled and said she'd come home for Christmas—she promised she would—and I believed her, rather than the doctors' worried looks.

Until, that is, the time came when I stopped believing her. Each time I visited, she was visibly weaker—she would fall asleep suddenly, even before I'd said goodbye—she looked strange, and our conversations went round in circles. When at last I realised how quickly she was going downhill and that there was no question of recovery, I forced Sissi to go and see her.

For a long time I had let her put me off with talk of all the practice she had to do for the young musicians' championship, but I wasn't having any more of that. The competition wasn't until the spring in any case. But Sissi resisted. She suddenly had no time. She had a headache, or else she had a cold and didn't want to infect anyone. She wanted to buy a present, but the shops were shut. It wasn't worth going after school and music practice—it would be better to go another day when there was no school—the day after tomorrow, say. Twice she set out alone and both times she ended up going somewhere else because something occurred to her on the way—that she urgently needed to buy rosin, for instance, or that it would be best to drop in at the dentist's in person to make an appointment. In the end I collected her from the basement of the music school and refused to listen to her excuses.

I took her cello off her and stood it in a corner. I put her arms in the sleeves of her jacket and held out her hat to her. I took her hand and didn't let it go until we were sitting on the bus. At first she talked, grumbling and protesting, but when we reached the hospital she turned quiet and pale and pressed her lips together. She said nothing when we got off the bus—nothing as we walked into the building and took the lift up—nothing when we stood outside the door to our mother's room—nothing when we went in the room—nothing at all, the entire time. Our mother was so pleased to see her. She was coughing and could only whisper, but she was so happy that at last Sissi had come along too. Sissi stood at the foot of the bed and wouldn't sit down. She wouldn't touch our mother. I was incredibly angry with her, but also full of admiration, because the truth was that I too would rather have stood there stiff as a poker than made muted conversation about the weather, talked about what was going on at school and felt the cold, clammy skin of Mum's hand.

When it was time for us to leave, our mother cried. We left all the same. We had homework to do and needed to catch the bus, and I had frozen fish fingers and mountains of washing waiting for me at home.

◊

While Heinz is holding forth on the subject of sea cucumbers and the swarm intelligence of herrings, Kilian is skipping through the radio stations. He doesn't stick with any of them for longer than a few bars of music—nothing finds favour in his ears.

He opens the glove box, bends down to look under his seat, feels for hidden shelves under the roof and then says: 'You don't have any music.'

'I like to think things over when I'm driving, or practise my lectures,' says Heinz. 'But if it's CDs you're after, the back seat's the place to ask. There's sure to be a small supply there.'

'Really, Katinka? Do you have music with you?' asks Kilian, turning to me.

I hand him my bag. He takes out a stack of CDs and holds them up to the light one by one, reading the titles aloud: 'Bruckner's *Seventh Symphony*, Chopin waltzes, Bach cello suites, a Sokolov recital, *Twenty Favourite Christmas Songs for Children*.' He sighs. 'All these years on and you're still listening to the same stuff, aren't you?' He explains to Heinz that lovers of classical music never evolve: 'They get stuck in their musical adolescence and insist that a new interpretation of an ancient piece is as good as a new composition. It's a kind of mental disorder they're not even aware they have. Lovers of classical music keep repeating the same patterns without getting anywhere. If you point this out to them, they tell you there have been huge changes in this area or that, but really they're talking about minute variations on the same old thing.'

'I see,' said Heinz. 'I know the type.'

'So what's it to be?' Kilian asks.

'Something with words,' says Heinz. 'Music without words bores me.'

Kilian pushes a CD into the player and Matthias Goerne begins to sing, accompanied by Vladimir Ashkenazy: ''Twas in the lovely month of May / When all the buds were blowing / I felt within my heart / The flower of love was growing.'

Kilian's right. I love hearing the same songs sung by different people, with different accompanists. I never tire of it. And I don't give a damn what Heinz would say.

We listen to the music in silence. Goerne sings about the rose and the lily, the dove and the sun, but this time I don't think of Dante and my student days—I think of a sheared-off wing mirror, Helli's nose, the cold in my car and Mrs Neumann or Kaufmann or whatever her name is. This morning's world.

'Is that love, all that?' Kilian asks. 'Flowers and the merry month of May and choirs of nightingales? Or is that kitsch?'

'Oh, no,' says Heinz, 'love's like that. Sometimes, anyway. At least it is for me. No idea what Theo thinks.'

'It's nothing like that for me,' says Kilian. 'How about you, Katinka?'

I don't reply, but take the bottle of vermouth he's holding out to me and help myself to a swig. I'm afraid of the moment when the alcohol begins to wear off and I can see clearly again. Who knows what I might see then?

'Stupid question,' says Heinz. 'After all, it's for Katja's sake that we're driving all the way to Berlin on icy roads in the middle of the night. I'd be very disappointed if good old romantic love didn't have some part to play in all this. I wouldn't go along with this nonsense for anything less.'

We hear *Dichterliebe* all the way through and even Heinz manages to keep his mouth shut. Around us it is dark—there seem to be no more villages and no light. Now and then we pass a service station, harshly illuminated, then for miles there's only darkness again.

We make it to the last song. Then Kilian can bear it no longer, and turning to Heinz he blurts out in the middle of the piano's closing bars: 'But you're really a woman, aren't you?'

◊

I shut my eyes and try to work out what I'll do when we arrive. I ought to make a plan, think of something to say, maybe something involving lilies. But my thoughts won't do as they're told—they're not interested in the future.

I suddenly recall an afternoon on the beach, only hours after Costas and I had held a positive pregnancy test in our hands for the first time. It was so foggy that we could see only the sand around us, although we could hear the water—the soft, steady lap of the waves, making the sound they make when there's no wind and the water is hardly moving. We walked for a while and talked—then we sat down on the damp sand and looked out at the fog. I knew that in front of me was the sea—I could hear it and smell it. But I couldn't see it—that was a strange feeling. And inside me a child was growing, a child of whose existence I knew only because I had peed on a strip. I hoped it would live and flourish.

Not long before, a woman I had studied with told me how she had lost a baby in the first weeks of pregnancy. She was doing an internship in Munich at the time and a doctor there had found out that the embryo in her belly no longer had a heartbeat. She decided to have a womb scrape because it could, apparently, be weeks before her body ended the pregnancy, and she wanted to be able to focus on her work without constantly having to worry about bleeding. She made an appointment at the university hospital in Lübeck because she wanted to be in familiar surroundings, and she got the train home for a few days.

I was so disturbed by the thought that she had sat on the train with a dead baby in her belly that for a long time afterwards I had trouble taking public transport without looking at the people around me and wondering what was going on inside them. I don't mean mentally—what was running through their minds. I mean physically. Was it possible that there were other women travelling about with dead embryos in their bodies? People with donor hearts from accident victims? With kidney stones or inflamed appendices? With damaged livers, atrophied lungs, water retention in unthinkable places?

I didn't yet know it was Alex I was carrying in my belly. I felt nothing at all and longed for the day when I'd notice some change, because of course changes had already

236

taken place—everything was different since that morning—
everything, in fact, had been different for a while. It made
me nervous that the changes had taken place so long before I
could even guess at them.

Costas held my hand and stroked it with one finger. I was
quivering and trembling inside and I think it was the same
with him. We were so full of anticipation. If anyone had asked
me what I wished for, that afternoon on the beach, in the fog,
I couldn't have said. Everything was fine the way it was, and
what lay ahead seemed so thrilling and interesting, so mysterious and yet at the same time so clear and simple that I
wasn't afraid. Life lay ahead of me, life with Costas and a
baby.

Costas let go of my hand and got up. He looked down
at me and said earnestly: 'I'm going to walk into the fog and
keep on straight ahead, because I think today's the day to walk
across the water. I'll be in touch when I get to Sweden.'

Then he took a few steps towards the white wall of fog.
I saw his shape fade to a silhouette and heard a splash. I folded
my hands on my belly and lay back on the sand, smiling,
waiting for him to come back with wet trouser legs.

◊

In Berlin it's snowing—the roofs are white and the snow is
falling thick and soft. Here there's no west wind to drive the
swirling flakes along and slap them against windowpanes and
into people's faces. Here snow is something romantic—at least
as long as it's coming down. The hotel where the Christmas
party's being held is in the south of the city—Heinz has a sat

nav. The roads it directs us along are winding and I'd be hard put to retrace them if I had to find my way home by myself.

When we reach the hotel, Heinz parks the car on the snowy pavement directly outside in spite of all the no parking signs, and I'm grateful to him because I don't know how steady I'm going to be on my feet. It's almost one o'clock—we've taken longer than expected because of the weather. Kilian and Heinz get out with me. We leave our coats in the car, but I wind Anja's scarf around my neck and the three of us make our way to the entrance.

'Off you go then, girl,' says Kilian, giving me a push.

'Good luck,' says Heinz, 'with whatever it is. *Omnia vincit amor.*'

No one stops us as we walk down a long corridor, following signs printed with the logo of the construction company Costas works for: two letters topped with a pointed roof. Eventually we come to a large room full of people. The noise level is formidable—music is coming from a CD player although there's a stage with instruments and an amp. The musicians must have come to the end of their program—or maybe they've gone for a break. I look around for Costas. I don't know what I'll do when I find him, but I suppose I'll come up with something. I don't have a master plan—how could I? No one knows how to tell people she has a something in her breast and will soon be lying bald and shaky in an adjustable bed, ready to depart this life.

Almost twenty years ago I was standing in Lübeck, staring at a sports shoe on a bench, and suddenly knew that love can bring things together and make sense of things. I had this feeling that as soon as I was face to face with Costas, I'd know what to do, and I have the same feeling now: all my emotions are going to fall into place—everything will be clear. Then I see him. Kilian gives me another push—Heinz strokes my arm. Costas is right at the back of the room, and appears to be surrounded by women. I raise a hand and wave. I call out to him. I jump up and down to make myself seen above the crowd, but he doesn't notice me—and why should he? It's not as if he's expecting me.

I try to squeeze my way through to him. It isn't easy. I keep stopping to wave and jump up and down and call out, each time struggling to keep my balance. But still I can't get through and panic rises in me, like in a nightmare when you know you have only to reach a certain point and all will be well, but try as you might, you can't get anywhere. I shove people aside—there's dancing in the middle of the room—and behind me, Kilian jostles impatiently. Then a path opens up in the crowd and I decide to strike out in a different direction and move towards the stage.

'Where are you going?' calls Kilian, but I'm already at the short flight of steps up to the stage—I'm on the stage, at the microphone. There's a little switch to turn it on.

'Hello,' I say. But my voice is inaudible. Confused, I flick the switch again—it makes no difference. Then I see that Kilian has followed me on stage and found the mixing console, half hidden behind swathes of curtains. He gives me a nod and busies himself with the knobs and dials. The music grows quieter and then stops altogether. The dancers stop dancing and look about them. I blow cautiously into the microphone and a loud puff echoes around the room. Kilian has turned on the amp for me.

'Costas,' I say, 'it's me. I'm here.'

All heads turn my way, but I look only at Costas. I'm not interested in the others—they're mere walk-ons. I want him to see only me, hear only me, and it's as I thought—I suddenly know what to do. Costas's mouth moves, but I can't hear him. There's a roaring in my ears. Costas begins to push his way through the crowd towards me.

'I know this is embarrassing because I'm so drunk,' I say into the microphone, 'but never mind. I'm here because I have something to tell you and I don't know how. I suppose everyone might as well hear it. No good whispering at a party like this. The music's too loud—you have to shout. The reason I'm here, then, is that I can't stand to keep this from you any longer: I'm going to die. You see, I have a something. And I don't know what to do. Nothing's the way it should be anymore. Nothing has turned out the way I planned— nothing—and now here I am having to listen to myself say: *Well, Katharina, what did you expect? You knew all along—it was obvious.*'

I feel tears rising. I glance at Costas, who is standing in the middle of the crowd, his shoulder gripped by a woman who's pointing at me and telling him something, talking into his ear so that no one else can hear. That makes me furious. God, it makes me furious. At first I try to swallow my rage, to breathe it away, but I can't—too drunk, too angry. Never have I felt such anger. It swells, filling me, taking over my brain, making the tears run, making my mouth keep talking, whether I want it or not: 'As for you, woman who's man-handling my husband, I bet you'd like to have a good look at me, wouldn't you? I bet you'd like to see someone who's as much of a mess on the inside as I am. Well, let me tell you, freaky woman, there's nothing to see. Everything's normal on the outside. Let go of my husband and look at me—then you can see for yourself.'

I unbutton my wool jacket—it takes a while but I manage. I let it fall to the floor, extricate myself from Anja's long scarf and pull my T-shirt over my head. The crowd reacts, but I ignore the noise. And at last I hear Costas calling. At last. Now I'm unhooking my bra—I'm not going to be put off.

'Look closely, woman. See anything? No, exactly, there's nothing to see. Maybe *your* insides are full of somethings and lumps and unresolved conflicts too—maybe you sing the song of the truffle, or the potato, or whatever it is you sing here in Berlin. None of that's visible from the outside. And you too, Costas. Have a good look, because I'm not going to exist in this form for much longer. Soon everything will have been cut out and irradiated and contaminated and poisoned and broken down, until in the end there's nothing left at all—only the song of the earthworm.'

I get out of my trousers like a spider shedding its skin. To my right, Kilian is giving me an enthusiastic thumbs up, while down in front of the stage I see Heinz shaking his head and moving his hands to and fro like windscreen-wipers. There must be security people somewhere in this room, either from the hotel or from the construction company, but no one climbs up on the stage to stop me. The moment is all mine. The bouncers may not approve of what I'm doing, but they don't dare mess with me. They sense the anger seething inside me—and indeed, if anyone tried to lay hands on me just now, I think I'd punch them hard in the face.

I take off my knickers too, for the sake of completeness, because I'm sick of always being interrupted and leaving things half-finished. The only thing I can't quite manage is my socks, but I try all the same, hopping about on one leg and steadying myself at the microphone stand. I'm crying shamelessly now, and over and over I shout: 'Look, don't be afraid to look. This is me—I've had three kids in my belly, been around for forty years and won't be here for much longer.'

Then, at last, Costas is with me and for a split second I sway and think I might faint into his arms. But the moment passes and I know that never again am I going to let anyone catch me when I fall, not even him. I can stay on my own two feet. I didn't come all this way to be propped up by Costas— I came to honour an agreement vital to our marriage. I came to inform him of what was going on with me. Maybe I didn't do it in the most diplomatic way. We stand before one another and I'm not sure what he's going to do, but of course he takes me in his arms and pulls me towards him and at once my anger is gone. Kilian turns up the music again.

Through the material of Costas's jacket I hear the unmistakable voice of Bob Dylan singing that he's only passing through. I know the song. What was the title again? It doesn't matter. Inside, I feel a peace that I haven't felt for a long time.

IT ISN'T CLEAR to me how we all ended up back in the car together. We must have walked along the hotel corridors, out through the entrance and over the pavement with its fresh covering of snow, some of us more dressed than others. I have my coat on again now, but I'm still freezing, huddled here on the back seat. Beside me, but too far away to warm me, is Costas.

We are both strapped in—the seat between us is empty. Heinz is at the wheel, and Kilian is lolling beside him, smoking—God knows where he got the cigarette. Costas directs us through the city; we stop outside the building where his little flat is and wait in silence while he packs a few things. Then he's back in the car and we can head for home. The wipers sweep snow from the windscreen unremittingly.

'You don't know what it is,' says Costas, turning to me as best he can with his seatbelt on. 'It might be something quite harmless.'

'I know. And then what happened this evening will be an embarrassing anecdote that you can dish up at awkward moments for the rest of my life. Reason in itself not to live too much longer.'

'Come here, Kat, come and sit next to me. My legs will go to sleep if I sit in the middle, but I can't bear to see you sitting there all sad in your corner.'

I unstrap myself and move over to the seat in the middle. As the lights of the city flash past, I grope around for the seatbelt. But there's no need—it won't be a car accident that kills me. I cuddle up to Costas. He puts an arm around me and we sit in silence. After a while he kisses my head—it's the last thing he does before his breathing slows and steadies. Soon his arm on my shoulder is so heavy that I lift it down.

◊

After passing Costas several Tuesdays in a row on my way to the music academy, I was so used to seeing him and being greeted by him that I felt almost like one of Pavlov's dogs. I sometimes had the feeling that my hand rose automatically when I got to the bench. It's certainly what happened on that one day that was the last and the first, a day of drizzle, as so often in these parts—that constant drizzle that settles on your scarf and hat like dew.

My hand rose in greeting, my eyes turned to the bench, my mouth pulled itself into a smile, but this time there was no Costas. I stopped in my tracks and the pain I felt in my guts immediately made me see what I hadn't wanted to admit before: that I was irremediably lost. This was no flirtation, no passing romance—Costas had crept into my life and made himself so much at home that his absence left a painful gap. At that moment I wanted only one thing: I wanted him sitting there on that bench right then—nothing else mattered to me. What if this were the end? What if he never again sat on that bench and said hello to me? Or, far worse: what if he were sitting on another bench today, saying hello to another woman? The thought was unbearable. I felt sick. Life was unthinkable with no Costas on that bench—not worth going on with. That's how my love for him felt. Only I wouldn't have used that word yet. Love, as I had known it until then, had always, however passionate or romantic, been under my control. I had determined whom I loved and when and for how long—and I'd been happy. Now I felt terrible.

On the bench was a shoe—a sports shoe, size forty-five. It looked fairly new and was sitting exactly where Costas usually sat. I picked it up and set off in the direction it had pointed, until I found the second shoe. This one was on top of a litter bin, pointing to the right.

I had been on my way to a lecture about musicians and medicine, and after that I was supposed to be going to the station to meet Ann-Britt, who was coming to spend a few days with me. When I found the second shoe, it only took me a few moments to decide against the lecture and in favour of Costas—and already I had an inkling that I'd end up deciding against going to meet Ann-Britt. She'd find her way to the flat on her own. I picked up the second shoe and turned right.

I had been living in Lübeck for several semesters and traversed the old town on its island every day, but I always took the same route: past Costas and his bench, and then up and down the straight streets to the academy of music. I didn't really know my way around at all. The next thing I found was a tie, knotted around the post of a street sign. I undid the knot, took the tie and turned into the street, a narrow alleyway I must often have passed without seeing it. The houses on both sides were old and crooked, but well-preserved and nicely kept. In the windows—so low that the tops of them were at eye-level and I could look comfortably into kitchens and passages, living rooms and halls—were little statues, pottery vases, glass ornaments and plants. The people who lived here seemed to have made an immense effort to make their houses as pretty as possible. No blinds or curtains kept out prying eyes, as if it were all right to pry—as if it were expressly permitted. And so I looked my fill. I looked into all those houses—other people's houses—and for the first time I grasped something of the bewildering fact that there's a different life for each of us—that no life is like another. I had grown up on a terraced housing estate, my schoolfriends had followed apparently preordained paths, and the students I had got to know all had similar backgrounds and aspirations—and until that day in the alleyway, it wasn't fully clear to me that although there were strong similarities and substantial overlaps in our lives, it was, if you looked closely, the differences that predominated. Each life was different—it was presumably for that very reason that we looked instinctively for similarities and attached so much importance to them. After all, to acknowledge the differences was ultimately to acknowledge that we were on our own and could understand

246

one another only superficially.

Hanging over a hydrant was a white shirt. I took it up and examined it. It was very big and very crisply ironed. I used it as a laundry bag to give myself a free hand. The hydrant stood by an archway, the entrance to a low, dingy tunnel leading to a courtyard. There was a belt lying on the ground, showing the way. I ducked my head and walked through the tunnel. On the other side I straightened up again and was met by a kind of backyard idyll, of whose existence I had been completely unaware. The little crooked houses had backs as well as fronts, of course, and it was clearly here, on this side, that the true lives of their residents were played out. There were little gardens with tables and chairs, washing hung out to dry, rolled-up parasols, wooden sheds full of toys, and lovingly decorated summerhouses. In the grey of this drizzly day, dahlias and rambling roses vied for brightness and there was even a plump cat draped over a little wall, dozing under an overhang. I followed the little path through this backyard world until I came to another tunnel that spat me out onto a bigger road on the other side, and there I spotted a hat on top of a public phone box.

I followed a scarf, a T-shirt and a jacket through Lübeck's old town. There were more backyards, more alleyways, more windows to peep in at—it was as if my eyes had been opened to a city full of people and their lives and fates, where I had previously seen only facades and thought it enough. Was that what Costas had wanted to show me? He may not have such ambitious intentions, but there's no doubt that he tends to focus on people when he looks at things. An object isn't interesting or beautiful to him until he knows who made it, who bought it, who's used it. He doesn't like houses until they are lived in. He despises office buildings that have to be functional, and where one workplace is distinguished from another only by a few figurines or family photos.

My wanderings culminated in an old church that had been turned into an art gallery after the war. A sock pointed the way. The exhibition was closed, but you could take a lift up the tower and there was already an elderly woman knitting in the ticket booth, although the lookout platform was officially closed for another half-hour. She gave me a nod and when I approached her to buy a ticket, she said: 'You've already been paid for.' So I climbed the few steps to the lift and went up the tower. By now the shirt that I was using as a bag was heavy and cumbersome.

When I stepped out onto the platform at the top, I was met by a cold wind. I must have been more or less directly beneath the spire, in a kind of gallery that overlooked the city and the surrounding countryside. In the middle of the tower, walls prevented you from seeing across to the other side, but you could walk all round the gallery. I followed it around and there was Costas sitting on a picnic rug, looking up at me. In front of him were two cups and a thermos flask. He got to his feet and then stood there, his hands dangling at his sides. I didn't know what to do. What I wanted was to charge at him and fling my arms around his neck, and stay there for the rest of my life, but instead I said: 'I'm glad to see you've got something on—I've found pretty much the entire contents of your wardrobe on the street.'

My heart was pounding in my ears and everything was a blur to me. I desperately needed to sit down, so I staggered past Costas and his dangling arms and dropped onto the rug. I didn't know whether I was doing the right thing—I was probably behaving like a rude cow, but Costas didn't seem to mind. He sat down beside me, poured out two cups of tea and handed me one. Then he spread a corner of rug over our legs and said with satisfaction: 'Now I've got you at last. Have some tea, then we can talk.'

'What about?' I asked in a squeaky voice.

'About our future,' he said. 'And whether we shouldn't kiss at some point.'

◊

The countryside is as dark as ever. From my seat in the middle of the car I can see the tiny piece of road that's lit by the headlamps, while the snowflakes whirling towards us grow finer and finer. The road stretches out ahead and it feels like pure happiness—we drive on and on with a mixture of hope and experience.

I picture Alex in five or ten years. I see him on stage in his (frankly ludicrous) cat costume, singing in his beautiful, well-trained voice into the tiny microphone on his forehead. It has cost him a lot of sweat and tears to land the role of Skimbleshanks and he is happy—the stupid music and the absurd plot don't bother him, because the songs melt the hearts of the audience who come in their droves from all over the world to see the show. More than anything they come for the perfection inherent in everything that happens on stage.

And Alex is thrilled to be part of this extremely successful concept—it only rankles with him slightly that no one out there knows his name—only that of his cat character.

In the dressing-room, he takes off his make-up like every evening, whether he's sick or well, whether he's in a good mood or a bad mood. Putting on and taking off make-up, getting changed—these are routines he has internalised. At home, his wife is waiting for him. Their two children are already asleep, a boy and girl with carefully chosen, fashionable names, marked out by their slightly unusual spelling. His wife looks like a Barbie doll, but he isn't aware of it. All his girlfriends have looked like Barbie dolls and he married this one because it was time he got married and he likes to do what's next on the agenda. And why shouldn't he? There are reasons for the conventions and so far he's always done well out of sticking to them. Or maybe it wasn't like that at all—maybe his wife looks him in the eye when she talks to him, and that's why he married her rather than any of the others.

At Christmas he'll think of me, you may depend upon it. He's keen on tradition and certain occasions offer themselves to remembering loved ones. He's a devoted father, almost bursting with pride, and an attentive husband. He's at the centre of a big, happy circle of friends—no one turns down his invitations without reason. He sits in the middle of his web—a fat, contented spider happy with his lot.

Helli, meanwhile, may end up dropping out of school. But who knows? Her ADHD and puberty might, it's true, prove an explosive mix that blows apart our best-laid plans. On the other hand, she might find that when she starts taking meds, she's suddenly able to do things she'd never have thought possible. Even then, though, she's unlikely to metamorphose into someone who always knows what she wants and how to get it. I picture her moody and chaotic—she's pregnant and doesn't quite know how it happened. Her boyfriend's a gamer and is okay with her moving in with him as long as he can sit undisturbed at his computer. She quit her first vocational training course because her boss was an idiot. She didn't even start the second because it was at the other end of town, and no one can expect her to get up early and sit on the bus for three-quarters of an hour, whatever the weather.

She's pleased about the baby. She likes babies. When it's bigger, she'll go to uni—why else did she bother ploughing through grammar school? She'll definitely choose a course that has something to do with people, maybe sociology or ethnology. Students don't have to get up especially early, and her boyfriend's at home anyway and can look after the baby when she has to go to lectures. She's wondering whether to marry him. He doesn't yet know his luck. But she likes his surname—it's short and pithy, and she saw such a great white dress in an online shop the other day that she just had to order—she can always send it back if he says no, or keep it for another occasion. One thing she does know—she definitely wants loads of babies. Maybe she'd be better off working as a childminder or a kindergarten teacher. She knows that the baby's going to be a girl—she just *feels* things like that.

She thinks of her mother and of the sister she never saw, whose name she couldn't stand. She'll call her little girl Tessa—she likes the way it sounds and it's not Greek. And if it turns out to be a boy, then Franz, but a girl would be better. Her boyfriend doesn't know yet—she's waiting for the right moment to break the news. If he doesn't react the way he should, she'll move out. Either he's properly excited or it's over. She'll manage on her own with the baby. She doesn't need anyone—never has. If she wants anything, she'll buy it. If there's anything she doesn't know, she'll ask. You don't need vocational training for that. It's possible that her web's a little threadbare, that the design is on the chaotic side and rather flimsy in places, but she's a spider, isn't she? If there's a hole somewhere, she can spin some more thread and patch it up. Spiders never have to worry.

And Costas, who is breathing over the top of my head, dreaming perhaps of zero-energy homes? Where will he be without me? I don't know. Maybe he'll find someone to cook for again.

On the passenger seat, Kilian is snoring loudly and steadily. I can feel Costas's warmth on my left—only my right side is still cold. Heinz drives doggedly at an even speed through the dark and the flurries of snow. In my head I hear Schumann's *Ghost Variations*. The fourth variation is the most beautiful. I'm too tired to shake my head. Schumann will have to do.

I can't get at my notebook from where I'm sitting and it's too dark to write anyway. Otherwise I'd look for my list headed *Pretty placenames I've seen with my own eyes* and add *Herzsprung*—heart leap.

My lids grow heavy. The fourth variation is the most beautiful, but it's the theme that sticks. There's a moment before you fall asleep when you just notice that you're about to drop off—that you're slipping over to the other side. There have been days when I've started looking forward to that moment as early as dinnertime, and it's so exquisite that I try to miss it as rarely as possible. A moment full of peace and contentment. I know nothing more beautiful.

If dying really is like falling asleep, I needn't be afraid.